By JWCouch

MIK3 D3VON
CONTINUING SERI3S

Discoveries
Disclosures
Disruptions

MIK3 D3VON: Discoveries

By
JWCouch

VC3 Publishing

Copyright © 2017 VC3 Books
Published in the United States by VC3 Publishing
www.VC3Publishing.com

ISBN: 978-0-9970354-0-7

Cover Art by Emily Masters
Cover Design by ViviAnne Brock
Virtual Assistant / Proofreading by Annie Lynn

DEDICATION

THIS book is dedicated to my family and friends, without whose support this book series would have never gotten off the ground. Our oldest daughter and my wife spent many hours editing. To those who cheered me on and to those who "always wanted to write a book": you were the fuel when I was running low. Thank you all.

TABLE OF CONTENTS

Now, I don't want to scare anyone, but there is more 'Science *Faction*' going on in the pages ahead than you may realize…

PROLOGUE

A girl's screams jerked young Mike Devon awake. He could barely make out human figures in the dim light. A shrill sound, carried by a low pulsation, had overpowered the room and blurred his vision. It sounded like a massive, wet finger was rubbing a giant crystal glass. Mike clamped his hands over his ears, but it did no good. He felt his eyes straining, then finally managed to focus on the scene playing out in front of him.

Several uniformed men were shouting and waving what appeared to be weapons, then a soldier struck an auburn-haired girl to the ground. The sickening thud of her skull striking the floor was felt over the chaos.

He saw an officer scramble toward the girl and felt a chill climb his spine.

Where is his face? Why can't I see his face?

Blood gushed from a gash in the girl's scalp and her eyes rolled back into her head. Her body convulsed, then went limp. The soldier stared at the girl for a moment, then drew a weapon from his hip and began to kneel. The officer dove at him, shoved the weapon aside and thrust a large knife up to the young man's chest. The soldier stiffened, as if expecting to die, but the officer pulled back the knife and cast him aside.

The noise crescendoed to the point where it was so loud it could only be felt, not heard and all went eerily silent. The officer knelt at the girl's side to hold her in a loving embrace. Easing one of his arms from beneath her, the officer brought the knife up to her neck. In one smooth motion, he cut into her jugular then placed his hand over the spraying wound. He cradled her and screamed in silent agony as the pool of blood grew around them.

The scene horrified Mike and he turned away to see scientists in dingy white lab coats staring at him. One by one, the soldiers spun around to see what was causing the new concern among the scientists.

Mike found himself staring down three gun barrels into the eyes of the soldiers who bore them. Time seemed to stand still as the soldiers looked back and forth between him and the officer holding the girl. The officer eased her onto the floor. He continued looking down at her until his trance was broken by an approaching soldier.

There was a tremendous shudder that knocked the scientists and soldiers off balance. Falling in slow motion, the three soldiers looked at Mike, then opened fire. The blinding flashes from the pistols appeared to be sprays of brilliant fog which dissipated into the air. The power in the room surged as the weapons continued to flash in blazing succession.

The closest soldier pulled at a handle on his hip. Where Mike expected to see the blade of a sword coming at him, he instead saw a hazy cloud trailing from the handle. The man dove toward him with death in his eyes. Mike covered his face, mentally reading the letters SAF as the image faded from his thoughts. He felt something strike him in the hip and his leg went numb, but he held his eyes shut.

Mike Devon fell backward out of his bed and onto the floor, unable to move a muscle. He was unsure if it was from fear, injury, or both. He lay there, awaiting his fate while horrifying images flashed before him. He struggled to block them out, but the sight of the girl being murdered was seared into his mind. He forced his eyes open to escape his thoughts and expected to face death. Seeing nothing, the quivering boy peered over the top of his bed. As the young officer's face came into view, the room jolted with a powerful intensity. Mike felt as if he would be crushed from the intense pressure, then all went dark and still. Mike lay motionless in the dark, trying to regain a sense of reality.

Is that me breathing? My pulse? He moved to get up, but felt his clothes sticking to him. *Is that water? No, not water—urine?*

* * *

UNIT 1: A NEW DISCOVERY

MIKE Devon woke, gasping for air, lying on the floor next to his bed. The familiar nightmare he had known since a young boy was both a dreaded and a welcomed event. She was always in it—the mysterious blue-eyed girl with the auburn hair. Often there were only brief images, but this time was different. He crawled along his bed, pulled down the tattered notebook and scrawled out some notes.

He rarely noticed new details in his dreams, even though he strained to find them. An odd haze blurred the boy's features, but for the first time Mike had seen his eyes and they disturbed him. Everything was more vivid, more real and far more emotional than any other episode in the past. His lean frame was shaking from the trauma and adrenaline overdose as he wrote.

"Uh … holy … wow," he murmured as he wrote in the old notebook.

The details were of the highest importance to Mike and he raced to capture every minute detail. Several moments went by. Then the stench of sweat and urine registered in his nostrils.

"Whoa! That was amazing!" Mike yelled out loud as he finished the critical notes. The excitement and the fear had pushed him to his emotional limits. He closed his eyes and envisioned the dream once more, forcing himself to ignore his shaking body. It helped a little. He added some thoughts that could help his propulsion development work. Mike scrawled out estimated frequencies and harmonics to his 'tune'. He had identified three new pieces to the puzzle. It was the most vivid he had experienced in the many years since that first night. He heard the sounds as clearly, but now he was able to capture their mysterious signatures.

"Yeah!" he said, trying to fend off the boyhood fear that crept in once more.

After nearly 20 minutes, Mike could no longer take the pungent air burning in his nostrils. He closed the old notebook and attempted to stand. He was startled to discover he had almost no feeling or control below his waist.

"Just like the first time it happened! Right where the soldier's weapon hit," he said out loud.

Mike pulled down the waistband to reveal a bruise the size of his hand.

Can't be real—I must have hit it on the floor.

The room shifted from left to right, in short jerky motions. Mike felt the room getting hot and nausea overpowered him. He fell sideways as his fingers released their death grip on his bed. The room flashed for a split second, then went dark. His sweat soaked, sandy blonde hair splashed on the floor as his head struck the hard wood.

* * *

A loud thud, coming from the apartment above her, caused Jillian to sit bolt upright in bed. *That's the last straw. Mike is out of his head if he thinks I'm going to let this go! His guest is going to get a piece of my mind, too,* Jillian thought. She grabbed a robe, stuffed her feet into her running shoes and stormed out of her apartment.

Boom, boom, boom. Mike's door shook from her repeated blows. She trained relentlessly for Ironman races and now every ounce of her lean body was ready for a fight. *Boom, boom, boom.* The hallway resonated with the pounding from Jillian's fist yet again.

"Mike, I know you hear me!" Jillian screamed. "Michael! Michael James Devon!" She knew that yelling at him like a mother would annoy him enough to make him open the door. A somewhat evil smirk twisted her otherwise pretty face. She would finally get to see the tramp he had dumped her for.

"Mr. moral high ground has fallen!" Jillian snarled under her breath.

***

Courtney zigzagged her way out of town on Friday night. She snuck through dark alleys and residential areas for hours as she made her escape. The six mile walk had gone by quickly as she watched for a tail and thought about the vacation ahead. She slipped into an apartment building's basement garage a few hours before sunrise and walked up to the coded doorknob on her storage room. Courtney punched in her numbers and opened the door. The lights came on and she stepped inside, pulling the door closed behind her. Courtney inspected the wall of boxes, making sure they were exactly as she left them. She then restacked the large boxes, leaving a path wide enough for her motorcycle to get through.

The real locks were at the back wall behind a false support in the corner. She slipped her fingers around back and waited for the thermal sensor to open the latch. It wouldn't open for gloved hands or even cold ones as she had proven last winter. Courtney worked the combination lock and a section of the wall opened into the dim inner chamber. Once she stepped inside the lights came up to full brightness. It revealed her bike, a collection of duffel bags, a few weapon cases, ammo boxes and a strongbox.

Courtney had learned a lot about secrecy over the years. She had been hiding caches of money, supplies and weapons long before she joined the DIA. Living her first fourteen years under the evils of Nazi oppression had given Courtney an advantage over her colleagues. She put it out of her mind whenever it tried to creep back in and barely believed it herself now.

Her pulse quickened and the excitement began to build as she stripped out of her street clothes. Courtney slipped into her tight, black Kevlar-lined leathers. She threw a leg over the motorcycle, balanced the bike and felt its weight.

"Hey gorgeous, it's you and me now. Ready to play?" she whispered, then rolled the motorcycle out of the back room. She climbed off, closed the secret door, then pulled on the black, carbon-fiber helmet. "Let's do this." She opened the outer door, rolled the bike out, then closed and relocked the door. When the engine came to life, she felt herself smile. The immense power of it was intoxicating.

For the next fifteen or twenty minutes she had to hold herself at bay. She had to clear the last set of street lights and cameras in town. Once in the clear, she laid down on the broad tank and the real fun began.

This was the newest and her favorite, in a series of crotch rockets. Courtney always acquired them the same way, from a different dealer. She was the rebel daughter of a wealthy family from New England off on a bender in Upstate New York, Maine, or Pennsylvania. By the time she returned from the dealership to her apartment north of the city, she knew the bike's behavior on every surface, wet or dry.

Courtney smiled as a thought crossed her mind. *I'm consistently inconsistent. Mike would find that amusing.*

As she ripped down the highway, Courtney's mind let go of her concerns and plans. One by one the corners were conquered, each with its own challenges and rewards. *Nice bank on this one, gonna feel some g's,* she thought, hearing the roar of her bike as she downshifted for maximum exit velocity. *Oh, yeah, that's nice.* She felt herself get heavy and the suspension squatted under her. Courtney kept accelerating as she neared a slight hump in the road. *One twenty five.* She eased off the throttle, feathering it to maintain tire speed as she glided above the ground. *That was nearly two hundred feet!*

Stopping only for fuel and water, Courtney continued her wild ride for the entire day. Right at nightfall she rolled up to the door of her storage unit. She shut down the engine, patted the tank and whispered, "That was the best ride ever."

After entering the storage unit, she stored the helmet, leathers and bike in the back room. She then moved the boxes in the front storage room back to precisely where they had been earlier in the week. She rocked the bike up onto the stand and made sure it was stable.

Back in her street clothes and stocking feet, Courtney stood on the seat. She slid the overhead light to the far side of its track, pushed upward on the ceiling tile and slid it out of the way. She then rotated a handle clockwise to disarm the security system. Courtney lowered the trap door and slid out a short ladder. Finally, she pulled herself into the room above and closed the trapdoor behind her.

Courtney Lewis slid out from under the heavy, king-size poster bed. She had reentered her safest world, the one belonging to 'Emily', the traveling saleswoman. Emily told the apartment manager she had a European territory to explain why she was rarely home. She made it a point to avoid her neighbors, not wanting to have any contact with them.

It was late Saturday afternoon and Courtney was chomping at the bit to execute her ultimate plan. She ate a small dinner, cleaned up, then lay down to get some rest before the late night return to her real life. Monday morning always came too rapidly after her rejuvenating trips. These occasional weekend getaways were her saving grace. Courtney felt the lack of sleep and forced herself to close her eyes. She relaxed and within seconds had dozed off.

Courtney lifted off her helmet with her back to the building. She zipped the jacket up to her chin and put on a pair of dark sunglasses. She ran her fingers through her hair, letting it fall across her face to provide even more anonymity. Comfortable with her camouflage, Courtney turned and walked in. She looked every bit the part of a black leathered rebel.

Not lowering her sunglasses, she said, "I'm here for the Kawasaki Ninja we spoke about last week. You did break her for me, correct?" She slapped down the title to her year old, low mileage Ninja from the previous year.

"Yep, factory spec break-in. That bike is extremely fast ma'am, but I suppose you already know that," the man at the counter said.

"That's what they told me when I bought this one," she said as she tapped the title on the counter.

"I see. Well, I suppose you'll be all right," he replied.

Courtney signed the paperwork, showed her counterfeit driver's license, then paid the difference in cash.

When the papers were finally in her hand, she said, "Thanks." Then she turned and walked out of the store.

The tech that brought it around began talking about the bike's controls as it idled. Courtney slipped on her helmet and without saying a word, straddled the new bike. She adjusted her jacket, slipped on her gloves and revved the engine. The roar drowned out his voice.

Looking at the temp gauge, Courtney saw the engine was warm. The young tech was still standing next to her as she slipped it into first gear. She looked at him and revved the engine almost to redline. He put his hands over his ears and took a step back. Courtney leaned forward, squeezed the front brake and lit up the rear tire. She backed off the throttle and let the rear tire get traction once more. Revving it several more times, she rolled toward the street, then glanced back to see the pleased young man in a cloud of tire smoke.

Courtney felt herself move and nearly woke, but was able to slip back into her exhilarating dream.

* * *

Terry and Bill were across the street in an apartment facing Mike's living room windows. They took turns watching Mike and the security camera footage from his building. They were used to pulling double shifts by now but looked forward to getting their lives back.

Terry and Bill worked for the Defense Intelligence Agency (DIA) in a Special Investigation Unit (SIU). They were recruited out of the military to work for the Department of Defense (DOD). Terry was an Operations Intelligence Specialist in the Air Force and Bill was an Army Ranger. If Terry was a scalpel, Bill was a jackhammer. Bill had only been out for a few months when he was assigned to 'Operation Marjorie' under Terry. The job was to monitor Mike and his technology for the DOD and make sure the designs didn't get out.

"I wish we could bug his place," Bill said.

"Yeah, I know, but that nosy maid sweeps the place at least once a week," Terry said.

"Courtney can take her," Bill said.

Terry smiled at the thought. "That would be too easy."

"You think she'd ever go out with a guy like me?"

"Why, can't you clean your own place?" Terry asked.

"That's not what I meant," Bill said, rolling his eyes.

"Oh. You think someone bugged you?" Terry struggled to keep his face clear.

"Not the maid, I mean Courtney!"

"Oh, I get you now," Terry, unable to hide his annoyance, watched Bill's face.

"She's a lifer, buddy, recruited right out of college. Something's broken with that one."

"No more than anyone else in our game," Bill said.

"No, I get it. She's beautiful, smart and fights like a badger. That's everything a boy looks for." Terry smirked.

"Pretty much."

"And if you ever make her mad, she'll slit your throat. You don't wanna get involved with anyone in this business."

"She's one of the best shooters we've got," Bill added.

"Another attractive attribute, I agree. Also, she's racked up several kills and likes long walks on the beach."

"I don't like helpless women," Bill said.

"I see what you mean, but don't let her looks deceive you. She's ruthless and if you don't think she'd kill either of us for a promotion, you're kidding yourself." Seeing his partner was becoming frustrated, Terry changed his tone. "You think she'd go out with you?"

"What?" Bill asked, turning to look at Terry.

"If she went rogue, could you pull the trigger?" Terry asked.

"Sure. Could you?"

"Not fast enough. She'd take us both down before we flinched."

Terry watched Bill ponder that thought.

"Jillian's in the hallway, looking torqued," Terry said. He pointed at one of the television monitors. "She's going to Mike's place." He glanced up at Bill. "Were they just on the phone or something?"

"How do you know she's going there?" Bill asked.

"The robe. Well, were they?" Terry demanded.

"Nope. Neither phone was active since earlier this evening," Bill replied. He rechecked their lines on another monitor. "Both are clear now, too."

"Listen in," Terry said.

Bill pulled on the headphones and tapped on the screen to enable the audio.

"There's some shuffling or something at Mike's place."

"She's up on his floor and cruising now. She heard something going on in his apartment," Terry said, immediately standing up. "We're going in! Mike's in trouble!"

Terry grabbed his phone and dialed. "Answer it!" he said, scrambling toward the door.

"What's up?" Courtney asked.

"We have a possible event, we need your assistance!"

"Roger that, I'm remoting into the system from home."

Terry followed Bill out the door of the apartment, making sure it locked behind them.

"Status?" Courtney asked.

"Unsure, but it looked like Jillian heard something in Mike's apartment," Terry replied.

"Jillian is outside his door now. Remember, no unnecessary collateral," Courtney said.

Terry knew collateral damage, like Jillian getting killed, was perfectly acceptable. Mike was their primary concern and Courtney only mentioned it to follow protocol. They rounded the back of the adjacent building and sprinted down the dark alley. In a matter of seconds, they were walking across the street at the crosswalk down the block. At the other side of the street they had some cover and sprinted into the alley behind Mike's building.

"We're almost there," Terry said as they tore across the pavement. "Kill the security feed to Mike's building. We need the rear door in five." He was unnecessarily calculating their exertion as the trip was far too short to tap into their conditioning.

"Done," Courtney replied.

They slowed long enough for Terry to open and close the stairwell door without banging it, then took the stairs three at a time. As the duo left the stairwell and entered the hallway, they each chambered a round and took in deep breaths.

"Prepared for interaction," Terry whispered.

"Roger that," Courtney said.

They headed down the hallway to the right, with their weapons drawn. As they reached Mike's corridor, Courtney's voice came over their earpieces.

"Stand down. I repeat, stand down."

"Acknowledged," Terry said, as if the previous thirty one seconds had never happened. Out of the corner of his eye he could see down the hallway and Jillian was standing at Mike's door.

"Write up your reports tonight. I'll review them in the morning before team two goes in to check Mike's notes."

"We will," Terry said, looking at Bill.

"Call me if you need anything, I'm going to try to catch a couple hours now," Courtney said.

"That sounds nice," Terry said calmly, knowing Jillian could hear.

Terry felt some jealousy creep in. *Let them collect the intel while we do the hard work.*

* * *

As they walked down the hallway to the back stairs, Terry remembered the first time they had to rush Mike's place.

He had never lead the team before and refused to leave his post until Courtney came back from vacation. Bill had been gone for half an hour when Terry had first noticed the intruder across the street. He was watching the FLIR thermal video of Mike's empty apartment, or he would never have noticed the man lurking in the shadows.

What are you doing back there? That door is locked and alarmed at night. He watched the man reach up to the top of the door and place a rectangular box on the steel frame.

"Oh, no! Don't you do it!" Terry said aloud.

The man then looked down at the lock and began to work with it. Moments later, Terry saw light come from the opening door. The man's dark gray clothes and black cap were illuminated.

Surgical gloves? He's a pro! Terry thought.

Terry ran out of the apartment, carrying the night vision in one hand and a pistol in the other. He glanced at the Kevlar vest hanging behind the door as he opened it.

"Bill, we have a visitor! I need you back here ASAP," he ordered into the com while leaping down the stairs.

"Wait for me, I'm two minutes out!" Bill said.

"No can do!" Terry said, sprinting across the street and into the alley behind Mike's building.

"You'd better watch your six!"

Terry could hear Bill's breathing and footsteps over the com. *Two minutes—that's nearly half a mile. He'd better pace himself,* Terry thought. He shimmied up the thin, steel support to the fire escape. Within a few seconds he had pulled himself over the handrail. He paused to push the emergency call button on his earpiece.

"Dispatch, this is Operation Marjorie, requesting backup, ASAP."

"Copy that, Marjorie, backup alerted. Location?"

"Use my GPS!" Terry said as he scrambled up the fire escape.

"Roger that, ETA twenty minutes," the voice replied.

He slipped in through Mike's bedroom window and lay in the shadows, opposite the bedroom door. He listened to every minute noise and tried to visualize what was occurring in the apartment. Terry was waiting to engage with his Beretta, an 87 Target with silencer. The gunsmith had widened the frame to double the pistol's capacity to eighteen rounds, at the same time he reworked the trigger and sights. With the subsonic rounds in the clip, Terry could empty the gun without so much as waking the neighbors.

Should have grabbed your body armor. Stupid decision. "He's in the living room, moving toward me. I'm in Mike's room," Terry whispered.

"Almost there," Bill said.

"Enter the front in twelve, eleven..." Terry counted down. He hoped Bill had detected the tension in his voice. They both knew Terry was not the right man for the job. Bill was much more capable in hand-to-hand combat and twice as strong.

Terry lined his sights up on the doorknob as he lay on his back, up against the far wall. He was a marksman, not a bar brawler like Bill.

He exhaled and released a soft, "Six, five...,"

Terry saw the knob rotate. The thermal vision showed him exactly where the guy was standing. He knew the twenty-two caliber rounds would not do their job through two layers of drywall, so he waited to fire. His heart was beating harder than normal as he held his breath. He would not breathe again until the first round left. After that, it was going to get crazy.

Really stupid to let this thing take off on you, Terry thought, as he realized the intruder had been doing recon under their noses. *He's good, quiet and careful.* The door had opened wide enough to allow passage, but the man did not reveal himself. Terry saw his gun barrel slowly move into view as the intruder scanned the room. *That was foolish, thinking you could sit here in the shadows and 'tap, tap' no more Mr. Bad Guy.* Terry sighted in on the gun hand of his intended target.

A click and soft hiss were Terry's only explanation of why his shoulder felt like it was on fire. Terry's own bullet had just left the barrel of his own gun and met its mark as well. He had shot through the wrist of the intruder, which was the only 'meat' he could see.

The bullet would have mushroomed to three times its size before exiting the man's hand. The searing pain of the ripped tendons and shattered bones had likely been what caused the intruder to tumble backward and fall.

Terry heard the intruder's pistol hit the floor.

"Coming in," Bill said.

"I'm hit," Terry whispered into the com.

Terry felt his confidence grow the instant he heard Bill inside the apartment and jumped to his feet.

"Fool number two," said the intruder, with a thick Asian accent.

Terry passed through the doorway, his sights resting on the man's chest. He saw the man's left arm in motion, trying to get something from beneath him. Bill was already too close for a safe shot, so he waited.

Two barely audible gunshots went off. One from Bill's pistol, the other from beneath the visitor.

"He's got a gun!" Terry yelled. "Did he—he did. He shot himself."

The intruder struggled to speak, as he lay on the living room floor, managing only to cough and wheeze.

Bill leaned down and poked him in the face with the barrel of his pistol and said, "Who's the fool now?"

The smaller man slapped Bill in the ear and gasped, "You!" He spit into Bill's face.

"He's pretty quick, Bill. Luckily, he didn't have a knife on him." Terry caught a quick glance from Bill. *Oops, that didn't help.*

Bill grabbed the much smaller man by the neck with one hand and lifted him from the floor, thrusting him into the wall.

"I was going to let you live until that! So that makes you the fool!" he screamed in the man's face. Spit and obscenities flew in his fit of rage.

Terry watched the last little bit of life jerk and convulse out of the would-be assassin's body. "Uh, that should do it," Terry forced himself to say, actually wanting to cheer Bill on.

Blood and urine formed a puddle on the floor around the intruder's second pistol, which was now lying at Bill's feet. He was regularly impressed with his partner's strength, but this had been one of the best displays of it yet.

"He's gone, put him down."

Bill laid the body on the floor, next to the growing puddle.

"Dispatch, cancel backup. Threat eliminated," Terry said calmly into the com. "We need a single cleanup."

"Backup canceled. Cleaning crew ETA ten minutes," the reply came.

"That's service," Terry said.

"Not my first rodeo," the voice replied. "Anything else I can do for you boys?"

"Negative. We're contained," Terry answered. "Strike that, we made a bit of noise. I'd bet at least one call went out," Terry warned.

"Two actually and I've taken care of them," said the agent on the other end. "Like I said—"

"Yeah, yeah, you're a bullfighter, we get it." Terry rolled his eyes, then glanced over at Bill.

"Buddy, you're breathing like a power lifter going for the gold." Seeing the color had left Bill's face, Terry patted him on the shoulder. "Come on, we need to get you to the toilet, pronto."

"I'm fine. I don't need to go—" Bill mumbled, as he followed Terry into the bathroom.

"Sit down on the side of the tub," Terry said. "You can't kill a man barehanded and keep a quickie mart grease-dog down. It can't be done." Terry started to chuckle as the look on Bill's face changed.

"Ayeeeee!" squawked Bill. The contents of his stomach gushed into the toilet.

"There, now you'll feel better."

Bill looked up at him. "For a second I thought he killed you."

"Nope," Terry said and smiled, still holding his bloody

shoulder. "You're one tough hombre, partner."

"Yeah?" Bill asked.

"You bet," Terry said and patted him on the shoulder with the back of his bloody hand. "The festering relish on that greasy pig rectum you eat would kill most men." He pointed down into the bowl. It had the exact effect Terry was looking for.

Bill turned back to the toilet and fired off another volley.

"Dispatch, how's that cleaning crew coming?" Terry asked.

"Verifying," came the response. "Coordinates show him less than five miles out."

"Roger that," Terry said, then went into the kitchen and pulled some paper towels off the roll. He walked them back to Bill and said, "Here, use these, not the hand towel."

"Thanks for the help," Bill grumbled.

"Just doing my job," Terry said, chuckling at Bill's grumpy appearance. He walked back into the foyer and pondered the night's events. Within minutes, he heard footsteps at the door.

"Knock-knock. Housekeeping. Anyone home?" the voice in his com asked.

"Not even a mouse," Terry replied trying to keep his smile from view.

The cleaner let himself in the front door, rolling a suitcase behind him. He was a contract cleaner and worked with the smooth precision of a true pro. Out came the supplies: chemicals, rags and two body bags.

"Pretty fast service tonight," Terry said.

"Yeah, I just finished up a job for the local PD in old downtown."

"Lucky for us," Terry said, annoyed at the odd smirk on the cleaner's face.

Bill finished up in the bathroom and the cleaner went in without saying a word. They did not like him and he did not like them. The tension was palpable.

The cleaner unzipped the suitcase completely, laying it flat on the floor, insides facing up. He then folded the body in half and rolled it onto the open suitcase. He folded the opposite side over and partially zipped it. He stood the suitcase up once more. The cleaner then shoved the bags with cleaning supplies in with the body and closed the zippers. He nodded to Terry, then left, leaving the suitcase behind.

"Six minutes flat, impressive," said Terry.

"Great, the idiot expects us to pack this out?" Bill asked.

"We need to take him to the lab, he may be papered through his embassy," Terry said.

"Who cares?" Bill asked.

"If he came in legit, we'll give 'em the body. If not, we'll burn it," Terry said.

The com came to life again, "You guys done up there? They're almost out of red lights to give the girlfriend."

"Give her the greens, we're on our way down now," Terry said.

Terry winced as he turned the keys in the locks and pulled them from their slots. He wasn't pleased with his performance and the bullet hole was his payment. He knew they had been lucky so far, but the bullet that went through the visitor's wrist had vanished. He paused in the hallway then reminded himself that the tiny, misshapen bullet was unrecognizable to the untrained eye. Terry turned and grabbed the handle on his end of the suitcase. With Bill on the other end, they were down the hall in moments and made quick work of the stairs.

"She's entering the garage in ten, nine..." dispatch warned.

"We're in the alley now," Terry said, slowly closing the

stairwell door behind them. "Bill, you wanna get something to eat? Maybe a corn dog or something?" Terry continued, leaving the com open.

"No, I don't."

"How about you, dispatch?"

"All good here," came the reply.

"Knock it off, before I snap your neck. It'd save the doc the hassle of plugging that hole in your shoulder," Bill grumbled.

"Reliefs are on scene, so return to the office for a debrief and checkup with the doc."

"Roger that," Terry said into the com. "Thanks, buddy."

"Yeah. Sure. Don't mention it," Bill grumbled. "I'll get the car. You wait here."

"Seriously, you saved my six in there."

"Now we're even," Bill said, as he walked away.

"Well, I wouldn't go that far," Terry said, chuckling.

While he waited in the shadows, Terry thought more about his report and how they would react. *They won't be leaving me in charge anytime soon.*

* * *

Mike was asleep on the wooden floor when he heard the auburn-haired girl calling for help. She was calling from another room and pounding on the door with such force he could feel it. *Boom, boom, boom.* The room reverberated over and over.

Wait, how does she know my name? No, please! Wait, wait, no! Mike pleaded, attempting to scream. Mike struggled to stay connected to his childhood dream, but it was over and he was devastated.

The voice kept calling for him.

Oh no, Jillian!

Mike was fully awake now. He called out, "Hang on, I—I

have a problem." He took another breath. He looked around for somewhere to hide. "I had an accident, I…" His voice trailed off.

His hands and feet were tingling but he could move them now, so Mike attempted to get up. It was futile. He crawled out of his room and made it far enough to see the front door before he collapsed. Defeated, he heard himself say, "I need your help. I'm hurt." *This is going to be mortifying.*

"Are you alone in there?" she asked.

"Yes, I'm alone. I'm sick, that's all, just sick."

Mike heard fumbling in the hallway and imagined Jillian retrieving his hidden key. When the key entered the lock, he tried to stand once more but only made it to his knees.

Jillian reached inside the dark apartment and flipped on the lights. She entered the doorway and stopped in her tracks.

"Oh, my," she said, covering her nose and mouth with one hand.

"Sorry. Food poisoning. Yang's," he said. Mike knew she would never believe the truth. They had both gotten sick once before on Yang's takeout, so it seemed like the best choice of lies he could concoct.

"Mike, this is awful! I…I…why didn't you call me?"

Don't answer that, don't even think about it!

"Forget I asked," she said.

Close call.

"Um, you're a mess," Jillian said, flipping her long, brown hair to one side. She straddled him, slipped her arms under his and stood him upright.

Jillian was fit and capable of lifting him by herself, but Mike strained to help.

Wow, she smells good, Mike thought, as the power of her scent struck him.

"Wow, you smell awful!" Jillian exclaimed.

"Yeah, it's shower week," Mike said, forcing a chuckle. Seeing Jillian's annoyed look, he knew it was the wrong time for a joke.

"Right," she said and helped him back into his bedroom. "I see the fancy bachelor pad hasn't changed much. Well, except for the puddle on the floor over there," she nodded toward his bed.

"Uh, yeah," Mike was afraid to say anything, knowing that no matter what he said, it would be wrong. They'd been separated for many weeks now and he didn't want to stir up hard feelings.

"Where's your latest girlfriend? Why isn't she here helping you?" she asked as they made their way into the bathroom.

"I'm single, Jillian. There is no one else." *Don't say anymore!* "Things weren't working out between us, that's all." *Oh, no!* Mike felt Jillian stiffen, then she released her hold on him.

"Here then, you don't need my help," she said, nudging him.

Mike stumbled, but managed to grab onto the marble countertop and steady himself.

"Thanks for coming, I appreciate it," Mike said. "Look, I'm truly sorry. But, I didn't love you the way I should. I wasn't crazy in love and you deserve that." He glanced in the mirror and saw the door behind him had closed. *Now that's a new reaction.*

Mike made his way to the shower and turned on the water. When steam started rising from the floor, he stepped inside and sat down on the heated corner seat. He then flipped the valve and turned on the shower head above him.

Half an hour had gone by when a much improved Mike finally emerged from his hot shower. He walked into his bedroom and noticed his tall, cherry wood poster bed was made. The smell was all but gone from the air and the floor was clean.

A new and improved Jillian?

He poked his head out of the bedroom to see her standing by the window in the living room.

"Hey, thanks for cleaning up. I owe you, huge."

"No biggie. It's not every day you get to clean up after a grown man who pees himself."

That's more like the Jillian I remember. "Uh, yeah, I feel terrible…"

"I can tell Maria is still caring for your every need. The kitchen is spotless and there's not a speck of dust on your bookshelves."

The old Jillian's back.

"Yeah, the company is still providing that service for me."

"Mommies for rent?" Jillian said.

"She's a housekeeper."

"Right. Breakfast in bed on Sundays still?"

"Well…" Mike felt nauseous and struggled to think of some way to change the topic. He dropped himself onto the couch. "Look, I don't want to argue with you. Sit down by me and let's talk about some of this stuff between us. Wouldn't it be nice to be friends again? You know, snuggle up and watch an old movie like we used to?"

"Yeah, of course it would and maybe a root canal afterward?"

"All right then, I'll see if there's an old Grant or Hepburn movie on," Mike said, reaching for the remote.

"Of course, your beloved Audrey Hepburn. So predictable. I'm going to check on the laundry," Jillian said and left the room.

So nice of you to remind me why I broke it off.

"Hey, Charade is on," Mike called out over his shoulder.

"Of course, it is," Jillian grumbled down the hallway.

* * *

Terry looked at Mike's apartment through the sight of the Advanced Long Range Acoustical Device, or ALRAD, from across the street. He switched to short wavelength thermal and the reflective glass of the windows vanished. He loved using the highly classified device. It could create false noises, make someone sick and induce paranormal sightings. His favorite was the ability to cause the loss of bladder or bowel control.

"Take your time, buddy. Jill is moving about, tidying up or something and Mike's on the couch watching a movie."

"I can hear it in the background, so he'll be out soon," Bill responded, heading toward Mike's apartment. "You sure we should move on this?"

"Yeah, we still have an hour 'til sunup."

Terry reached over and adjusted the audio from the sound dish he had aimed at the living room window. "He's about out already. You can get your pics of the notebook in less than ten—" Terry felt a vibration in the weapon and his heart skipped a beat.

Due to its classified status, the weapon had some unique features in case it got into the wrong hands. The onboard processor was programmable to a user's fingerprints, but only while docked at a station that linked to the DOD. If you happened to know this and liberated a user from their hand, the lack of a pulse would trigger lockout and destruct commands.

"We still good?" Bill asked.

"Yeah, just had to adjust my grip."

Bill chuckled and Terry knew he was remembering another SIU team that triggered a self-destruct. They rushed the costly gadget to Courtney's office, with only minutes to spare. She tried to help them, but had to toss it down the emergency incinerator chute.

"Don't worry, I'm not getting any extended assignments in Siberia today," Terry said.

"Almost to the top of the fire escape."

"Hold up, I think she's reading the notebook," Terry warned.

Jillian was not considered a threat, but he knew Courtney didn't want Jillian to see Mike's notes.

Terry moved down to the far window and could see the outline of Bill's feet. "Hold tight, I'll get her out of there." Terry fired off a shot from the ALRAD, sending a soft thud through the apartment.

The light went out in Mike's bedroom and Terry saw Jillian peek out the living room window moments later.

"Worked like a charm, she dropped it," Terry said into the com. "She's on the couch with Mike now. Get the new info and let's wind this thing up for the night since it's gonna be daylight soon."

"Roger that, going silent," Bill replied.

Terry moved again and watched Bill move across one of the bedroom windows. "I see you. Still clear."

Bill gave a deliberate thumbs up in sight of the window and moved out of sight, toward Mike's bed.

The buzz of a laundry machine rang out.

"Jill is on the move! Get out of there," Terry hissed into Bill's ear.

Bill slipped out the window and back onto the fire escape.

"Stay loose, you're doing fine."

"Got it," Bill whispered.

"Nice work, buddy. She went into the laundry room."

"There's a few new pages..."

"Get your pics?"

"Yep."

"Stay low, Mike got up. He's moving toward the bedroom," Terry said, feeling the tension rise. He caught glimpses of Mike passing the bedroom windows. "Uh, oh, he's looking for the notebook."

"I see," Bill whispered.

"Stay out of sight," Terry warned.

"I need to know where I can put it."

"He heard something," Terry said. He saw Mike lift his head up and hold still. "He's heading for you!"

* * *

Where could it be? Mike looked around his room, in the early hours of the morning. He opened the drawer on his bedside table. *She read it, but she wouldn't throw it out, would she?* Mike stood upright and froze for a moment, glancing out his doorway and down the hall to the spare room. *Door's closed.* He spun around and headed for the chair by the back window to grab his robe. Mike noticed the window was open and reached to lock it. *Wait, she had it open to air out the room.* He crossed his bedroom and headed for the spare bedroom. As he walked across the apartment, he glanced over and saw a stack of folded laundry on the chair next to the couch. *Not there.* After the revelations from his latest dream, Mike was concerned about his notebook. He never purposely let anyone read it. Although a few of his girlfriends had read some, they couldn't understand it.

He peaked through the bedroom door and Jillian opened her eyes. She gave him a drowsy smile that faded as quickly as she woke.

"Morning," Mike said and smiled.

"You look like you're feeling better. How's the head?"

"What did you say your name was again?" he teased, touching the knot he had on the side of his head.

"I'm your ex-fiancée, remember me now?" asked Jillian, with a trace of hostility.

You walked right into that one. "Well, I can't imagine why anyone but a fool would let you slip through his fingers." By the look on her face, he thought he'd been given a brief reprieve.

"Slip through? Don't you mean dropped? Remember, I'm beautiful, attractive and you love me, but I'm not *her.*"

Her words proved him wrong. Knowing he deserved it, Mike let her go on without saying a word. *Hell hath no fury—*

"So, what do you suppose a fool should do now? Ignore a girl's messages? Reject her calls? Maybe a fool should pretend he doesn't see her in the lobby?" Her tone was starting to take on an even more hostile note. "What happened to that sweet, boyish grin of yours?"

Pulling back, Mike said, "You know, I really am sorry, but I can't change it and I won't. I appreciate everything you did for me last night, you were great. I'm exhausted and have a splitting headache, so I'm not looking to cause trouble."

Mike walked into the living room and dropped down on the couch. *Let her cool down before you ask about the notebook.*

A few moments later, Jillian appeared. She walked up behind Mike and put her hand on his head.

"I'm sorry, but I needed to get that out. For what it's worth, it helped."

Mike's drowsy eyes stared out the window, but he kept his mouth shut. Jillian walked away and he listened to her footsteps moving around the apartment.

The whole thing was your fault. Jillian isn't her and you knew it all along, he thought, feeling his eyelids droop.

"I'm leaving now," Jillian said, unlocking the front door.

"OK. Thanks again for coming up to check on me," Mike said. "Say, you didn't see my notebook lying around, did you?" he asked, glancing back to see her expression.

"Nope."

"OK," Mike said. He listened to the door close as he saw Audrey Hepburn appear on the screen. Distracted, Mike leaned his head back onto the couch and relaxed, enjoying her smile. He welcomed the drowsy feeling as it overtook him, hoping the dream might return and reveal more.

* * *

"Are you sure we should be doing this?" Bill asked.

"It's much better to get the notes before daylight," Terry replied, ignoring his guilt. "We know this place better than anyone, who's better to do the entries? Our backups?"

"You don't think Courtney will rip you for this?"

"Don't worry, if anything comes up I'll call her," Terry said. He checked the security cameras on Mike's building once more. Terry looked back through the thermal sights and saw Mike's head had rolled even further over to the side. "He's asleep on the couch."

"Volume?" Bill whispered.

"Terry scanned the device toward the corner of the building and saw Bill's head peeking out at him. "Roger that. Sorry." He moved back to the living room window and checked Mike one last time.

"You're clear, go now," Terry instructed.

"I'm out," Bill said.

Terry moved the ALRAD to the far window and saw Bill easing down the fire escape. "I see that. Nice work."

Terry placed the device back on the tripod and connected both wires to it. Once again, he scanned through the building's cameras. Seeing nothing, he checked the external cameras. Some were placed by the team and some were from neighboring buildings they had hacked into. Hearing movement outside the front door, Terry pulled his pistol from its holster. He waited for Bill's noise, realizing he hadn't heard a warning over the com.

"Bill, is that you?" Terry whispered into the com. Hearing no reply, he released the safety on his weapon. Finally, the doorknob made two clicks, followed by a dull thud on the door and Terry felt himself relax.

"Sorry about that, my battery died," Bill said, stepping inside.

"No problem. Though, I was about to blow your brains out," Terry said. He clicked the safety on his gun and stuffed it into his holster. "Put it on the charger before you do anything."

Bill obediently removed it and placed it on the charging base.

"He won't know, right?" Terry asked.

"Nope, I dropped his notebook on the floor under the

headboard, against the wall."

"Excellent. It's bad enough we have to go in there, but tipping our hand could be devastating at this point."

"Understood."

"You keep an eye on the monitors and I'm going to skim through the pictures you got. Let's hope it was worth the risk," Terry said, connecting the camera to a tablet computer. *Good or bad, I'm going to catch heat for that.*

* * *

Mike was exhausted and elated as he lay on the couch dreaming about his invention. Memories of college and working long hours on directed energy in the lab played out as he watched on. He could rarely see the faces of others working with him, but he knew who they were and where they worked now. He enjoyed watching dreams of those days, since there were so many exciting discoveries. Other parts of his past nearly escaped him, fading into the background.

In school, he worked on sound wave technology and near light, focused energy. It was on a much smaller scale and this was the obvious next step for him and for science. The cost and waste of solid and liquid fuel rocket engines for stellar travel had proven too costly. They were old Nazi technology that had been 'done to death' and the intrigue of lasers had all but died.

It seemed like almost no time had passed since the Theoretical Applications Corp. recruiters had approached him at the university lab and offered him a $250,000 signing bonus. His very next thought went to the moment he realized the Audi R8 he saw at the dealership would actually be his. The sleek, sexy, silver Audi R8 Mike called 'Babe', 'My Girl', 'Gorgeous' and a few other endearing terms, was his. She had cost him roughly half of his signing bonus for joining TAC and was worth every penny.

Mike's dream skipped to his latest discovery. He felt

himself relax as if a great burden was lifted, knowing he had found the missing pieces.

Is it really my invention? Or my discovery? Why does it feel like it's being revealed rather than created? Mike felt a sense of guilt wash over him. *I didn't steal it, that's impossible. Unless my dreams are psychotic episodes...*

Mike felt his awareness taking over but forced himself to let the dream take him where it wanted to.

Soldiers appeared. They were rushing down the street, aiming their weapons at anyone in sight. Mike watched on, feeling the terror of a child.

Swastikas? I wasn't in World War II. The Nazi symbol is on everyone and everything. It's from ancient India, maybe that's what it means.

The military group stopped abruptly. Half of the foot soldiers took a knee, aiming their weapons in all directions. The other half ran into the nearby buildings and disappeared.

Mike felt horror wash over him. *No! No...*

When they returned, an officer stepped out of an armored vehicle and held up a bullhorn and announced, "There is a price to pay for deception!"

Mike felt helpless as he listened to women and children screaming in the distance. *Run! Fight! Do something, but don't just stand there!* He couldn't make himself move and saw soldiers drag dozens of men from the buildings. They made the men kneel in one, long line down the street.

"There is an even greater price to pay for rebellion!" the man yelled, raising his free hand as high as he could, spreading his fingers wide apart.

The men pleaded for their lives as the soldiers put pistols to their heads. The officer's fist clenched as his arm dropped to a powerful, bicep-flexing pose. In one, synchronized shot, the entire row of men was executed.

Mike turned and ran as hard as he could, but his legs were barely able to carry him and he stumbled. He kept stumbling, step after step, until he let himself fall.

Picking himself up, Mike looked around. Relief washed over him as he realized he was inside the safe walls of the lab.

* * *

Courtney had barely slept one hour when the light of her phone awoke her. She slipped her arm out of the blankets to retrieve it, then entered her passkey.

The text message read, *News on Marjorie, we have new intel. Looks like the new vitamins did the trick, please advise.*

Marjorie was the code name for the Mike Devon project. Courtney chose the name because Mike had written it several times in the margins of his notebook. In one case he had also written, 'What promise?' after the name.

Courtney was instantly alert when she realized that the experimental drugs they slipped into Mike's dinner had worked.

En route, ETA 7am, she typed, then slipped out of bed. Before setting her phone down, Courtney tapped the car icon on the screen, to have it brought out front for her.

Scrambling through her scalding hot shower, all she could think of was the word 'intel'.

What had Mike come up with? Was it the breakthrough she so desperately awaited? Had he finally put the missing pieces together?

Waiting was tantamount to torture; after all, she had so much riding on him. She had spent her entire career studying and monitoring the technology. Now, Mike and his team at Theoretical Applications Corporation were developing it. If the news was what Courtney was hoping for, her years of dedication had finally paid off.

No more watching Mike and his co-workers at Geek Squared. No more dual life…

Her unassuming Toyota Camry was idling in front of the downtown apartment building. As she got close enough to touch the door handle, the door unlocked and Courtney let herself in. She felt a slight uneasiness as she pulled the door shut. *Relax. No one has a reason to put a bomb in your car. Not yet anyway.* She considered electronic bomb detection for her Personal Protection Plan, but the others would have thought it excessive. She felt a slight tinge of regret for not investigating it further.

As she pulled away from the curb, another thought struck her: *No more worrying about every gesture and behavior. I could even shop at the same grocery store twice in a row.* She understood the time consuming efforts to mask behaviors and minimize predictability were necessary. But, the thought of a simpler life was intriguing.

Courtney's navigation on her phone spoke and she followed its command. She meandered through the streets and after a dozen unnecessary turns, was far enough off course to mask the purpose of her trip. She opted to use one of her memorized route variations to complete the journey. Courtney recognized her confidence and decided it wasn't misplaced. She was one of the best.

✳ ✳ ✳

Mike was still asleep on the couch when he thought he heard a noise. *Oh, no, Jillian!* He peeked out of one eye and saw she wasn't in the room. "Jillian? You still here?" He heaved a sigh of relief.

Remembering his missing notebook, Mike got up and walked into his bedroom. He paused to read a note on the kitchen counter. *I hope you're feeling better, Jillian.*

Wow, no guilt trip or scolding? Wish you would have figured that out a year ago, Mike thought as he crumbled the note and tossed it in the trash. He continued into his bedroom and started searching for the notebook. *I know I left it over here.* He pulled out the bedside table and it dropped to the floor. *Typical, careless Jillian.*

Relieved, Mike's focus turned to the sounds he could still remember from the dream. He went into the living room, got out his laptop and began working away.

It's not perfect, but an audible test on the waveforms will have to do for now. In the back of his mind, he doubted he would remember everything to recreate the sounds he heard. If there were other frequencies that were beyond audible range, he was only shooting in the dark. Something inside urged him on, as if it knew the answer was within reach.

Several hours went by as Mike struggled to get the frequencies and their sympathetic harmonics identified. He had near perfect pitch, or the task would have been insurmountable. One by one, he identified the tones, until he had assembled them into a complex chord. When he played the finished product, a big smile crossed his face.

But these cheap speakers just don't do it justice.

"That's it!" Mike said, as he reached for the remote on the coffee table.

Mike started up his overpowered, audiophile grade sound system by playing the usual Bach. He didn't want to overwork his prized speakers, until they were properly loosened up. Mike played it on his laptop several more times.

"Wait! That's a fifty cycle carrier, Euro-electricity, not American sixty cycle power!"

He made the change, then duplicated the complex frequency set at a second, higher pitch.

"I can add a lower set, too, if it needs more Oomph. I wonder…"

He checked the analysis graph and recognized that every major frequency used was divisible by fifty, twenty-five, or twelve and a half. Even more reassured that he was on the right track, Mike couldn't wait any longer to test it out. He picked up the remote, shut off Bach and uploaded the sound file to the receiver. Nothing came through the system. Refusing to accept the results, Mike turned it up to full volume.

"There it is! Just barely, but it's there!"

His heart pounded in his chest, knowing he was near a breakthrough. Mike ignored the slight swaying motion he felt, thinking it was his enthusiasm.

"The current draw is pegged at max load, but that's all I get? How?"

Mike forgot his confusion when he realized he hadn't powered up his dual amps. Though he loved his sound system, Mike had always believed he had gone overboard, until now.

He replayed the file, forgetting to turn the system down from the previous attempt. At first the sound was very quiet, but gained intensity until it was unbearable. Mike struggled to understand the events, oblivious to the world around him.

The amps are gonna trip, he told himself. But he turned the amps all the way up anyway. Mike had brief reservations about the damage he could do to his prized system, then decided to push it until something failed.

The room was full of energy, but the sound didn't seem loud anymore. The entire room appeared to begin shifting from side to side and he couldn't focus his eyes on anything. Also, the pressure in the room seemed to have increased, making it difficult to breathe. Realizing he was no longer safe, Mike tried to turn down the system, but the remote did not work.

It's interfering with the signal from my remote?

"Uh, oh," Mike uttered, but the words—and the remaining air in his lungs—were sucked out of him.

The lights dimmed, but the energy in the room continued to grow. *How can it be feeding? Off the other circuits? Or gravity? That's not possible—is it?*

He turned toward the receiver to power it down. Struggling with all his might, Mike could not close the gap between himself and the system. His oxygen starved body was beginning to shut down. He hadn't moved a step, then the amplifiers tripped and all went silent. The next instant, he slammed into the far wall and fell backwards onto the floor. Mike lay there, gasping for enough air to support his laughter.

"Eureka! I got it!" Hearing himself yell, Mike's focus broke for a moment, as he thought about his neighbors. "They're gonna hate me now!" He began laughing at the thought. He wiped the tears from his eyes and struggled to regain his composure. "Go ahead, try to evict me. I might buy the whole building, when they see what I have!"

***

"It was a massive buildup of Earth's gravitational and magnetic energy. He was focusing it, storing it within the audio bubble of the sound waves he was emitting. The satellites picked it up for nearly thirty seconds. The Pentagon was gearing up for a missile strike, for crying out loud! Can you imagine if magnetic reconnection had occurred and directed the energy like a solar flare? How many people would have died? We're very fortunate the energy was released in all directions. I can't believe I'm happy your boy set off an electromagnetic pulse, but I am."

"An EMP? Sir, we had no clue he was this close," Courtney began.

"Then why did you authorize your team for an entry this morning?" he demanded.

"Sir," Courtney paused, replaying the nights conversations in a split second.

"Actually, we knew something big had happened, based on Mike's reactions. Since we can't maintain full monitoring inside the apartment, Courtney wanted us to make entry and get an update."

"Who said that?" the Chief demanded.

"Terry, sir."

"Let your team lead speak for herself next time, Terry," the Chief ordered.

"Understood," Terry replied.

They went in without my approval? Now I'm really glad I didn't involve them with my other plans, Courtney thought, as her phone lit up. She switched over to the messages. *Seven new pages, technical details, he thinks he solved it,* Courtney read. *Nice, Terry. A quick message to save your skin? All that does is buy you a little time.*

"So, what did you find out?" the Chief asked.

"Well, sir, there are seven pages to decipher, when I get into the office. The short of it is that Mike himself believes he's cracked the nut. We'll have a report on your desk by eight hundred," Courtney said.

"What do you need from me?" the Chief asked.

"Authorization of funds and resources to bury this EMP situation," she replied.

"Done. Don't go over five hundred."

"Half a million should do it, sir," Courtney said.

"This EMP dissipated in a very short distance, we were lucky," the Chief added.

"It reabsorbed into the earth's magnetic field quicker than we expected," Courtney said. "That's probably since he was using the earth's own fields to create it."

"That's what my adviser tells me. She also says it's easily weaponized at this point."

"She's right, sir," Courtney said. "Whoever *she* is." Courtney had tried to get him to admit the woman's identity more than once. She already knew it was a girl from NASA—a math genius hailing from obscure Shawano, Wisconsin. The Chief wanted to keep up the facade, so Courtney continued to play along with him.

"The pulse went vertical for half a mile. She said it would have dropped any civilian aircraft in the vicinity," the Chief added.

You don't need Dr. L. at NASA for that...

"That's reasonable," Courtney said. She realized the Chief

was posturing to make a move on the project. The recording of the call will be his justification for action. "I expect we have a week or two to get operational on this," Courtney said.

"She thinks that's overly generous and I agree. I expect that report on my desk by eight hundred, like you promised."

"Roger that," Courtney said, redirecting her annoyance at the Chief's adviser. She was right, after all. "ETA five minutes."

"Done," the Chief said and the conference call went dead.

What a genius you are, hiring people to bring it down to your level. Courtney caught herself and shifted her thoughts back to the task ahead.

Courtney walked up to an elevator in the parking garage of the massive government building. She pushed the button, entered when the doors opened and simultaneously pressed buttons 'B1' and '10'. When the display blinked rapidly, she placed her hand over the 'G2' it was showing. There was a loud click and she turned to face the security camera lens. The elevator then lowered her from the 'lowest level of the building' to the tenth sub-basement level and she stepped off.

Her bag and attaché went into the conveyor and she walked down the long, white corridor. She slowed to pass through the x-ray scanner, arms over her head and gave the guard behind the camera a hand gesture. Courtney knew that the resolution left nothing to the imagination of its operator. She could do little more than make futile attempts to distract the operator while he stared at the screen. The metal detector alarmed as she passed through and the guard looked even closer at the screen.

Knowing it was likely the last time she would get a chance to even the score with the guard, Courtney decided to act. Pulling the metal pen from her pocket, she used her thumb and two fingers to flex the metallic shaft in one hand. At the point of breaking, she released the projectile toward the side of the man's head. It was a solid hit to his right ear and the man let out a yelp as the penpoint punctured the cartilage.

"I don't think this—oops I mean that—will make it through the detectors," she said as the red faced guard held his ear. She walked on down to the end of the security hallway, turned and collected her things.

"You did that on purpose!" he squawked.

Looking back at the glaring man with blood on his hand, Courtney said, "Sure glad you were so focused on the screen. That could have easily taken out an eye."

Courtney went through the last set of security doors and met a concerned look from a junior agent. He was begrudgingly 'doing his time' on guard detail and was getting an earful from the guard over the radio.

"I see he's involved you in my little mishap."

"What's going on here?" he asked.

"Nothing and watch your tone. I pulled a pen from my pocket and it flicked out, hitting the guard in the ear. I apologized immediately, of course," Courtney said.

"He says you—"

"I suggest you pull him from the roster. There's clearly some sort of anger issue with that one."

"Listen, Miss, you can't—"

"Jason, may I call you Jason?" Courtney asked, reading his badge. "Stop by my office in twenty minutes and we can discuss this with the Chief if you like, he'll be in there. But right now, I'm in the middle of something bigger than all of us." *Call me 'Miss' again, I dare you,* Courtney thought as she watched his eyes for a moment. "Super, Jason, I'll be in my office if you need anything else."

Walking toward her office, Courtney felt her phone buzz. *Secured files. Thanks, Terry.*

She went inside, sat down at her desk and docked her phone. Courtney placed her hand on the smooth black pad next to her keyboard, then leaned in to the camera on top of her screen.

"Hello, Courtney," the synthesized voice said.

"Hello, Courtney," she replied.

She read on screen, *Three forms of verification accepted*, then the main screen appeared. Courtney clicked on the icon that looked like a dented mailbox to her. Seeing the latest item in the list was from Terry, she opened the document it contained. Courtney scanned Mike's pages they had collected. She reread several odd phrases and made mental notes as she went, but knew there wasn't much left to wonder about.

You think you've done it, but you don't know what IT is, she thought.

Courtney heard a knock at her door. "Come in."

"Chief said you would need help cleaning up some mess your boy made?" the agent said.

Forcing an appreciative tone, Courtney said, "Oh, great, we sure do. Come on in." Stupid desk jockey slash wannabe IT pro.

"Right," he said, sounding bored.

"Log into the PC over there." Courtney pointed to her guest workstation in the corner. She texted Terry a simple 'THX' while she waited for the man to get into the system.

"I remoted into my PRL account via the two-thirty server, using—"

"Nice," Courtney interrupted. "Now I need you to get into the Public Utility's control system."

Courtney jotted the ID for the transformer that fed a four block area around Mike's place.

"Interesting," he said, typing away. "They reworked the interface a bit since last time I was in here…OK, got it."

Courtney transferred her screen to the large, flat panel on the wall in front of them. "Let's watch the fun in the control room." She got up and walked the paper to him.

He glanced at the four camera view she had up.

"I need the voltage to this transformer to go up to seventeen KV. Put the switchgear in maintenance override mode."

"Are you going to make the turbine run away?"

Courtney glanced at him, but remained silent.

"That'll give 'em a good scare."

"Perfect," she said.

"Oh, OK. You're sure this is the right transformer?"

"I got it from one of your pals. Maybe I should get him in here to help me?" Courtney asked.

"No, but that could scrap a multimillion dollar piece of equipment," he said, turning to look at her.

Courtney noticed he was looking intrigued and doubted he was actually concerned. "Then I guess they're going to earn their pay this morning." She knew she was right when he chuckled and spun back to the screen.

"Then I'll have to turn off this alarm and override the safety dump valves. This and this need to be in manual. Oh, and that, too," he said, clicking on several icons on the substation control system. "Override. Yes, I know I'm changing the limits. Yes, yes and confirm." He glanced over his shoulder with a sinister grin on his face. "I'm ready."

Someone has a little hacker left in him.

"Spike it."

"Seventeen KV? You're sure?"

"Yep, much higher and the turbine might come apart."

He tapped enter and they watched as the turbine speed started climbing.

"They'll catch it at fifteen-five."

Courtney chuckled. "This shift has two imbeciles at the helm and at least one is sleeping at all times."

"They are pretty still," he said. "How do you already know so much about the crews at this substation?"

"If I told you, I'd have to slit your throat," Courtney said, letting her face and eyes go cold. She almost laughed as he blinked, then slapped him on the back. He jumped when she made contact. *Our country's bravest.* "Just messing with you."

"Right. I knew that," he said, then laughed nervously.

"There—the other transformers tripped offline." Courtney pointed. "You're going to have to bring it back down," she said, as the alarms started going off.

"I'll do it at seventeen KV, if they don't," he said.

"They can't hear anything."

"Now how do you know that?" he asked.

Courtney pointed. "Earbud cords hanging off both of them, see?"

"You have to be kidding me!" he said.

"Nope."

"Your transformer is screwed up. It tried to trip repeatedly. Look at the error codes the gear is throwing," he pointed.

"Perfect. You're done," she said.

He moved the cursor back onto the turbine speed control and throttled it back. "They don't even know something happened."

"Like I said," Courtney turned and walked back to her desk. "Now most of my work is done for me." *Fast and clean. That's exactly what I needed.*

* * *

Thoughts bounced around in Mike's head as he lay on the floor in his living room. After all, this was the day he had worked toward for six years. It began when he started working at Theoretical Applications Corp., or TAC as they all called it. He joined the aerospace propulsion lab to work field technology and directed energy. Directed energy had been around at least since Archimedes' mirror focused sunlight to burn ships. Field technology was even older, but much less understood.

Mike's complex package of frequencies and harmonics was another system to harness and focus great amounts of energy. It was theoretical and only those on the fringe of current science would openly discuss its possibilities until recent years. History has shown that a scientist who is too far advanced for their time is often ridiculed and even ruined. Mike had been working on the edge of advanced science most of his career and now he was to be leading the mainstream into new technology.

Georg Friedrich Bernhard Riemann's work on the n-ply dimension proves correct, Mike thought. It nearly overwhelmed him as he realized he was treading where giants had been. *I wonder if they'll use my full name after I'm gone?*

Mike picked himself up off the floor. He was shaking and somewhat disoriented, but elated with the early morning's outcome.

I have to be more careful, or I'm going to get the wrong kind of attention. I triggered a chain reaction, a summing of energies that far exceeded the momentary energy input from the amplifiers. This could be dangerous in the wrong hands. A thought struck him, *I can't play with it here ever again.*

He shuffled over to the couch and started to lower himself, then froze in place.

Mike was certain he had unlocked one of the key forces of the universe, that GOD himself had kept locked away. It was so efficient it could be utilized as a weapon, or propulsion system. But, it only required a small portion of the energy needed for current pulse energy, plasma, or light-based technology. It focused and collected the energy from Earth's magnetic field and gravity.

If you bottle up too much, the energy release would be extreme. The craft would have to maintain a safe distance from stars or risk attracting solar flares. *What about large planets? Do they have strong enough fields to actually flare? Need to test that one. A transfer from one set of planetary fields to the next and you might hopscotch your way through the solar system.* He straightened back up and stared out the window, seeing nothing but envisioning volumes.

Mike knew he could finish the propulsion system now.

* * *

Courtney knew her control over the project was slipping. Her assignment was to watch Mike's technology. Both to keep it from going too far and from falling into the wrong hands. As an EMP alone, it was a completely viable weapon the Department of Defense could lock down.

I need proof, before I make my move. Courtney realized the evidence she sought would push the DOD into immediate action. *It's not the message as much as it is the delivery.* Her mind raced to find a plausible opinion to deliver to the Chief. It would have to provide her with more time and not raise any suspicion before it was time. Once the DIA figured it out, they wouldn't need to wonder if she had gone rogue; they'd know it.

First things first—I have to deliver my report to the Chief. She sent a simple message, just as he liked them. "Breakthrough." Within a few seconds, her phone lit back up.

Secured incoming conference? That was quick. Courtney thought for a moment. *Too quick.*

"Go ahead," Courtney answered, as protocol dictated.

"Please hold," said the voice on the other end. There was a several second pause on the line.

"All present, connecting you now," the operator said.

Courtney heard a click on the call.

A moment later, an anonymous agent said, "We have important information to discuss regarding Marjorie."

"We'll do it here," the Chief said. "ETA O-nine hundred. Get breakfast called in." There was a loud clunk on the line, followed by another click and the line went dead.

Someone at the office already sent out an alert. I should have known —

The thought of being blind-sided by some mediocre agent who couldn't survive outside a cubicle made her angry.

I'll have to make my move soon.

Courtney's mind immediately went back to her secret apartment outside of town where she kept everything she might need for an emergency. The DIA had a string of them, mostly in major cities, but she would need her own when the situation changed. This was the sixth incarnation of a plan she had been perfecting since her late teens. It was there she felt the safest, though her visits were few. The underground garage housed her car and the storage room where she kept a fresh Kawasaki Ninja. Her pulse quickened when she thought about the jet black, six speed, traction controlled two hundred horse power rocket. It was capable of keeping up with any production car on the planet, even with a second rider onboard.

Made his R8 look like a toy, she thought as her face involuntarily pulled up on one side. *That was the best night,* she chuckled to herself...

"You're closing fast, better slow up," Terry warned.

"I'm good," Courtney said, referring to the fake plates on her bike as she roared down the freeway. "All he'll know is that some *chick* smoked him tonight."

"The owner of that thing has probably turned it in by now."

"I *borrowed* it from some rich punk across town. He's not even around to miss it," Courtney lied.

"If he's still alive."

"No one was hurt when I acquired it."

"Of course not," Terry said. "You should see Mike at your twelve o'clock now."

"Yep, but not for long," Courtney replied, downshifting and twisting the throttle hard.

The bike lurched forward and she felt her weight easily double in the seat. The roar of the engine was exhilarating, but the feeling of hard acceleration while approaching one hundred and fifty miles per hour was the ultimate. Courtney shifted into sixth gear and at the same time saw the tail lights on Mike's Audi squat slightly.

Of course, you want to play.

She felt the R8's engine straining over the howl of the air as she moved past the rear bumper. Courtney slowed and glanced over to see Mike's face as she passed his door. In front of his car, she felt herself chuckle.

Someone's not happy.

The two shared a competitive yet euphoric moment as they touched one hundred and eighty miles per hour.

Sorry, Mike, you're topped out.

Glancing at him again, Courtney saw Mike double take out of the corner of her eye.

Yes, Mike, I'm a girl.

Staying tucked, she reached her left hand across, under her right arm and wiggled her fingers at him.

Mike's left hand released the wheel to return a wave then quickly reattached itself.

Courtney twisted the throttle once more and pulled away from Mike as they entered a sweeping corner. She felt the G-forces making her bike lower under the additional downforce. Courtney's bike lifted as she left the corner and she shifted her weight for the next one. At this speed the nearly straight freeway turned into a curvy racetrack. She checked her mirror and saw Mike's headlights were falling further behind. A sudden red and blue streak on the left median startled Courtney, but she held on to the throttle.

Yeah, I know you'd like to chat and all, but that's not gonna happen.

"Cop," she said. The lights went dark again and Courtney knew the officer had only done it to spook her. "I'm clear and I think Mike had enough warning to slow down."

"That's great news," Terry snapped.

"I'm going to pull off and make sure he's not in trouble."

She braked hard as she left the next corner and immediately took the exit. She parked on top of the overpass and shut off her bike, smelling the hot brakes as they cooled in the night air. Almost immediately, Mike's car came into view. A moment later, he rolled past on the freeway beneath her. Relieved for both of them, she started it back up.

"He got through," Courtney said.

"Plain luck," Terry said.

"But it was fun."

"No, that was stupid. What got into you?" Terry asked.

"I needed a little stress relief, that's all." Courtney felt herself breathe a sigh of relief. "OK, let's get back on his tail again. Where to?"

Courtney sat up in the chair and looked around her office. *Daydreaming? When you're this close? Get your head in the game, Courtney.* She felt the girlish grin fade, along with the brief warmth within her. Courtney checked the security camera feed at Mike's building and saw nothing of interest. As she jotted down her plan for the coverup of Mike's EMP, she caught sight of him entering one of the frames. Mike's facial expression changed as he neared his car.

"Good morning my beloved car, may I caress you?" Courtney mocked. "You look at that machine like you're in love with it."

She watched as he pulled the remote from his pocket, then suddenly stop. He pointed it at the car and turned his head. She watched as his face went from disappointment to worry, then he mouthed something. "Sorry, Babe? See ya, Babe?" she said, trying to determine what he had said. "Good grief, you look like you're going to cry. Grow up already, you big baby." Courtney felt awkward, but pushed the emotions out of her consciousness. *He's a big baby.* She picked up her phone and dialed. "I need a car removal, ASAP. Two of them, actually," said Courtney to the agent at the office and gave him Mike's address. "They need to be destroyed. The damage done to the electronics is classified. It needs to look like theft and it needs to happen ASAP."

The voice on the other end asked, "Can't they be stolen and dumped somewhere?"

Annoyed by the question, Courtney said, "Not with any of the electronics in them."

"I need an R8, at the same address, pulled in for repairs."

"We can have it torched, too," the agent suggested.

"No, that could interfere with our primary. We can't have him upset or distracted right now." Courtney imagined Mike's face when he saw the burned-out shell. *He'd definitely cry over that.*

"The guy is that fragile?"

"He's not fragile, but it would distract him." Realizing she sounded protective, Courtney added, "He's definitely in love with it."

"Roger that," he said. "What next?"

"I want all of the electronics in the R8 swapped out today. Get me one of our chop shop specialists, but make sure he knows it's an R8. I'm sure you'll need a donor car to make it all happen in time."

"A used R8?" She could hear typing in the background. "They're a hundred grand."

"Fine. The National Guard base has a Helo big enough to hold one. Use it if you can't find a local car."

Hearing no answer, Courtney added, "The chop shops can strip one of those cars to the bare frame in two hours. All I want is some electronics swapped out."

Courtney knew that burning the car up would have been easier. Admitting to the agent, or herself, that she was doing it to be kind to Mike was not an option.

Time to finalize the report on the EMP coverup and get back to business. She paused for a moment and put herself into the Chief's mind. *Get him thinking about Mike's invention and he'll sign off without batting an eye.*

* * *

Within an hour, a team went through Mike's building. They took inventory of dead electronics that were not plugged into wall outlets. By noon nearly all were replaced, save for a few, older devices. Those were purchased online and being flown in.

* * *

Mike sat in the cab, almost scared that he would forget what he had discovered. He could barely wait to get the test file into the sonic propulsion design system. After that, he could begin work on morphing it and test the effects. The twenty minute cab ride went by in a flash and before he knew it, Mike was at the front entrance to TAC.

He hurried his way through the four levels of security, checking his watch. *Forty-five minutes since I left home and nearly an hour to get to the workstation,* he thought. *Fifty-two weeks per year, no, two hundred and sixty times per year.* "In five years that's six hundred and fifty hours getting to work and another six hundred and fifty getting through security!" Mike heard his own voice echo down the security hallway. Looking up he saw two guards and several other employees looking at him. *You said it, you own it.* "Sorry about that, folks, but someone should streamline this process a bit. Don't you think?" Seeing several nods, he felt slightly less embarrassed for his outburst.

Mike dropped the test file off for data screening. He waited impatiently for Gloria, the administrative assistant, to deliver it on a secured card. The readers were encrypted and coded to the cards they used, made in pairs with twenty cards and a storage unit. Only three cards could be out of the storage unit at any given time. One for each drive and one for a courier. If a card was lost, the data would be transferred to a new set and the old set destroyed. It was expensive and tedious, but necessary to keep the data secure.

"Good morning, Mike," Gloria said, more cheerful than usual. "What brings you into the lab so early? Skipping your meetings and email?"

"Yeah, good morning. That." Mike pointed to the data card in her hand.

"Fine, but I need one back."

"Right, but I'm in a bit of a rush." He pulled the chip from her fingers. *Oops, hurt her feelings.* "You look extra nice this morning, Gloria."

"Uh, thank you," she said.

Mike looked down at the 'Do Not Disturb' sign as he reached to open the door, then stopped. "Oh, one more thing, my car wouldn't start this morning. I need you to talk with the dealership about a loaner if she won't be ready by tonight."

"I'll call them now."

"Thanks." Mike went inside and sat down at the workstation to convert the audio based data into a wide-spectrum file for the propulsion computer. He had been working for several hours when the non-stop pangs in his stomach caused him to look at his watch.

Nice, my lunch has been sitting out there for nearly an hour. Mike retrieved the bag from the outer office and tore it open.

He all but inhaled half of the now cold, roast beef sandwich, forgoing the partially congealed au jus. He gulped down a bottle of water and went right back into the lab.

He sat up straight in his chair. *Oh, no! I still need to write up a test plan and send it upstairs for approval.* Mike looked around to see if anyone was watching him while he wrestled with the rebellion inside. *No. I can't wait another day, not for some annoying procedure.*

* * *

Courtney grabbed her tablet PC before heading to the conference room. They had taken it over to process Operation Marjorie's twice daily meetings. She had a few minutes to spare, but the team had already assembled. Courtney assumed they were discussing the reasons for the morning's impromptu meeting. The room went silent as she entered and Courtney knew why. She had heard the Chief's stride and his breathing, coming up from behind. As she turned to take her usual seat at the right hand of the Chief's chair, she acted surprised to see him.

"Eat." It was the only word out of his mouth, then he motioned for Courtney to follow him, with one grumpy finger.

She was up, with a breakfast sandwich in hand, heading for a quick pre-brief, briefing. The rest of the agents knew to grab food whether they were hungry or not. It was clear to everyone that they would be stuck inside for a while.

Courtney walked into the Chief's office and closed the door behind her.

"This event almost dropped Mike's apartment building and set off hundreds of seismographs. Also, the EMP damaged a lot of devices and affected quite a few people. I want it cleaned up enough for plausible deniability and reasonable doubt, that's all."

"Chief, we've killed most of the seismic reports and edited the data at all facilities within a hundred miles."

"Excellent. An earthquake with an epicenter at 'Mike Devon' would be problematic." The Chief raised an eyebrow.

"Exactly," Courtney said. "Plus, we kept him from realizing what he has."

"Nor do we want him to." The Chief paused.

Courtney remained silent as she believed he was on the right track.

"We have some time then," he said.

"Mike will apply this to his device within a week or two,"

Courtney said, certain he would do it in half that time.

"I like your story, I do, but…"

Courtney felt her stomach fall and had to force herself to let the Chief finish.

"I liked another idea, too, so we went with it."

"Sir, you understand we're already invested in this other story. We've been feeding it the local media." *You overconfident fool!*

"Yes, continue with it," he said, watching her eyes. "We had to act quickly and you did."

"Then, they aren't mutually exclusive?"

"Correct. The second story is about an underground water main leak. It created a cavern that is believed to have collapsed. An investigation will reveal that the collapse of the cavern was the root cause."

Courtney replied, "Nice. It will explain away any remaining grumblings in the seismic community, too."

"I know it's not perfect, but give me something other than a terrorist bombing or a nuke to explain the EMP with a seismic event and we'll publish that instead."

"Actually, sir, it covers all the angles. After a few days go by, the locals won't even remember it happened."

"Well—" he began.

"We could have the power company issue an apology and pass out a few free electronics to sweeten the deal. Though, I don't know a better way to cover it all," Courtney added. *You finally pull off a truly good suckup on your last day. Nice work, Agent Lewis,* Courtney thought. *Though, it will help if you stay and they make a big deal about the security guard's ear.*

"Well, all right then," the Chief said.

"I wonder if he figures this out the next—"

"This is the mag-field and resonance technology the DOD has spent billions on. When he solved the issues with his own device, he tripped over the recipe for it, too. We can't let him test it again. Clear?"

"Absolutely sir, you're crystal clear." Courtney knew she was fortunate the DOD had not stepped in already and cleaned everything out.

These events were painful for both sides and usually ended up in months of closed door negotiations. They were followed by some large deposits wired to shareholders' private, offshore accounts. Publicly, everyone knew that something had happened, but the spin doctors made sure that they never knew what. The DOD's reputation for costly coverups that often ended with casualties kept most from uttering a word in public. They could claim just about anything was related to 'National Security' and then it was hands off.

She took a deeper breath than she meant to, but was otherwise able to maintain composure. "Excellent, we'll be ready to clean up when the time comes." Courtney hoped he would leave them on the project for a little while longer, but knew she would have to make her move very soon.

"One more thing, there's a project down in Texas that we may need your team to take on," he said. "Someone is leaking information on NASA and JPL's Magnetospheric Multiscale mission project."

You only need twenty four more hours. Don't push back too hard, Courtney reminded herself. "Yes, I'm current on the MMS project. Someone got paranoid last year, so I spent two weeks reading hundreds of documents between JPL and other players. Anything that resembled NASA's magnetic portal monitoring satellite tech was fair game."

"Verdict?"

"They didn't have anything as promising as Mike and I was returned to my current assignment."

"The competing project by the two MIT dropouts was quite impressive."

"I agree, but Mike is creating electron diffusion X-points, while the rest of these folks want to hang out in orbit and wait for one to appear. I mean, come on, do we really have that much taxpayer cash to burn?"

"Don't be so cynical," he said.

"Mike's propulsion tech has a real world value. Hyper spacing down an unstable portal, that could put you next to the sun, or a random star somewhere, seems a bit less valuable." *You're too ignorant to realize Mike shifted space-time in his apartment with that low powered, version of his device, so why am I wasting my time?*

"You have to admit, it's pretty intriguing technology," he said.

"Sure, but watching over the MMS project is not going to get us where we need to go," Courtney said.

"Well, that's very difficult to know for sure."

"Even if it does expose dimensional anomalies, the MMS project doesn't do anything. They are still having trouble calibrating the four satellites' instrument arrays. After that, even if they find and document X-points, they aren't going to use them. It will take two or three years more, if not longer, before they'll take action." *Here it comes—you have a great point there Courtney.*

"Hmm. You make a good point there, Agent Lewis." The Chief looked toward his screen, but Courtney saw his eyes never focused on it. "I have something I need to address." He looked at her then nodded toward the monitor.

Bingo, he's stumped. "Oh, sorry, sir, I didn't mean to hold you up."

"Well, I'm glad we're on the same page, but ultimately, it isn't up to us," the Chief said, turning away.

Courtney noticed he was actually looking at his screen this time.

"Besides, we still have a little time on that other one. It seems their funding has dried up," he said.

Yep, you've reached your highest level of incompetence. I'm working right here, under your nose. I can read you like a book and usually get you to do what I want in thirty seconds or less.

"Dismissed," the Chief said, as he turned to face his monitor and began typing.

Courtney got up and walked out without uttering another word. *I'll show you dismissed.*

***

Sitting back in her chair, Courtney closed her eyes to rest as she waited on information from the teams.

What if you're crazy? You imagined it. You were young. That's what they'll tell you, but you know that's not true. Remember the war, bomb shelters and the bodies? The memories are too vivid. You know that was real and it's worth the risk.

She forced herself to remember her childhood. The decades of war had taken most of the men from the families she knew and many of her cousins had died in the fighting. When she reached the age of fourteen, she realized she would be old enough to be a champion's bride in a few years. She needed to do something to protect herself from the SAF warriors and from the Nazis. If she wasn't betrothed to someone who could protect her in the next year or two, she would have to be able to do it herself. Only a few of the young girls who tried before her had succeeded. It was the way of their culture. They married young and they died young, often before they reached the age of thirty.

She remembered the young Corporal who had her assigned to the Special Attack Forces Research and Development Division. She thought he might try to arrange to marry her. Thankfully, the new job had given her a glimpse of the freedom she had always desired. For the first few weeks at the lab, she thought it may work out for her. Everything changed when she volunteered to help test the crystal altar that was discovered in a captured base that summer of 1995. It was her last summer at home. She understood that one had to have strength of the soul to have victory against the evil of the Nazis. They were hell-bent on world domination and control. They capitalized on religious, financial and governmental means to achieve their global domination. They had repeated the Egyptian successes that were proven centuries before.

The altar was clear crystal and looked very old. It was ancient Sumerian most likely, even though the Egyptians had made their marks on it now. It was built for someone small, being five feet in length. Captured documents told of girls being able to see future events. The SAF had discovered that the Nazis had been using it experimentally with the young girls. They had been operating under the guise of making sacrifices to their gods. Hitler and the SS believed they had opened a window in time. They said it was a gift from the ancient German tribal gods Odin and Thor.

Lacking knowledge of the power source for the vibration exciters, the first SAF tests were done with low power. They assumed the ancients excited the crystal with chanting and music, but no one knew for sure. The Nazis had destroyed their operation procedures, so the first tests were shots in the dark.

Growing impatient and with SAF troops dying every minute, the decision was made to accelerate the trials.

Since Courtney had reported only slight effects at low power, they doubled it. The jump cost Courtney her whole world. The overwhelming vibration and noise immediately produced shadowy figures. They dressed differently, so she deduced they were somewhere deep in Nazi territory.

Courtney felt sleep overcome her and eased her head over to one side. As the resonation continued to increase in intensity, the vision became very clear. She could see the inside of a room. It was nighttime and there were strange decorations all around her. Without warning, everything became still. She was in a strange bed in that room. It smelled so clean and wonderful, she almost forgot how terrified she was. She lay there quietly, analyzing the smells, trying to understand what had happened. She heard loud footsteps thundering nearer; her hearing exaggerating every sound.

The door flew open and her light flicked on, "Dear Lord! Courtney? Are you OK? Is someone in here? We heard strange noises, voices and—Courtney? What happened to you? Your hair is short. Wait, you look dirty."

"Court, that's not nice."

"Danni, look at her."

They look like mom and dad, Courtney thought.

"I see her. Sweetie, what's going on?"

"I'll tell you what's going on—she snuck out tonight!"

"Court!" Danni barked. "Say something—talk to us sweetie —we want to help."

"Where am I? Did you bring me here? Or—" Courtney asked.

"You're home and of course we brought you here. Are you on drugs?" Court replied.

"Oh Court, seriously? She's fourteen!"

"Well…" he said.

"If I'm home, then why don't I know this place? And why do you have that funny accent?" Courtney asked.

"Your accent is a bit off too," he replied, with a distrusting look in his eye.

"What happened, sweetie? Tell us something." Danni reached out toward Courtney's face.

"Your hands and nails are too clean. My mom's hair is barely longer than my dad's, but yours is much longer. You look a lot like them, but I'm not falling for your trick!" Courtney closed her eyes and tried to fight off what she thought was a dream. Is this a Nazi trick? Or has something gone wrong with the experiment? When she reopened her eyes, nothing had changed and she felt her heart sink further.

Court reached out toward her.

"Don't touch me! Stay away, you Nazi impostors!" Courtney screamed.

"You're having a bad dream, or something," Danni said.

"You're not my mother! Now leave me alone!"

The rest of the night was a blur for Courtney. The disturbing events had taken their toll on her. She spent the rest of the night locked in the bathroom with the fake Court and Danni taking turns talking through the door. Finally, she collapsed from exhaustion. When she awoke, Courtney found herself back in the strange bed. Looking around in the daylight, she saw pictures of herself and other young girls. Sneaking up to the pictures, she was shocked to see herself looking back.

It can't be, can it? But she looks so much like me! How could this happen?

"Courtney? Are you awake?"

Courtney jumped and let out a yelp. "What are you trying to do to me?"

"Sweetie, I want to help. We know something is wrong, but we have no idea what to do," the impostor said, with tears in her eyes.

"How can you help me? This isn't my home and you aren't my parents!"

"You may have had a nervous breakdown. Did something happen to you at school?"

Courtney grabbed some shoes and tied the laces, refusing to speak.

"Court! I need you!"

Courtney heard footsteps pounding up the stairs.

"What are we supposed to do?" he asked.

"We're taking her to see that specialist my sister recommended."

He walked up cautiously, then took hold of Courtney's arm.

"Come on, we are going to see someone who can help you," he told the struggling girl.

Realizing she was no match for the man, Courtney

surrendered and immediately began plotting. *Save up your energy, then run when you get a chance.* "Fine, let's go then," she said, trying to sound calm.

They went out to the car and he loaded Courtney into the back seat. He watched her for a moment, but she didn't even glance back. *Stay calm for a little while longer. You can do it, you have to.*

"Buckle it," Court said.

Courtney reached down and latched her seat belt.

Court climbed in and began driving them away from the house.

This must be far inside Nazi territory. The cars and the houses are all so different. Why would these fools think I would fall for this?

As the car got up to higher and higher speeds Courtney slipped her seat belt off, coughing to cover up its noise. She noticed a large garbage truck lumbering toward them and saw her chance. *There it is, you can do it. Kill these Nazis before they kill you.*

Courtney dove over the seatback, past the man and yanked the steering wheel hard to the left. She felt her elbow hit his head as she pulled herself back, then she fell to the floor. The noise of the impact was deafening, then everything went black.

Why does it hurt so much? What happened to me?

"It's all right, sweetie, I'm here. It's me, Auntie."

Courtney recognized the voice of her dead aunt and fought to open her eyes. When she got them open and finally focused, Courtney was amazed to see her aunt. "What—happened?" she managed.

"You were in a car wreck, sweetie. You have broken ribs, bruises all over and some stitches on the right side of your head. It's nothing your hair won't cover."

"Where am I?"

"You're in County General Hospital, a few blocks down from your school," her aunt replied.

"School?" Courtney asked.

"Yes, sweetie and some of your friends are waiting to see you," she answered.

"My parents?" she managed to ask.

"Sweetie, not now," her aunt said.

"They're dead," Courtney whispered.

Putting her head back on the pillow, Courtney saw tears stream down her aunt's face. "But…I thought you died last year. In the war," Courtney said.

"Goodness, no, sweetie. The car wreck has your memories all jumbled up. The doctors warned me you could be confused when you woke up."

Courtney wanted to argue, but couldn't find the words.

"You need some rest now, please, we'll talk in the morning. Now close your eyes." Her soothing voice eased Courtney back to sleep.

Over the next few years, Courtney healed and eventually accepted her new existence. It wasn't until her freshman year at college when she started to grasp what had likely happened to her. That was where she first learned about the physics behind solar flares and wormholes. She read everything she could find, devouring her first class on quantum mechanics. She finally felt like she had a plausible explanation. It was unthinkable, but there was no other option. Someone had gone back in time and changed the course of history, or she had moved into a parallel universe. Either way, if it had been done, then it could be undone. It was at the moment of this revelation that Courtney dedicated her life to finding a way to return home.

* * *

Seven p.m. already? The janitors will be chasing me out of the lab again. Mike looked up and saw a cleaning cart rounding the corner by the elevator. *Yep, right on time.*

They were on a tight schedule and only allowed access to sensitive areas at very specific times. It annoyed Mike at times like this, but fighting procedures would only take him away from his project.

Seeing his favorite janitor, Mike felt the frustration leave him and opened the door for the kind man. "Hey George, how's your wife doing by now?"

"Evening, Dr. Devon, I mean, Mike," George said. "She's doing all right, considering the third miscarriage is only two months behind us."

"Did you call that specialist I found for you?" Mike asked. He was pleased George had remembered to use his first name.

"We went to see him the other day. I've been saving up since insurance only covers half," George replied, as he emptied the trash.

Mike winced when he heard those words. *You forgot to call and tell the doctor you were covering the rest!* "Right, I forgot about that insurance you have. Sorry."

As George walked the dust mop around the lab, Alec opened the door and grimaced at Mike.

"Thanks, George," Mike said, ignoring Alec. "Thirty seconds and I'll be out of here."

He had disliked Alec, the head janitor, since they first met. Alec was obnoxious, demanding and constantly complained at the cleaning staff. He felt his anger toward Alec spike. *Keep your mouth shut or I will rip off your head and use it for a soccer ball!* Mike cringed at his own morbid thoughts. He logged off his workstation and gathered up his things. "Thanks again, George. Have a good night."

"You, too, Mike."

Mike felt Alec's eyes staring at him as he passed, but neither said a word. He walked toward the elevator and his mind flashed to the empty evening ahead.

He had several relationships over the years, but none of

them quite measured up to *her*. After each of his failed relationships, Mike would pour himself deeper into his work. She had died many times while Mike helplessly watched the tragedy repeat. He told himself that even if she had existed, she was dead, but that didn't ease the pain. The girl he never knew had taken some of his heart and though he knew it made no sense, it haunted him.

Maria is right, you need to take a few days off and clear your head. This supposed obsession might fade if you actually had a life. Mike felt saddened by the thought. His mind shifted. *Why is it everyone says you should take some time off, yet each time it gets close, they ask you to postpone it?* As he stepped into the elevator, Mike remembered being in college and the excitement he felt. He loved meeting people and learning. It seemed like that was only yesterday, but now he was in his thirties and burning out. *What is it all for? Do you want to blow another ten years of your life so you can make a name for yourself?*

The bonuses were nice, but the money was piling up now and his life was flying by. Mike's boss, Arlen, told Mike that if this project was successful, there would be an obscene bonus. Mike knew Arlen thought this would motivate him, but it had the opposite effect. *Just wrap this thing up and you're free. Quit, take a month or two off, whatever.*

As Mike exited the elevator, the security guard reached out and took hold of his arm.

"Sir, I'm sorry but I've been instructed to detain you," he said.

"What?" Mike asked, his heart pounding.

"You have a phone call."

"Oh, I thought you meant—"

The guard looked at him for a moment, but Mike pretended not to notice as he walked toward the counter.

"Here you go," he said as he reached over and pulled the phone receiver up for Mike to use.

"Mike?" Gloria asked.

"I thought you left over an hour ago."

"I ran an errand for you. Your ringer must be off or something. I've been trying to call you since you got on the elevator."

"Oh, yeah, it's been acting funny since this morning when…well, I must have dropped it," Mike said. "So, are you about done up there?"

"Almost. I'm trying to get some of our paperwork caught up. There is a division review at nine in the morning," she said.

The elevator dinged behind him and Gloria called out, "I have something for you."

Mike turned and handed the guard back the phone. "Me?"

"Your car key," she said and dropped it into his hand. "She's waiting for you out front."

"Super! They got her all fixed up then?" Mike asked.

"He said it was something to do with the computer."

"Oh, they probably wiped my custom programming out then."

"He didn't mention anything about that," Gloria said, shrugging her shoulders.

"That's fine. Well, don't stay too late."

"If I'm still wearing these clothes when you get back, you'll know why," she said with a tired smile.

"Order dinner and charge it to me."

"Already did," Gloria said, then turned and headed back to the elevator.

Mike glanced over at the guard who was watching him.

"She's amazing," Mike said, loud enough for Gloria to hear.

"Yes, she is," Gloria called over her shoulder.

"She's single," Mike whispered.

The guard stared back at him without an expression.

"Great. Well, thanks for the help," Mike said. *And folks think the geeks are bad?* He walked away from the guard and out the front doors. Mike pushed the start button on his remote and the engine growled to life. Mike felt a twinge of excitement as he opened the door, then the smell hit him in the face.

"So, you got a full detail and an oil change," he said. Mike picked the tiny sticker from the windshield and closed the door. Touching the stereo buttons on his steering wheel, Mike noticed the new feel was back. "Wait a second, this isn't my—" He leaned forward and checked the seat for a small gouge made from a pen he left in his pants pocket one evening. "Never mind, Babe, it's you. Take me home."

* * *

Courtney was sitting at home on her couch, monitoring the feed from Mike's phone and car on her television.

I swear, he'd marry that stupid machine if it was legal.

As the silver sports car rolled away from the front of TAC, Courtney watched to make sure nothing was out of the ordinary. She toggled through the feed from the security cameras, as well as the cameras and computers on Mike's R8. Courtney then switched over to his apartment building and toured the surveillance there. If someone wasn't following or watching him, then she was. Jillian was declared safe, but Courtney didn't want her near Mike anyway.

Her phone rang and Courtney checked the number. "Hello?"

"I'm tying off before I head home," the specialist said.

"He's pleased with the car and everything seems fine. Thanks," she said.

"I'm guessing he'd pop a cork if he knew we put his seats, wheels and tires on a different car," said the agent.

"You have that right," Courtney replied.

"Though, it only showed three thousand miles until we tweaked it up to thirty-eight," he added.

"Wouldn't help. That was his baby," she explained.

"One of those—"

"Well, thanks again for your help today. You're free to go."

"Roger that," he replied and the line went dead.

Courtney checked the time and noted the whole project had taken less than twelve hours.

"Courtney, you did a fine job!" she sarcastically praised herself, knowing the Chief wouldn't. "Why thank you, sir, but I have to give the credit to the team."

Glancing at the GPS on Mike's car, Courtney realized that he was less than ten minutes from his apartment.

Plenty of time to get a quick shower before his workout, but I'd better hurry.

Some evenings Courtney would sit and watch Mike exercise. It wasn't to see his lean muscles ripple, though his rippled abs always caught her eye. It was during these times he let his guard down and she could see the whole Mike Devon in his face. Her instincts and intel told her he suffered like she did, and poured it into his workouts when no one was around. It made Courtney feel like she knew him better than anyone else. She felt a strange closeness to him that she would never allow to go beyond her occasional fantasies. Her plans had been far too important to allow personal interference. Now that everything was coming together, she was certain she made the right decision.

* * *

An exhausted Mike arrived home that night after eight. He grabbed one of the ready-made dinners Maria left in the refrigerator for him and put it in the microwave. When it was warm, he retrieved his notebook from his bedside table and went into the living room. Falling into his easy chair, he read through his most recent pages as he ate. He felt his eyes grow heavy. *Only close them for a minute,* he thought, but immediately dozed off.

He jolted awake. *They've come for it!* Mike flung himself to the floor and peeked around the chair.

"Good morning. Oops, I'm sorry sweetie, I didn't mean to —" Maria paused. "That must have been a scary dream!"

"No, I thought someone…" Mike stood up.

"Someone giving you trouble around the apartment?" she asked.

"Nothing like that, I thought I heard someone break in." Mike felt his heart slowing. "That's what I get for sleeping out here in my chair," he replied with a groggy smile. He got up and headed toward his bedroom. "I'll be out of the shower in ten."

Mike thought of Maria more like family than a housekeeper. She had cared for him since he had moved in, right out of college. She cleaned and cooked three days a week. Mike had once calculated it freed up about thirteen hours per week. She was well worth the meager cost and gave Mike the occasional scolding he needed. He had tried to give her raises more than once but she refused them.

"I'll have breakfast ready when you get out."

Mike rushed through his shower and returned as she was putting his breakfast on the counter.

"This looks great, Maria," Mike said. He picked up the plate and took a bite. "Thanks."

"Now you sit down," she instructed, pointing at the barstool.

Mike smiled and obeyed.

"Is there anything else you need me to do today?" she asked, as she wiped down the counter.

"My bedroom floor could use a mop. I was sick the other night and Jillian came to help, but it still smells funny in there," Mike said.

"Why didn't you call me sweetie? I would have come and helped."

"I couldn't call you for that. Besides, it was pretty bad," Mike winced at the memory.

"Your biggest fan would have gladly come to help," she said, patting him on the shoulder.

"Breakfast was excellent. You're too good to me," Mike smiled and got up from the barstool. "Off to work!" He put an arm around Maria's shoulder. "What would I do without you?"

* * *

Maria had retired from the FBI with twenty-seven years of service at age fifty-two. She wanted something to keep her busy until she was ready to fully retire, so she took a private security job with TAC. She was a specialist in finance and did most of her years from behind a desk, but had seen action once or twice per year. There were some perks TAC didn't tell Mike about and Maria was one. The monthly sweep for electronic surveillance equipment in his apartment was another.

She walked through the apartment with her cell phone out in front of her. Watching the screen as she meandered around, she made her way into Mike's room. Laying it down for a moment, she made his bed and straightened his alarm clock. Picking it back up, she walked over and closed the blinds. She dialed a number on her phone, then walked into the bathroom and closed the door.

"Any news for me?" the man on the other end asked.

Turning on the faucet, she answered quietly, "Looks like there are a few new entries. I'll send them in a few minutes."

"Excellent. What about the Chinese and the Americans?" he asked.

"I haven't seen the Chinaman snooping around since Mike found that bullet fragment. The American team could have done something and it would explain the bullet."

"You're still clean?" he asked.

"I'd like to believe they haven't figured me out. But, if that's the case, then why haven't they tried to bug him?" Maria asked.

"Bobby?"

"I'm still here," he replied, "re-reading your notes on that little Chinese character. He's the one that scares me. I think he's going to make a play for Mike."

"I agree. He could be working with the crew across the street, but I doubt he is," she whispered. "We should come up with an excuse for me to stay here for a week or two."

"Meet me at the cafe in one hour," Bobby said.

"I'll be there, sir." Maria hung up the phone. She made one last pass through Mike's apartment. She adjusted his blinds so the team across the street couldn't see in, then pretended to tidy things up.

At first, Maria thought only she was monitoring him. After Mike found the bullet fragment lodged between scarred books in his bookcase, Maria knew she was also his protector. From then on, she redoubled her efforts to protect him, knowing his life was in jeopardy.

If he ever finds out about all this, he'll never forgive you.

* * *

Bored and exhausted, Courtney sat in front of the four screens that made up the conference room's west wall. The systems were all running and flagging potential concerns to be reviewed. These were called *Potentially Valuable Data*, or *PVD*. It was being performed by the eleventh generation A.I. program, or *Eleven* as they called it. Eleven was good at weeding out chatter while collecting and prioritizing the rest. It had taken years to fine-tune its algorithms to understand the subtleties of speech and now it successfully used speech patterns and word choices to detect anomalies. These were flagged as PVD so a human could discern if the speaker was lying or passing hidden meanings. It saved agents countless hours every day.

The teams would review the PVD list each day as part of

their normal routine, usually first thing in the morning. Each of the team members would get a piece of the file from the previous day and it was easily manageable. They would then clean out any remaining fluff and return their portion of the file to the server. Data that was seen as *Operationally Valuable Data* was tagged *OVD* for further consideration. This data was often too technical or cryptic for the agents to understand themselves, but they knew their cases well enough to recognize OVD.

Courtney had audited team performance and was content that they caught the important details. Even still, she would often sit and watch the raw, live video feeds and Eleven's stream of PVD on Mike's case.

When she was certain she would not be interrupted, Courtney liked to zoom in on Mike's face and listen to his voice. She would watch his lips and eyes as they moved with the intonations of his voice. Her favorite moments were those when he was frustrated, especially by his personal failures. It was these times she could feel his desire to succeed. It was also when she learned how he would react under duress. It gave her additional insight into Mike Devon. Courtney knew she needed this understanding to interact with him, especially if he unlocked the true power of his technology.

At first, she was amazed that he could sustain twelve hour days, for weeks at a time. Later, he began working sixteen hour days and the entire team had to readjust their lives to keep up. Thankfully, he started taking one or even both weekend days off again and the team had some time to rest. Courtney was the only one who missed the weekends. These were the times when she could sit and watch him work, uninterrupted for hours at a time, just the two of them. She would laugh when he burned the back of his fingers on the soldering iron and feel his frustrations when his latest test went up in smoke. She occasionally caught herself offering him advice.

Courtney's thoughts drifted back to a time when Mike forgot to shut down the power supply and took hold of the power leads. She yelled at him that day, jumping out of her seat as he lurched back from the voltage coursing through his body. He fell backwards, onto the workbench behind him. Courtney's heart was pounding as she grabbed at her phone to call the security team a few floors below him. She was confused by the horror of telling her daughter—their daughter—her daddy had died. The vision was amazingly vivid. She watched on as his eyes blinked at the lights above him. When he rolled over on his side muttering to himself and laughing, she dropped the phone. Irritated at him for making such a dangerous mistake, Courtney went for a walk to calm down. Later, she convinced herself that the strange thoughts about a daughter were due to a lack of sleep. After all, it was ridiculous for her to have feelings for someone who did not even know her, much less dreams of a child.

Courtney opened her eyes.

It's too late to become attached to this place or anyone in it. Besides, you'll have to steal it from him someday. If he—or anyone else—gets in the way, they're expendable. You've either wasted the best years of your life, or you haven't. Stay focused, it isn't long now.

* * *

I think a speeding ticket would be acceptable this morning.

Mike tapped on his phone and sent Babe the command to start so she would be warmed up for the ride to work. One way to ease his anxiety was to hear the howl of the R8 and feel her acceleration in his chest. He could get completely through third gear, if he took the freeway and this morning called for it. Grabbing a hard shift and chirping all four tires, Mike was on and back off the freeway, in a matter of minutes.

"One hundred and forty on the way to work? That's a new record! Way to go, girl!"

Talking to his car was one of the things that had annoyed almost every one of his girlfriends, but Mike didn't care. He loved his car and what she could do. If someone didn't get it, that was too bad.

Forty minutes later, Mike was in the lab, excited to continue refining the system.

Some of the team were working on issues with the miniaturized, extremely high power supply the spud needed. They had to get the efficiency above ninety nine percent—a near impossibility. They vaporized thousands of dollars each week, but were only at ninety five percent. The ceramics, liquid nitrogen and hyperconductors were pushing the limits of modern science. Without the power supply pushing the levels required, the spud couldn't be proven.

Mike made a few changes and had the newly modified program loaded into the system within an hour. He moved into the hardened test lab and dialed the maintenance team.

"Guys, I'm going to be pulling some heavy bursts off HV-X after lunch today," he warned an unhappy technician. He was referring to the high voltage transformer that delivered 13,800 volts to their lab. "I'll make a few easy pulls this morning, but nothing major until later."

"Thanks, we'll call the control room at the plant," the tech said.

"I thought you guys needed to do something here on site," Mike said.

"Nope. Since our capacitor banks are offline, we have to warn the substation what you're up to."

"We aren't using that much power, why would you need to do that?"

"If you'll remember a couple of years back, before we had the cap-banks online? You browned out a thousand homes."

Mike could make out another voice in the background.

"Right. Larry just reminded me that you almost knocked a turbine offline twice before that," the tech said. "Why don't you call them yourself? Here's the number," he grumbled and read it off to Mike.

"Uh, OK. So, are you calling? Or is that my job now?" Mike asked, as he scribbled down the number.

"I suppose I will," the tech answered.

"Good answer," Mike shoved the phone into its cradle and exhaled. "Jerk."

Mike knew it wasn't the best time for it, since the local substation was heavily loaded at the start and end of each business day. The problem wasn't the amount of energy the propulsion system consumed, as much as it was the repeated bursts. He would wait until after nine tonight before any full power tests. That was when the power plant turbines went idle.

Mike turned on the lab recorder.

"Sonic pulse harmonizer drive trial fifty three."

The idea behind the SPHD, or spud as they called it, was to fire focused energy bursts from either end. These highly complex electromagnetic beams were nearly identical to the sounds he had played through his home system. The difference was they were replicated in both extremely low and high frequency, with numerous harmonic sets. Emitting the frequency sets in this way, through the platinum tipped focal points, created almost no audible sound. While this was occurring, the secondary field generators would create a high energy, magnetic pulse on one end and the opposite field on the other. This caused the first end of the spud to push toward the second end. The primary beams firing from each end of the spud kept it from spinning in space. It acted as an invisible cable for the spud to travel along. Mike believed the vacuum of space and its low gravitational forces would enable the spud to reach half the speed of light. Doing this in earth's atmosphere and fields required infinitely more energy.

This was due to field interference, natural insulation and friction.

Previous trials had been modestly successful, with the last trial being the best on record. The spud had not only moved, but it had moved with measurable force—two ounces. Mike needed to see something near a hundred pounds of force to prove it was commercially viable. So far, they had consumed massive amounts of energy and funding, with minimal results. He needed and expected to see an exponential rise in output like he had at home.

Set to the lowest level, Mike engaged the spud's newest power supply, using the modified program. It lifted off the rails, suspended by the invisible magnetic fields and moved toward strain gauge until it rested against it. The strain gauge meter moved.

"Yes! Oh…uh, the test is successful. Level one netted eleven ounces with no adverse temperature or vibration. Level two is deemed safe at this time. Power source switched to level two. The twenty five percent increase in power netted a two hundred percent increase in force. We are over two pounds, the gauge limit has been exceeded, or I would be more precise. Stepping back down. Power off. Noticed an anomaly when powering down. The gauge held for a few seconds after the power supply had fully drained." Mike's heart was pounding.

They'll be mad if you don't stop to tell them what you're up to.

He knew he had already gone too far, but any further would be inexcusable. Mike stepped out of the hardened test lab and fell in the first available chair. Through the glass he could see some of the team members scrambling toward him.

"I'm fine. Everything's good," Mike told Ray and Chilli, with a sheepish grin.

"What was that?" Ray asked.

"Well, we just had a bit of a breakthrough. The efficiency increase is significant. It was a ninety percent drop in consumption. I maxed out the two pound load cell with the power clear down on level two. I need to swap it out for a fifty pound cell before I try it again."

"So, the current power supply might be enough?" Chilli asked.

"It could be," Mike said, then filled them in.

"There was no trial authorization. We have to go tell Arlen before he rips your head off," Ray said.

Ray and Chilli were the power supply techs Mike had been working with for many months now. They pulled him up to his feet and rushed him out into the hallway. Their boss was going to be ecstatic, they all knew it. It was the news the team needed. They had all been making minor step improvements each month, but it was many months since they made a significant one. They hurried up one floor to deliver Arlen the news.

"Knock-knock," Mike said, as he tapped on the open door.

"Come in. I can tell from the stupid grins on your sidekicks' faces, that you have something exciting to tell me. Well? Let's have it."

Repeating the events, Mike tried to hold back anything that would seem dangerous. He didn't want anything to slow them down, but was sure Arlen would find a reason to.

"Wow," Arlen finally said. "The spud is operational then?"

He appeared overwhelmed by the news, which was not what Mike had expected at all. Arlen called up the video footage from the labs and found the video of Mike testing the spud. He watched it in regular speed, then half speed and then turned and stared at Mike.

Finally, after what seemed like a minute had gone by, Arlen exclaimed, "Mike, you did it, didn't you? This one's almost in the bag now! Lunch at Bella's, on me."

* * *

Courtney entered the main office building as her phone vibrated. She looked down at the screen and read the message.

Something big has happened, she told herself and rushed to the Chief's office as instructed.

The Chief was staring at her as she opened his door.

"He solved the issue with the spud's exponential rise in power consumption. He's harnessing gravity and magnetic fields, through synchronized resonation. All with minimal added energy. They're only days, or even hours away from completion," the Chief said.

Courtney showed a concerned reaction and gasped out loud, though she felt ecstatic upon hearing the news. This was possibly the most important turn of events in her life, since arriving in the USA.

"You're to make contact. Proceed as detailed in your contingency number twenty one," the Chief said, dropping the familiar packet on the desk.

She and the team had spent weeks developing twenty three contingencies. They had reviewed and rehearsed so that any of them could be implemented at a moment's notice. Twenty one was one of her favorites, though she lead the team to believe she despised it.

"Refresh your memory and get out of here. You'll be going to lunch at that Italian restaurant downtown that Mike loves."

"Bella's," Courtney replied, "Roger that."

Courtney started to feel nervous. She planned for this moment for several years and quietly hoped that one of the boy meets girl plans would catch the Chief's eye. *Boy and girl are finally going to meet.*

* * *

"Do you know what TAC is going to do? Will they let us keep working on it? Will this go to NASA, or Lockheed's Skunkworks?" Ray asked.

"Down boy. This may or may not go any further for us.

You know the big boys decide that. I know you want to keep developing this, but we have to get a trial proposal written up and submitted to the brass ASAP. Plus, we need to take a step back to recheck everything before you go any further.

"That was my fault Arlen, but it wasn't that serious," Mike said.

"Don't kid yourself, that stunt you pulled was very dangerous. You risked the lives of more than a dozen people on a hunch. Look, this is awesome stuff, but we don't fully understand the recent changes you've made."

Ray leaned forward and opened his mouth to speak, but Arlen didn't let him.

"I know it's resonating gravitational and magnetic fields. I know it's a magnetic field that pulses and emits plasma like solar flares, so don't even start." Arlen's face turned serious.

Ray sat back in his seat.

"You weren't going to—" Mike started to ask.

"Yes, he was." Arlen looked at Ray who nodded in silence. "This report better have some details and I'm not talking schematics either. You all know what I mean. Go over the system, give me a test plan and make some reasonable predictions of the results."

No one said a word.

"Guys, I'm dead serious about this. Mike, we need to get the patent boys back in the loop first thing tomorrow. I'm going to try to keep this thing in house for a while, but it may be gone by morning. You could go with it, but it's out of our hands at this point. I don't like it, but that's the way it works."

"Got it. Sorry sir, I got ahead of myself. It won't happen again," Mike said.

"Yes, it will. You geniuses have a way of getting yourselves into trouble and that's why I'm relevant." Arlen laughed. "Enough of this serious business, let's get some drinks on the way."

"Don't look now, but that babe is scoping you out," Chilli

said to Mike.

"What? We're talking about a scientific breakthrough that will change our careers and that's your observation? I need to get you guys out of that lab more often, before it's too late," Mike teased.

"No, I'm serious, there are two women over there by the bar. The hot one has her eye on you," Chilli said, indicating her position with his eyes.

"Uh, Mike, he's right. Would you go get me a whiskey sour, or do I have to go myself?" Arlen asked.

"Aye-aye captain, you're the boss," Mike said, with minimal interest. He stood up and placed his napkin on the table. He turned around and nonchalantly scanned the room for the siren his comrades had noticed. When he saw the gorgeous brunette and her stunning blue eyes, Mike paused. He started to move toward the bar, but almost forgot to take a step and stumbled over his own feet.

"Strike one," he mumbled under his breath. *Where's the finger, come on, you're thirsty...excellent! No ring. You girls...no, ladies...I noticed you ladies...nope, that isn't going to work. Dang, I can't have a second strike this early on. I'd better go to the bar first.*

At the bar, he ordered a whiskey sour and sat down to wait.

"Hey there, a bit early for drinking don't you think?" The blue-eyed girl broke the ice for him. "Emily," she said, as she reached out.

Mike felt his eyes blink twice. *Strike two.* He reached out awkwardly and took her hand, "Uh, Mike."

"You sure about that?"

Go for the honest approach. Chuckling, he said, "Yeah, pretty sure it's Mike." *Last chance.* "I was trying to figure out what I could say to you that some schmuck hadn't already tried."

"Oh?"

"Then you came over here and caught me with absolutely nothing in the queue. I know you know, since I had the ol' *deer in the headlights* thing going on there for a minute," Mike said, managing to relax a little.

"Well you did it. That one was unique."

"Really?" Mike pretended to be surprised.

"Oh, yeah. No hormone flushed schoolboy has ever tried that line on me before. So, you're a real man after all?"

Single, beautiful, an amazing smile—I wonder what's wrong with her. "I sure hope so." He returned the smile. "So, I need to wrap up the meeting at my table. Can you ditch your friend and talk a bit, in say, twenty minutes?" Mike heard himself say. *Geez, I told you not to push your luck! She's not the kind of girl to sit around and wait.*

"Uh, yeah. Yeah, I'd like that, Mike. I have about an hour before I need to be at the office," she explained.

"Then I'll see you in ten," Mike said and stood up with Arlen's drink.

"Ten it is," she said and walked toward her table.

* * *

Terry and Bill were sitting in the surveillance support van, monitoring Courtney's conversation.

"That is one easy mark," Terry said with a smirk.

"Poor guy's getting played, but thinks he's the player." Bill chuckled. "He's way out of his league."

"That cute, blue-eyed monster can chew 'em up and spit 'em out," Terry mused.

Their radio started blinking to warn them of voice traffic. Terry reached over, muted his mic to Courtney and keyed the other mic. "Go ahead."

"We have a possible ten seventy nine in progress over on Wabash and Lake," came back the dispatcher.

"Are you sure we should be involved?" Terry asked.

"Affirmative. The team is forty five minutes out and there are foreign dignitaries on scene."

"Roger that, en route, ETA nine minutes." He released the button. "Unbelievable! Call her and tell her we have to roll," Terry said, as he scrambled up to the driver's seat. "She stays. No matter what, she finishes this or the Chief will kill us all."

* * *

Her phone buzzed on the table and Courtney looked to see Bill's cell number.

"Hi, Mom, what's up?"

"Nothing more than a little bomb threat up the road. We had to pull out, but we'll be back as soon as we can," Bill said.

"Oh, I should come to the doctor with you, Mom," she said, making sure to sound concerned.

"Nah, it's basically traffic duty. We'll be back as soon as we get free."

"OK, but you'd better call me if something comes up," said Courtney.

She put her phone down about the time her companion's phone rang.

"Uh, huh. Yep. OK, I'll be over there in a few minutes," said the fellow agent next to Courtney. "You're staying then?"

"Unless I get told otherwise."

"OK, thanks for lunch," she said and walked off.

Courtney felt a twinge of regret as she watched her coworker walk out of the restaurant. *You're in deep now.* She stood up, walked over to the bar like nothing was wrong and ordered an orange juice. *You have a tight window, make the most of it.* Courtney glanced over at Mike's table, smiled, then looked toward the bar. She watched the men get up and Mike headed toward her. Part of her wanted to stick to the rehearsed routine and savor the early moments of a friendship, but she was annoyed with herself for entertaining the thought.

Mike smiled as he approached.

Good, he's nervous.

"Hiya, Emily, I didn't expect to see you in here," he said.

"Yeah, what a coincidence," she replied. *There's that smile again.* "I know this will sound crazy, but it's not a coincidence," Courtney said quietly, motioning him to follow her to the table.

"It's not?" Mike asked.

"No, it's not," she said, as she sat down.

Mike sat down across from her, looked into her eyes and Courtney was struck with a strong sense of déjà vu.

"Mike, we don't have much time, so I'll be brief. I need you to smile from time to time for the security cameras. There are people watching us and they would like to interfere with your project."

"Wait, you—" Mike began.

"So, you'll know I'm for real, there is a bomb threat about a mile away from here right now. You'll hear about it on the news later today. It'll turn out to be nothing more than a threat text, traced to a throwaway cell phone."

"A bomb threat?"

"Yes, but hold on to that for now. I have reason to believe that the spud is a much more capable device than you realize. Smile for me," she smiled at Mike, but she knew her eyes did not. "Thanks, but that wasn't very convincing."

"You said spud?"

"Yes. You've tapped into something that is both very important and very dangerous. Neither you, nor I, want this thing to fall into the wrong hands," she said.

"Who do you work for?"

"I work for an agency that keeps folks like yourself safe. We handle things in and out of our borders with a great deal of anonymity. Smile again for me, Mike."

Mike forced a smile.

"Do it like your life depends on it." Noticing the veins in Mike's neck, she said, "Relax as best you can and listen carefully.

Your research will be out of your hands in less than forty eight hours. You need to be sure you save a copy of the important data for yourself. Keep it safe, there are some who will do anything to get it. Smile again, Mike, you're looking disturbed."

Mike grimaced. "Yeah? Well I am. You seem to know quite a bit about me and yet I have never seen you before."

"That you know of." She went on, "I don't want you to tell me anything. Besides, I already know basically everything you might want to hide. What I *do* want is for you to be ready to lose access to everything that pertains to your new discovery. Imagine what that would be like, then make a detailed list of everything you need. Keep it in the vault at work if you like, but don't keep it with the rest of your files. Do not—"

Courtney noticed Mike's face had fallen somber again. "Smile again, Mike, we're still having fun here."

"Loads," Mike said.

She smiled at him once more. "Follow my rules. Do not act suspicious. Do not ask anyone about me. Do not mention our conversation to anyone. You're under level one surveillance. We get your garbage and laundry first."

"How many others are working with you?" he asked.

"Several, but I don't want them to know we're having this conversation, which is why I texted in the bomb threat." Courtney took his hand and slipped a small, cheap cell phone into it. "From this. Now your prints are on it, but mine don't seem to be." She rubbed smooth fingertips across the back of his hand and saw a startled look flash across Mike's face. "Now, go into the men's room, read the bomb threat text I sent, then delete it. Mike? Are you following this?"

"Yes—yes, I suppose so."

"Good. Next, there's a combination to a padlock on the storage unit next to yours, under the phone's battery. Remove the note with the combination and other directions. If you can't memorize it, keep it in your wallet. Third, individually wrap the cover, battery and phone in tissue paper and flush them, one at a time. You don't want any evidence to turn up, now do you?"

Mike stared at her.

"Still with me, Mike?"

"I sure am," he said in a wry tone.

"You think I'm nuts, I get it. But once you get home tonight, hear the news and peruse the storage locker—well, you'll feel a little better then. I'm going way out on a limb here for you, Mike. This will end my career and both of our lives, if you screw this up." She leaned in close and kissed him on the cheek. "I promise you, this will be the ride of your life." She grinned widely at Mike's boyish blush.

"Well, I sure hope you're right. But from where I'm sitting right now, it seems like a bad dream."

"I know. Hang in there for a few hours and it'll all start to make sense. I promise. Besides, I'm your biggest fan." She chuckled after using Maria's line.

"What if I don't buy in?"

"You think I'm delusional and even a bit scary, but you've only seen my good side so far." Noticing Mike's expression change, Courtney added, "I can read minds, too." *That wiped the smug grin off his face.* "Oh, yeah, one more thing that may help you to believe my outlandish story. Remember that little chunk of lead you found in your bookcase? That got lost one evening when we bagged and tagged a Chinese national in your apartment. He was with the *Guo an bu* or the *Quing bao bu*, their version of the CIA and DIA."

Courtney watched Mike's eyes dart around, then fix on an imaginary spot. *There you go...*

Mike very thoughtfully said, "It *was* a bullet, wasn't it? I remember that well. What I don't remember, however, was you being there."

The look in his eyes changed and Courtney didn't like it.

Before she could answer, he asked, "So, you work for the

SAF then, Emily?"

The grin on Mike's face infuriated Courtney. It was as if she had forgotten her training for a moment. She just stared at Mike, forcing herself to hold back the anger.

"Deer in the headlights, Emily." Mike jolted her back with his smart remark.

Change the subject, you're letting him get to you. No one gets to you. "What do you know about that? You think you're smart? Are you trying to work me? Man, you are brave or crazy if you think you can play in my league." *You're losing it, Courtney. Get hold of yourself!*

"I guess I'll take that as a 'yes'. Do you have one of those weird swords as well?"

She remained silent and focused on regaining her composure. She held up one finger when Mike opened his mouth to talk and he obediently closed it. *He knows more than you thought. Get him on your side now or this is going to blow up.*

"My real name is Courtney Danielle Lewis. I was named after both of my parents who are with the *Special Attack Forces*, or *SAF*. Well, *were* with them, in the intelligence division. I briefly worked as an assistant for the SAF in research and development. I can't tell you anything more because I haven't been there, nor seen my parents, since I was kidnapped at age fifteen." Courtney felt her eyes burn slightly.

"Now that was honesty." Mike reached out, took her hands in his. "I'm glad you're being truthful with me now. And, I'm very sorry about what happened to you. What a horrible thing to go through and at such a young age."

Perfect response, but is he working me now? Why can't I control my feelings?

Mike's concern almost brought tears to Courtney's eyes and she realized he had lowered her wall. She felt as if she had awakened, as if a weight had been lifted, but she also felt vulnerable. Courtney had not discussed her parents or the SAF for many years and talking about them now brought back an unwanted flood of emotions. She fought back the feelings, knowing they jeopardized her opportunity to put things right. Everything she did was for one reason, to return home.

Implementing her plan had about a sixty five percent likelihood of ending in death. Not implementing it resulted in guaranteed failure to return home and help free her country. Based on her instincts and Mike's psych profile, she knew he would never trust her again if he caught her lying. She also knew she could not give him much latitude or he would flounder.

"What exactly is the SAF, Courtney?" Mike asked.

"It used to be a large, global group that fought the powers bent on world domination. I don't know if it even exists anymore."

"I've never heard of it," he said.

"Correct and you shouldn't have. Mike, you need to call me *Emily*."

"I'd like to help you, but you have to be straight with me from here on out, or I'll take my chances with the authorities."

"Do you believe they have good intentions?" she asked.

"I think some will weaponize my device, but I'll die before I let it fall into the wrong hands.

"You didn't want to create a weapon?"

"No, I wanted to make intra-stellar travel possible for everyone. I don't think these hands want to make a weapon either, but I'm not sure about that yet," he said as he turned her palms up.

As he ran his fingers over the smooth coating on her hands, Courtney wished she could feel the touch with him.

"Trust but verify. I like that in a man," she said, looking down at their hands, then back up at Mike. "I don't want it for a weapon, but I can't tell you anything more. Not yet."

"Can't? You mean won't."

"Look, even if I did tell you, you wouldn't believe me. It's better to leave it where it is, for now. The note and storage locker won't be much of a surprise at this point. I've stashed things in there that we may need if this thing goes south. I've also given you several sets of instructions, with contingencies, so we can work together."

Courtney squeezed Mike's hands then let go and sat up in her chair. "I have to go now. They'll be back for me anytime. Go to the men's room and take care of the phone. We'll be in touch later tonight."

"OK, you have me for twenty four hours, but I'm going to need a lot more after that."

"Understood," Courtney said and turned to walk toward the front door. She noticed a table past the front door. She smiled as she envisioned sitting there with Mike and the little girl for dinner. Once again Courtney felt herself jolt out of a trance.

There is no little girl! That never happened! You're working hard and spending too much time watching him. It's messing with your mind and causing these emotional reactions. Focus, you're almost there.

Courtney stepped out into the sunshine and dialed Bill's number. She could feel herself return as the seconds ticked by.

"Hey Bill, I'm out now. Should I come your way?"

"Nah, it's a false alarm. Besides, there's over a hundred people working the scene already."

"Roger that. I'll head back to the office and see what our boy is up to."

"Got it. We'll see you there in a bit."

Courtney sat down in her car and turned the key.

Probably the last time I'll be safe to do that.

Arlen let Chilli and Ray off the elevator at the third floor then continued to his office on the fourth. When he opened the door to his cherry-adorned quarters, he found one of the trustees, R. David Chase, sitting at his conference table with Bobby, the chief of security.

"Mr. Chase, Bobby, to what do I owe this pleasure?"

Mr. Chase grumbled something under his breath but didn't turn his gaze from the window.

"Let me rephrase that. Judging by your demeanor, Mr. Chase, it appears we have something very serious to discuss?"

Bobby's presence added weight to the severity of the visit and it made Arlen uneasy.

Still looking out the large window, toward the landscaped parking lot, Mr. Chase began, "We have come to understand that Mike's team made serious headway today."

You're going to take a hit on this one. Arlen sat down in his chair. "Yes, they did, sir. The guys are writing everything up as we speak."

"How could that be? There is no record of any such trials approved for today. Were the tests conducted without following protocol?"

"I didn't know I needed to get the board involved for simple trials." *That was pushing it.*

"I suppose it could have been innocent enough, if your team hadn't immediately disappeared for over an hour."

"Sir, I can—" Arlen began.

Turning to glare into Arlen's eyes, Mr. Chase continued, "I didn't pause to hear you talk."

The room was silent while Arlen returned the gaze. *A stare down? After everything I have done for this company and he treats me like this?*

Mr. Chase went on, "We are in this for over fifty million dollars and it's climbing every day. You were burning thousands of dollars every day in failed tests, so we agreed you would follow this new protocol, that *you* designed! So, without clearance, you run a test that could have cost us millions and when it pays off you go out for lunch?"

The team screwed up, he's right. Damage control today—Mike's bonus tomorrow. "Sir, you're absolutely right. We did make mistakes today. You hired me to keep unique individuals motivated and on task. That requires a great deal of thought and finesse. It seems that in my drive to deliver, I gave the team a bit too much slack and I acknowledge that. We ask for a few hours to gather our thoughts so we can document and deliver this monumental breakthrough to you and the other trustees."

"I didn't come here for an apology, or a sales pitch, Arlen," Mr. Chase said as he looked back out the window.

"The SPHD really works sir and we are anxious to show it to you. Mike had an idea and tested it, completely underestimating the outcome. He already apologized to me for his mistake and not taking the time to fully analyze the potential." *It's on Mike now and Chase is coming around; you might get a promotion out of this after all.*

Turning to stare at Arlen for several seconds, Mr. Chase appeared to have calmed slightly.

"I want to have a chat with Mike, alone," he said firmly.

"I will have him up here within an hour." Arlen's confidence welled up.

"Now. Call him in here now," Mr. Chase demanded.

"Well, you see, sir, we were at lunch and there was this attractive young lady, so Mike stayed at the restaurant for a few extra minutes. He'll be here shortly."

David Chase turned toward Arlen and growled, "Describe her."

Here we go again, Arlen thought, trying to hide his irritation. "Maybe five-eight, long, auburn hair and blue eyes. Why?"

Bobby tossed a picture on the table. "Maria snapped this a while back. It was taken at the rear entrance of the building across the street from Mike's apartment. She caught a glimpse of the lady a few times, but this is the only picture she's been able to get. This lady seems to come and go at different times, from different directions and changes her appearance regularly. The only reason Maria caught on was that women kept slipping in after dark, through the back alleys. Turns out to be one woman—one *cagey* woman."

"The clothes and hair are all wrong." Arlen curled his finger and laid it over the lady's hair. His chest sank as he focused on her face. "I think that's her."

Mr. Chase screamed, "You fool! Are you truly that stupid?" Spit flew from his mouth. "She's a blasted professional!"

"This is Bobby's world, not mine, I'm a—"

"You're a worthless fool, that's what you are!"

That tirade even caused Bobby to twitch. Just keep quiet or you're out on the street, Arlen told himself.

Bobby said, "Maria made a Chinaman casing Mike's place a few months back. We were watching for him to make a move and when he did, another group stepped in. These people were pros, stationed across the street from Mike's and armed to the teeth."

"How long—" Arlen saw Mr. Chase glaring at him and stopped talking.

"The same people have leased the place for two years now, but we never noticed them before. This is a dedicated group with serious funding. I mean silencers, multiple operatives. They killed a Chinese attaché to the embassy and no one makes a peep? Arlen, they brought in a professional cleaner, for crying out loud."

Arlen felt the blood rush from his face. "Who are these people? Wait, are we in danger as well?"

Bobby replied, "It reeks of the feds to me."

A furious Mr. Chase interjected, "The problem with that theory is Uncle Sam gets first right of refusal on any and all technology TAC develops. The government wouldn't steal this from us, they don't care how much of the taxpayers' money they waste!"

Bobby went on, "This was the absolute worst time for you guys to deviate from protocol. Now Mike is AWOL and possibly being forced to spill his guts to one of our competitors, or even worse. Are you getting it now?"

"Enough!" yelled Mr. Chase as he rose from his chair and stormed toward the door. "Bobby, take this idiot with you and get Mike back here, if it isn't already too late!" He yelled, then flung the door open so hard it struck the stop and shook. He stood with his outstretched arm pointing down the hall. Bobby and Arlen hurried through the door, each trying to get through before the other.

"If he does not return to work by morning, you can kiss your sorry—"

Arlen was pleased he made it past Mr. Chase first but let Bobby lead the way toward the elevator. Neither of the two men said a word on their descent. When the doors opened at the executive garage, Arlen asked, "Yours or mine?"

"We'll take your company car," Bobby said.

"They haven't gotten you a car yet?"

Arlen could tell by Bobby's silence that he had accomplished his goal, but he held back a grin.

As soon as both car doors shut, Arlen looked over at Bobby. "Is there anything showing up on the tracker?"

"Tracker?" Bobby asked.

"Look, I know you have the ability to see where any TAC employee phone is, at any given time. I also know that folks up the food chain had vehicle tracking systems installed on all company cars and a few *key* personnel too. Well, Mike is key to this organization so pull up the tracker utility on your phone so we can go get him."

Arlen knew more than he should, but the 'big boys' weren't the best at keeping secrets, so it shouldn't have been much of a surprise. Bobby handed his smartphone to Arlen and the tracker was running already. It showed Mike still at the restaurant. Arlen had tried calling him twice already and tried again as the BMW roared out of the facility.

"Still no answer. Do you really think something happened to him?" Arlen asked. "No, wait, he's moving." Arlen's eyes were glued to the screen. "He's heading this way. Pull into that gas station, right there."

Bobby did as he was told and they silently watched the little dot on the screen coming up the road for nearly a minute.

Arlen looked down the street and saw Mike's car. "There he is now."

As the R8 rolled by, they recognized Mike's profile through the tinted windows. Both of the men let out a sigh.

"Wow! You and Chase had me going!"

"Yeah, well something's up, so don't get complacent yet. We were just plain lucky, this time," Bobby fired back.

"That probably wasn't even the girl in the picture," Arlen said.

"We'll see about that, but for now we treat her like she is. No more unnecessary risks, Arlen."

Arlen thought about making another comment, but changed his mind. *Mike is in for a rude awakening.*

* * *

Courtney received a message as she stepped onto the elevator. *Conference ASAP—Marjorie.*

Bill and Terry were just leaving the scene of the bomb threat with their two backup teams, so it was either one of the analysts who was watching Mike remotely, or Mike himself. There would have been a welcoming party in the garage if they were on to her already.

There's no way they're on to you, so get in there and wrap it up.

The Chief, Bill, Terry and the analysts' supervisor were in the conference room when she walked in.

"Hey guys, glad you made it back," Courtney said to Terry and Bill. She felt her senses heighten as she casually watched for hints on their faces.

"You didn't miss a thing," Terry raised an eyebrow.

"So, bring me up to speed," said Courtney as she sat down.

"There's a big to-do over at TAC and they started to move on Mike. They're very concerned about some girl he encountered at lunch. Sound familiar?" the Chief asked. "They have assigned two, individual freelancers to shadow him, on top of his existing security."

Courtney asked, "Are they any good?" *Looks like I still have the upper hand.*

"One is a retired spec-ops, counter-intel specialist from our beloved Rangers. He won't miss our nighttime ops, much less daytime. They already found the nest across the street from his apartment, so we had to run a diversion and strip it. No boots on the ground. Period. We go one hundred percent remote now and by that, I mean utilize existing systems only, none of our own hardware. Absolutely none. I'm not going to have any dead agents *or* freelancers until I give the order."

Courtney synchronized her facial expressions to the Chief's tone as she thought about what Mike might be doing. She picked up a pitcher of water from the center of the table and poured a glass, trying to distract the others slightly.

"This technology has matured to the point it is nearly out of our hands. We have to keep Mike alive and the data secure, remotely, for a day or two while the extraction is prepped. Your faces are known, so you're all confined to your offices when you're on duty." He pointed at Courtney, Terry and Bill. "Do any of you think there is any gray area you want clarification on?" he asked, looking around the room.

Courtney felt her head shake 'no' slowly. *He's not leaving any wiggle room; the time line for the extract must already be decided. Mike will be pulled out soon—maybe tomorrow?*

"No questions then? Well good. You've all done outstanding work so far. I could not have asked for anything more. Remember, the next few days are key to our success. If we fail now, the last two years are in the garbage."

The room was silent as the thought sank in.

"On a more positive note, everyone gets two weeks off and a ten percent bump into their 401K when we are officially off the case, providing it ends successfully. Now, go back to your desks and keep yourselves sharp."

As they filed out of the room, each of the agents appeared to have a renewed interest in the operation.

Courtney quickly reassessed the threats they posed to her. She felt a smile try to cross her face. *Nah, they're too far behind now. Just stick to the plan.*

***

Mike sat down at his desk and immediately logged in to his PC to check the local news for an update. The radio had been vague, but he knew details would be coming out soon. An aerial video of city buildings was rolling by and Mike read the caption, "Bomb threat made from nearby cell phone!"

Mike jumped as the door opened beside him.

"Hey Mike, we need to talk. Are you all right?" Arlen asked.

"Sorry, you guys spooked me!"

"You're scared of us?" Bobby asked.

"No, of course not. There was a bomb threat in town just now. Makes me nervous, that's all."

Mike saw Bobby and Arlen exchange a quick glance. *They know something.* He felt nauseous as his heart pounded in his chest.

"You sure you're all right?" Arlen asked. "You don't look like it."

"No, I'm fine. I mean, yes." Mike heard his voice waver. *Calm yourself down!*

"Good," Bobby said. "So, it seems we haven't been clear enough about security protocol. With today's events and all, we feel we need to review some things with you."

That sounded rehearsed, Mike thought, forcing himself to relax more. *This is not a coincidence, right after meeting her.* "Sure, where should we go?" he asked.

Both of the men answered, "My office."

"We'll use my conference room," said Bobby, looking at Arlen.

"Right, that would be better," Arlen agreed.

Arlen playing second fiddle to Bobby? They know. Mike's stomach turned.

Bobby turned and lead the way while Arlen waited for Mike to pass.

What do they know? Mike's mind raced. *Wait! Maybe she was a test to see if I could be trusted? No, that's ridiculous. They wouldn't do something like that, especially outside the building.* He followed Bobby, noticing how awkward it felt to walk. *She was worried about the security cameras. Maybe she got caught and her boss called TAC?* Mike noticed the door to the stairwell and felt himself being drawn to it. *She was so careful with her expressions and posture, though. Maybe it was me? Did I give it away?* Mike followed Bobby into the elevator and Arlen joined them.

The video will look like I was innocent—I am innocent!

Mike forced himself to stop thinking about all of the possibilities. After all, the worst they could do was fire him. Mike was able to relax a little as they stepped into the hall of the executive offices. He knew Bobby had an office up here, but was unaware just how extensive Bobby's piece of the organization was. There were several assistants, each with an office of their own and at least two conference rooms.

Maybe they would do something outside, he thought to himself. *If there's a mirror on the wall.* Amused at the silly thought, Mike smiled, until he crossed the threshold and saw video cameras in each corner of the room. *They are far more capable—*

Trying to break the tension, Mike said, "Wow, what a great place you have up here Bobby. I didn't realize they took such good care of you."

"Thanks. So, who was the girl at Bella's today?" Bobby asked, his eyes focused on Mike's.

Bobby did not beat around the bush, ever. Mike thought back to all of the times they had joked about Bobby and how seriously he took his job. *Not so funny now, is it?* "Yeah, well I guess I'm not so sure why you're asking that, but her name is Emily. Nice girl, some sort of office professional, white collar type here in town. I just met her today so I haven't filled out the security contact sheet on her." All of the annoying security measures he had endured at TAC were starting to make more sense now.

"When are you going to see her again?" asked Bobby, not taking his eyes off Mike.

"Not sure—she was a bit too interested. I think she figured I had money. It can get in the way at times."

"Oh?" Bobby said.

"Maybe she or her friend saw us drive up? Or maybe they saw my watch and were just digging for gold," Mike suggested.

He lifted his Swiss made, Richard Mille RM208, diver's watch. Mike knew Bobby had noticed it before and was curious enough to ask the brand when it first showed up on his wrist. Bobby was visibly jealous of Mike and Mike hoped it would give him an edge now. *Why doesn't he look up from that stupid phone?*

"Did she mention the watch, Mike? Because, it seems a bit far-fetched to me. I think she had other things on her mind."

They could have had someone watching security cameras, or maybe from the street, through the glass in the front. Everything you give them has to fit any video they might get, so keep it simple. "Actually, she did hold on to my hands at one point. Felt a little awkward, too."

Bobby watched his phone a little more closely with each question.

He doesn't seem distracted—what is he watching? Video from lunch? Mike realized he was letting his imagination get the better of him.

"So, no second date?" Bobby kept looking down at his phone.

Mike looked to Arlen who just stared at Bobby. *He looks like a pawn in a chess game.* It was a new look for Arlen. Mike had new insight into the limits of Arlen's power and the depth of Bobby's. "Nothing planned, but I gave her my number. I needed to get back to work, so I cut it a little short for today. And, if I don't get back to it, we won't have anything to guard."

Mike felt himself twitch when Bobby leaned forward, but noticed Bobby's phone had tipped slightly. *He has a camera zoomed in on my face!*

"Well, genius, that pretty blue eyed, auburn-haired cutie you met today is definitely white collar. She works in corporate espionage and is trying to steal a lot more than your precious watch! You'd better watch your back and your front, because we won't be making any exceptions to our disciplinary policy if you screw up again! Do I make myself vividly clear to you?"

"Absolutely. Yeah, *vividly* clear. Do you have some additional security to help me out? This whole thing is starting to make me uneasy." Mike hoped he sounded sincere, but he felt his loyalty to TAC had all but vanished.

"Don't worry about security. That's my job. You do your job. We've already stepped things up a notch, so you don't have to worry about anything but your own behavior."

They are active outside of the building!

"Understood. So, are we done then?"

Arlen spoke up for the first time, "You can go back down now."

Mike left the interrogation room feeling like he had just been punched in the stomach.

I have a bad feeling about this—

✳ ✳ ✳

After Mike left, Bobby and Arlen walked into Bobby's personal conference room. Mr. Chase was waiting for them, watching the replay of the feed from the conference room.

"Well gentlemen, I saw what your *Hal 9000* had to say about his story, but I want to hear your thoughts," he demanded.

Arlen knew he was poking at Bobby for the large investment in the 'Athena' system.

"Using the *Hal 9000* as you put it, my team has dissected the video from the interview and processed it through Athena," Bobby began.

On the right side of the video being displayed was a four part graph from the lie detector system which monitored nervousness, tone fluctuations, eye movement and thermal data to provide statistical analysis of a subject. It was the latest and greatest interrogation analysis system on the security market, requiring a license to own and operate.

"They also retrieved and processed the security video from the restaurant," Bobby explained. "They were able to corroborate every one of Mike's statements with imagery from the, albeit average quality, video. He was nervous, we all could see that, but he didn't seem to tell any serious lies."

"And *your* thoughts?" Mr. Chase demanded.

Bobby took a deep breath, as if to calm himself, then answered, "I think the girl is a plant and the same girl Maria photographed, but I'm not certain if she's government or private. I'm leaning toward government at this point. That whole group across the street from Mike was very professional."

"I agree. Continue." Mr. Chase continued to stare at Bobby.

"Well, I think Mike is innocent, for the time being at least. He did not lie to us, not that my gut, or the Athena system could detect. The thing we noticed was that he appeared to have several reactions that didn't fit her gestures. She was leaning in and touching his hands, so that could explain it, but the guy is used to being hit on from time to time, by some fairly attractive ladies I might add," Bobby said. "They'd like to keep Mike around, but he's no longer *critical* to the success of this project. We've brought on two private specialists, some of the best in the business, to make sure there is no leak."

"They won't *actively* stop a leak, will they?" Arlen asked.

"They'll stop any and all leaks, however they deem necessary. Need I remind you national security is at stake?" Mr. Chase glared at Arlen.

"The DOD won't like us going cowboy, besides, it could be them," Arlen said.

"I already contacted the DOD and they assure me they are unaware of any covert operations around Mike. I received clearance to take necessary steps to secure the technology." Mr. Chase stopped abruptly, as if something distracted him.

"Maria has been warned and authorized to use deadly force to protect Mike and his designs, with the full backing of TAC," Bobby said.

"Shouldn't we keep Mike on-site until this blows over?" Arlen asked.

"Maria will be staying at Mike's place around the clock for a while. She'll tell Mike a water line broke in her building today."

"But he'll still be at risk when he's off-site," Arlen said.

"We may not be able to keep him alive, that is acceptable. But, we'll know when and where he falls and take down anyone that gets close to him or our information."

Mr. Chase held up his hand and said, "Enough. Arlen, I think you're finally getting just how serious this is for all of us. You are both incompetent and let this situation go too far. For your sake, my hunch had better be wrong and if I *am* wrong, you just might survive this."

He got up and reached for the doorknob without a single hint of emotion. Bobby and Arlen watched in silence as he opened the door and stepped out of the conference room. The door shut with a resounding clunk, then Arlen turned and looked at Bobby for a few awkward seconds.

"Did I misunderstand him or did he just threaten us?"

Arlen asked, not sure if he should be afraid or irritated.

Bobby stared across the table, looking right into his eyes with a cold, lifeless gaze and said, "I will personally put a bullet in your head if I think you are even partially to blame for any failure to maintain secrecy."

As he leaned forward to stand up, Bobby's jacket opened toward Arlen. He got a good look at the oversized grip of Bobby's pride and joy—a fifty-caliber Desert Eagle. Bobby was always careful to keep it covered, until now. Arlen looked away, staring out the windows and did not turn back until he heard the door latch shut. As he tried to stand up, his legs shook beneath him and sweat trickled down his back.

"Idiot. Hiding behind a gun," Arlen said aloud, trying to regain some of his confidence.

His phone rang; it was Bobby.

"Go somewhere else and call me names. Now get out of my conference room," said Bobby.

His heart was pounding in his chest as he lunged for the door. *What has Mike gotten me in to?*

* * *

When the elevator door opened, Mike saw Chilli and Ray staring at him.

"Mike!" They both exclaimed in loud whispers.

"Hey guys. Everything's fine," Mike said, reading their faces.

"One of Bobby's henchmen came down here and interrogated us. He asked a bunch of questions about you and the girl from lunch," Chilli said.

"What happened? Who is she?" Ray asked.

"Nothing happened. They asked me a bunch of questions, too, but everything is fine."

"Something must have happened to cause all of this," Ray

said.

"It's all because I side-stepped protocol this morning, it has nothing to do with Cour—Emily."

"Cor-Emily was amazing! Did you get her number?" Chilli asked.

"It's just Emily. She might call later tonight, but we have more important things to think about right now."

"No way! We want to hear all about it," Chilli started.

"Not now," Mike interrupted. "First, let's get all of the documentation caught up. While you guys work on that, I'll log all of my notes in, put together a plan and meet you back in the lab."

"Are you sure everything is fine?" Chilli asked.

"Yes, now get back to work." Mike smiled and shooed them away. He went back to his office, dropped into his chair and took a deep breath. Mike closed his eyes and saw Courtney's face smiling at him and felt a smile cross his own lips. *Wait. Bobby is probably watching to see if you do anything suspicious. Maybe she is too?* Mike sat up and glanced out his window at the security camera. *Don't look at it!* Mike regained his composure and pulled himself up to his PC. He was not sure if he could pull it off, but he had to get his thoughts together.

Mike wrote out a plan to run through the various parameters that influenced the process, so they could isolate the most influential components. Suddenly, he realized how to get a copy of his files out of the lab.

"Gloria, are we up to date on our compliance requirements?" Mike asked over the intercom, knowing full well he was behind on several things.

"Um—seriously?" she asked.

"Seriously. I've been reminded that I'm not sticking to protocol as well as I should, so I need your help to get caught up." Realizing his tone was off, Mike quietly added, "The jerks upstairs put some pressure on me, so I need to get right on this."

Mike smiled to himself, pleased with his performance and

the likely effectiveness of his ploy.

"So, are you available now? I can get you started on a few items right away," Gloria offered.

"Sure, but I don't have much time. We hope to begin some tests in an hour."

Mike knew Gloria would be quick to help since she had direct responsibility for the data backups. He was always at least a day behind on his primary copy but rarely did the secondary copy. The third copy he was to create at the end of every week had been done twice since he started working at TAC almost seven years ago. Gloria was the gatekeeper and had been frustrated by his procrastination, but no one had ever physically checked, or enforced the policy.

Mike's door opened a minute later and Gloria reached out with two backup cards, "Here you go, these are the secondary and tertiary backup cards. Can I have the primary?"

Mike was nervous, but this was his only chance. "Great, thanks. No, it should still be in the other drive, or maybe the unit."

"You don't have it? Are you sure?" Gloria's face fell.

Mike knew she would be agitated. He remembered watching Gloria scramble around, looking for a card she misplaced once. She didn't return to work in the secured lab for nearly two weeks. She cried as she described the interrogation, the full body scan which revealed it in the cuff of her blouse. Mike felt badly knowing he was bringing up painful memories, but it was his only good option.

"Card three? Really now Gloria, I didn't want to go overboard here." He gave her his best, flirty smile and Gloria blushed slightly.

"It is protocol. If they're checking up on you then I'm not going to get in the middle of it," she replied as her smile slipped away.

Mike reached out and put his hand on her hip as if they had a more intimate relationship. "I will do it, for you." He looked into her eyes hoping he had not lost his touch. It worked perfectly.

"Uh—OK then. I'll be back in ten to swap you out," Gloria said with a slight tremor in her voice.

Mike placed card two in the class 5 drive at his workstation and the pop-up asked permission to run the backup utility.

Let's hope no one figured out you left my USB ports on. Mike remembered the IT tech who had installed device drivers via a thumb drive.

When the system chimed at him, Mike removed card two and placed it on the table and then picked up card three. Careful to keep the USB drive out of sight, he inserted it and card one simultaneously, initiating two more backups. His heart pounding, Mike organized his desk, blocking the camera's view while he waited. Just as the progress bars showed 100 percent, Gloria walked in and looked right at the computer.

"Hey, that was fast—just finished up," said Mike, as he carefully pulled out the card and handed her card one stacked on top of card three. Softly holding her hand open from beneath and keeping her palm out of camera view, he made sure she could see that he gave her the missing card. He mouthed 'Found it' to her and watched Gloria's demeanor change. "I'll keep card two in here for now." *Now hurry back to your computer and delete the log file before it goes to the server and it becomes part of history.*

"Oh, good." She closed her fist, concealing the cards.

"All right, I'll be stopping by your desk with card two and if I don't see you when I leave—"

"Oh, you'll see me. I'm staying late tonight," said Gloria.

"Feels nice to be getting caught up," Mike said, looking up at the clock."

"Thanks, I owe you one or maybe you owe me one?" Gloria smiled as she opened the door.

"Sure, let me buy you lunch on Sunday. I'll pick you up around one?"

"Sure, I'm game," she said, as the door closed behind her.

Mike was relieved, but had to be certain she wasn't suspicious, or even turning him in. As he turned the knob, he could see Gloria's face. *Nope; not suspicious.*

She turned and looked at him and he opened the door.

"I forgot to ask, did you get a call for me while I was out to lunch?" he asked.

"No, were you expecting one?"

"Yeah, but maybe the vendor forgot. I'll call them in a bit. Thanks," Mike said and returned to his desk. Mike closed his eyes, taking deep breaths to slow his pounding heart and clear his head for the spud tests about to take place. His hands were shaking and he felt like he could explode. *What a rush. This could be addicting!*

* * *

Courtney sat silently in the surveillance room in the covert DIA office building downtown, watching the feed from TAC's own security system.

Courtney watched as Mike did a series of backups on his computer. She noticed him leave his hand in front of the computer when he slipped the final card in.

Fidgeting? That's uncharacteristic, she thought. Courtney watched with concern as Gloria entered Mike's office. *What's he up to now? Is he—flirting with Gloria?* Courtney felt a tinge of jealousy, as she noticed the front USB cover was open on his computer. *Ah, so that's what you were up to earlier. You have your own copy now, but you left the USB cover open. A rookie mistake and exactly the kind that can get you caught,* Courtney thought. *He is following the plan, though.*

She watched Mike get up to leave his office, then glance back at his workstation. Reaching with some papers in one hand, he placed them just under the little door and went for the stapler with his other hand. He stapled the papers, then flicked the USB door shut as he picked them back up again. *Like a pro.* She caught herself as feelings started to reappear. *He's right in the middle of this and might get himself killed. Heck, you might need to do it yourself.*

Closing her eyes, she imagined how she might kill him. Mentally, she snuck up behind him and started to slit his throat, but he turned and kissed her. Then she tried it with a pistol, but when he looked at her, she hesitated. He smiled and nodded approvingly at her, but she was unable to shoot. Furious at her inability to complete a simple mental exercise, Courtney set herself up several buildings away from his apartment. Maria was in the room so she waited for the two of them to line up with the reticle before she squeezed off the perfect two-for-one kill shot.

There, that's more like it, she told herself.

But then, the little girl from her dreams entered into the vision, ran over and fell on top of Mike's body. Courtney felt devastated.

Frustrated by the repeated emotional interference, Courtney slammed her fist down on the big, wooden table in the conference room. A moment later, a tech poked his head in through the door looking concerned.

"Got it," she said and smiled, wiping her hand off toward the floor like she had just killed an insect.

"Ready for me to take over for a while?" he asked.

"Perfect. Looks like our boy is back to work after that ugly meeting with Mr. Chase and his flunky," she said as if nothing was wrong.

"Good news," the tech said, looking at the screen. He settled into a chair and donned a pair of headphones as Courtney stood up.

"They are being actively monitored from inside. Arlen's PC has been accessing the cameras around the lab for a while now," she pointed to the desktop view she had in the lower right side of the large wall display. "That's his screen."

"OK, thanks." The tech glanced at her, below the neckline and said, "Nice!"

"Excuse me?" Courtney demanded.

"The Sig, it's a P226 Dark Elite, right?"

"Oh, yeah. Sorry." Courtney pulled the weapon from under her arm, dropped the clip and checked the chamber before handing it to the younger man.

"Threaded barrel too; I love it!"

"For those occasions when a girl wants to be seen but not heard," she said holding out her hand.

"You field agents get all the cool toys!"

"We take all of the risks, too," she said, taking her sidearm back, "so don't think it's all fun and games." Courtney turned and reached for the door.

"I've seen a few good agents get themselves hurt already," he said.

"Yeah, you techs make mistakes and we pay the price." Courtney noticed him wince slightly, then stepped into the hallway with a smile on her face.

* * *

Mike joined Chilli and Ray in the lab and they began the tedious but necessary process of documenting every detail. One hour later, they were done and Mike called Arlen's desk.

"Arlen, we're about to try a few runs with the spud."

"Excellent. I'll log in now," Arlen said.

Mike could hear abnormal tapping on a keyboard, then a few, loud mouse clicks. *Yep, Arlen was watching.*

"I'm in now, so you can do your thing. Just be careful so no one gets hurt. Got it?"

"Absolutely. We'll be as careful as we can."

Mike hung up. *How much more have they been watching? The apartment?* He realized he had been naive before Courtney had opened his eyes. *What is she really up to?* Mike briefly remembered gazing into her alluring eyes and her eerily familiar beauty. Fighting within himself to break the trance, Mike felt himself twitch. Remembering the surveillance, he gathered his thoughts and spoke into the microphone, "Sonic pulse harmonizer drive, trial fifty four. Attempting to duplicate trial fifty three."

Mike looked at Ray and Chilli, "Well, it's time to clear the lab guys. Take your places." He pointed through the near bombproof glass into the observation area on the other side. "This should net just over eleven ounces with no adverse temperature or vibration. The second test will also be a repeat, but with the new, heavier cell."

The two obediently headed for the door.

"After the first two tests, I want to make Chilli's adjustments to the power supply for the mag field generator, Ray's fluid system mods and I'll do some more fine-tuning of my own."

Mike knew they were getting tired, but without their help, he would have to wait until morning. He reached out for the spud's power supply and switched it on, then nudged it up to the first increment. The strain gauge read just over twelve ounces.

"Step one successful. The two pound strain gauge has been changed for a fifty, which probably accounts for the additional ounce of force we see now. Rolling into step two, spud power at five percent."

"We have three pounds of force. The power was doubled and the force it returned was tenfold." Mike said, glancing back at the guys staring at him with their mouths open. "It appears that the first few percent are consumed in field excitement and atmospheric insulation, as a fifteen percent increase in power netted us over one hundred in propulsion force. Unless it's exponential, then we're in for another, major surprise," he recorded.

The phone rang and Mike read Arlen's number on the display. He powered down the spud and watched the gauge slowly drop to zero. Ray and Chilli joined him in the lab as he answered the phone.

"Yes, sir?"

"Mike, you guys have hit this one out of the park."

"Thanks, Arlen, we've put a lot into it."

"I hate to leave, but I have to get to a five o'clock recital for our eldest and I'm already late. Document everything, but don't stay too much longer. I want to be here when you blow that door off its hinges," Arlen chuckled.

"I think we're pretty close to that now. We'll finish these adjustments, then call it a week."

"Don't you think we should come in tomorrow?" Arlen asked.

"No. The team is beat and needs the weekend to recharge. Let's go for the real trials first thing Monday," Mike said, glancing at his watch.

"Monday, huh? All right then, Monday it is," Arlen said. "Enjoy your weekend."

Mike hung up and wondered if Arlen was suspicious of his decision at such an important time. "OK guys, do your worst. We'll finish our adjustments, then call it quits," Mike said. He pulled up the local news on his phone and read the headline.

Bomb threat proves to be hoax. Authorities are looking for a person of interest. If you recognize this man, please call.

Mike felt like someone had punched him in the stomach. He slowly scrolled down and saw his own hair. *Oh, no! No, no, no!* His knees became weak and he felt light-headed. Mike's heart was pounding as he stepped over to a chair and sat down. He forced himself to look back down at his phone, rolled the face up into view, then let out a groan. "That's not—"

Be quiet, you idiot!

Ray looked over at Mike.

Mike felt his entire body relax, then begin to shake. *Cut it out or they'll know something is up!* He pulled his tablet over to the counter in front of him and acted like he was reading some notes. After a few minutes went by, he felt his mind clear and began to focus on the spud once more.

The three of them poured over the devices and programming for almost two hours, barely saying a word. When Mike realized they were done, he yawned out loud a couple of times, then leaned back to stretch.

"Guys, I don't know about you, but I'm wiped out," Mike said and yawned again.

"Man, you are killing me with that yawning! I can barely stay awake as it is," Ray said.

"Sorry, it's been a long day," Mike said, rubbing his eyes.

"Looks like we're done. Should we stop here?" Chilli asked.

"Yeah, this looks like a good place to stop," Mike replied.

"Otherwise, we're signing on for another couple of hours?" Ray asked.

"Yeah, about that I guess. At least an hour if we start on the next round of tests," Mike answered.

"Then I'm done. See you two on Monday," Chilli said as he stumbled out of the lab.

"I'm with stupid," said Ray, chuckling at Chilli's glare.

"Thanks again for all of your help guys. I'm twenty minutes behind you," Mike said.

After his conversation with Courtney and his new understanding of TAC's methods, Mike was convinced that something serious would happen. He had no intention of stopping until something broke or he achieved the gains he expected. Mike paused for a moment to make certain he was prepared for the consequences. *There's no turning back.*

* * *

Courtney was sitting in her office, watching Mike and the guys in the lab. It didn't have the massive displays of the conference room, but she had access to the same tools.

The guys knocked off—what's your plan Mike? Why so still? Courtney zoomed in on him to try and guess what he was thinking.

Mike spun around and stared right at her. His stare was so piercing and analytical that, yet for some reason she was amused. *Do you think I'm watching? Or someone else maybe?*

Mike stared at the camera long enough to arouse suspicion in anyone, then turned back toward the counter. He picked up the phone and dialed.

Who are you calling? Courtney wondered as she moved her mouse and muted the audio feed from Mike's cell phone. She then turned up the tap on the lab phone and checked the surveillance feed. Eleven fed the numbers he dialed onto the screen as she watched. *I know that number—*

"Control Room," said the voice on the other end.

Of course, the power plant. Courtney told herself.

"Hey, this is Mike Devon, I just wanted to let you know we'll be running an experiment down here at TAC that will draw pretty hard bursts on our transformer," Mike said.

"Hey, Mike, thanks, but I'm going to need about twenty minutes to spin up a turbine. We're all but idle after the evening draws go down," the technician explained.

"No sweat. Ring me back at this number when you're ready."

She watched as his head drooped slightly and Mike stared down at the counter.

Seriously, Mike? You know they'll come down on you tomorrow—so it happens tonight?

* * *

As he waited for the substation to call him back, Mike's thoughts went from his experiment, his responsibility to TAC and the strange encounter with the mysterious Courtney. *She definitely had resources. She knew far too much and the bomb threat played out just as she predicted. A bomb threat.* He felt doubt and mistrust creep in. *So, the real question is whether or not she's good or bad?*

Mike's mind jumped back to the project. He knew the Defense Department would pay TAC handsomely and the entire project would be moved out.

But what happens to me? I'm intimately close to the technology, so they could offer me a position to continue with development. What if they already have the technology? Wait—maybe I know too much? Is that what she knows?

Every scenario he played out ended with him being a liability—at odds with TAC and the military establishment. For the first time in his life he was starting to regret his career path. He had chosen it because of the dreams and her...the girl in his dreams. Had he actually chosen? Or, was fate playing itself out?

Mike forced himself to clear his mind and relax by closing his eyes. After several minutes of listening to his own breathing, he dozed off and conjured up memories of the girl and her eyes, her hair, her face...

"Mike, help me please! Help me!" Courtney screamed at him as the guard knocked her to the ground and her head split open. Blood sprayed all over him and trickled down his face. The liquid in his eyes blurred his vision and he could no longer see the horror unfolding. The metallic tasting liquid was in his mouth and eyes, but he was frozen, unable to wipe it off. It pained him to hear her gurgle his name one last time, as her life ended.

Mike jumped in his seat and gasped for air. Frantically, he wiped his burning eyes and checked his hands. *How could I have been so blind? It was Courtney all along! But how? How did she survive?* He spun around in his chair and looked up at the camera again. *She knew who I was all along!*

Mike's phone buzzed in his pocket. It was a text from a blocked number. *Hope you are OK. Can't wait to see you, have lots to talk about. Em.*

He replied, *probably not wise to continue.*

The cameras are looping. They think you're being a good boy.

Mike looked inquisitively at the camera and another text came in. *I'm keeping my eye on them.* He was so relieved and impressed, he couldn't help but smile.

Mike turned back to the counter, then a thought struck him. *If you go any further, there's no turning back.* Mike let it sink in for a moment, trying to convince himself it was too dangerous. Instead, he felt an overwhelming sense of desperation. *No, I can't lose her again, not now.*

Mike picked up the tablet PC and noted the latest changes. He had to capture every detail. He wouldn't be coming back to TAC ever again. When the phone rang, he nearly jumped out of his seat. On the second ring, Mike had calmed himself enough to talk.

"Lab." He heard his voice crack.

"Mike? We're ready here at the substation," said the technician.

"Thanks. I'll let you know when I'm done," Mike said, regaining some of his composure. He took several deep breaths to calm himself. He then put in earplugs and placed a set of earmuffs over the top, just in case it went audible.

"Sonic Pulse Harmonizer Drive trial fifty five. Testing the adjustments we made to see if the spud is still operational." *That sounded innocent enough.*

He reached for the controls, engaged it, then set it to five percent. The strain gauge rose to nearly five pounds.

"The adjustments appear to have had no adverse effects." Mike struggled to maintain his composure, but screamed inside. *We did it! The changes netted more than double the output. Double that should get me around ten or maybe even fifteen pounds?*

He leaned forward and spoke into the mic, "Going to ten percent now." Mike watched in disbelief as the meter jumped.

"Twenty three pounds," Mike was both startled and pleased. Closing his eyes briefly, Mike notched it up to fifteen percent, expecting the gauge to max out at fifty pounds. Instead, there was a vibration in the room as the spud started banging against the load cell, pegging it out repeatedly. Against his better judgment, Mike turned the knob to twenty percent. It struck the test bed with such force that it snapped the entire end off and sent pieces clattering to the floor. The spud itself stayed just off the end of the guides, suspended in space about a foot past where the gauge had once been. He felt a growing reverberation in the room and a familiar hum engulfed him.

"And that, folks, is what magnetic reconnection feels like!" Mike said, as he switched off the lab recorder.

Mike knew that nothing he did now could make things any worse, so he continued on. At twenty five and thirty percent, it maintained its position in the middle of the magnetic field. Mike reached over and adjusted the field, extending it to nearly twice its length but nothing happened. On a whim, he reached out with a Kevlar-gloved hand and delicately touched the levitating object. He could feel a slight tingling sensation work itself halfway up his arm and the room came alive with the vibration. If it was not for the isolated floor the laboratory rested on, the entire building would have been shaking and he would have been discovered.

He sent her a message: *It's stable, but there's a strong vibration.*

I can hear it, she replied.

Not much privacy these days, he texted.

Not for some people.

Her answer made him smile. Mike slipped his phone into his shirt and spoke loudly as he reached for the power supply. "We are holding stable at thirty percent load on. I don't think I can exceed eighty without tripping the building's HV-X, uh, high voltage transformer. The noise in here is actually quite low, but I can definitely feel the energy in the room. I've felt much stronger before, so it's safe to continue." Mike paused for a moment, then continued. "I'm going on up in five percent increments until something changes, or the HV-X trips out on me. Wish me luck."

He suddenly felt guilty. *They're gonna be so angry! They'll have Bobby at the apartment by ten in the morning.* Mike became angry with himself. *Get a backbone! Why do you care? You're in huge trouble no matter what you do, so get on with it!*

Another message arrived and distracted Mike from his thoughts. He read, *I'm here if you need something.* "Like a place to hide, maybe?" he said out loud.

The reply came in, *Sure.*

All right then, here we go, Mike thought.

Mike eased the power up another notch. The energy in the room jumped drastically and the familiar noise from his dreams consumed the room. Another notch on the power supply was too tempting for Mike to resist and then another. "Forty five percent now!" he yelled, but the test was beginning to saturate the lab with energy. He raised his hand for her to see four fingers, then all five; *forty five percent,* knowing she would understand. Looking at his screen, Mike saw the HV-X was near tripping at eighty nine percent.

That's drawing enough energy to power the entire building, on a hot summer day, five times over!

It had never sustained such high loads and Mike was pleased everything was holding together. He nudged the spud's power to fifty percent knowing that he was nearing the limits.

This could damage it, or even the building, he told himself, but continued anyway.

At fifty five percent Mike once again held up his hand for Courtney and showed five fingers, closed his hand and showed five again. Toward the door, there was a wall of haze. It looked like a round, foggy mirror and was centered off the tip of the spud. With a quick glance at the screen, he could just barely make out the HV-X was at ninety three.

One more step up, that's it.

Sixty percent on the power supply caused the room to disappear from view and the round, mirror-shaped anomaly grew large enough that the bottom of it was flat across the floor. It had moved toward him, within twelve inches of the spud. Expecting the HV-X to trip at any second, Mike stuck out a foot to quickly touch the circular pattern. He felt an impact, then pain throughout his body. All went still.

Mike lay there, elated, unable to open his eyes. He couldn't hear anything, nor move a muscle and struggled until he felt his leg twitch. The only thing he could feel was his weight, laying on the hard floor.

Fear started to creep in, *Was there an explosion? I don't remember a flash or anything.* Mike struggled to understand, but couldn't. His excitement had given way to terror.

* * *

UNIT 2: REVELATION

COURTNEY lunged forward, jumping from her chair. *It works!*

She quickly ran through her mental to-do list as she dug through her top drawer and grabbed a key. Then she pulled a can of cleaner and spray latex out of her bottom left drawer and quickly cleaned her hands. Courtney blew on them to make sure all of the cleaner had evaporated, then generously coated both sets of her fingerprints and palms with latex. She glanced at the video feed from the lab and noticed a man in a military uniform in the hallway. She scrolled through the other cameras so she could get a better look at the soldier and noticed he had an odd tilt to his head with a hand on the wall steadying himself. She zoomed and panned the camera, but his face was turned away from view. Courtney moved the camera down to better see his uniform.

He's SAF!

Then she gasped. The name on the uniform read, *COL DEVON*. She nudged the zoom back out, as his face turned toward the camera. *It is Mike! But he looks different, older even. Did he go and then return years later?*

Courtney struggled to maintain her composure. Ecstatic, she rushed across her office to the cabinets where she kept her various outfits and disguises, along with other professional and personal items. In the bottom of the armoire section she kept a variety of feminine products partly hidden from view. She smiled knowing that her office had been combed numerous times but no one had moved those little boxes at the bottom. Placing them on an upper shelf, she quickly removed the makeup mirror and light that was suction-cupped to the full-length mirror on the closet door. Using the suction cup to lock onto the bottom of the compartment, she tugged up and lifted out the panel. After replacing the small mirror,

Courtney worked two, identical hard cases and a short, black nylon rifle case out of the compartment. She replaced everything to avoid arousing suspicion any sooner than necessary, then turned to leave her office for the very last time.

The glance around to double check was unnecessary. She had rehearsed her evacuation plans countless times. She rarely made even a slight change to them now, they were nearly perfected. As the door closed behind her, Courtney felt the few connections to her employment slipping away. Her identity was transforming with each step. She made her way out of the building, continuously checking the video feed of Colonel Devon on her phone. She switched apps long enough to initiate a system reset to the rear corridor and garage entrance surveillance server.

Ninety seconds without video surveillance, they're going to have a meltdown over this. Courtney smiled. *This will tie them up for hours and by the time they figure out what happened, I'll be long gone.*

***

What happened just then? The man wondered as he stumbled along the wall. *It sounded like the crystal altar. Wait, where is this place?*

An angry man approached him. "Mr. Devon, we just finished your office," he nodded across the hall. We are not done with the hallway, however." Looking down at the man's chest, he read out loud, "*Colonel* Devon?"

"Yes, Alec, I can read nametags, too. Now move."

The gap between the two men closed to mere inches, but Colonel Devon didn't stop. "Get out of my way you imbecile!" he snarled.

Moving out of his path, Alec yelled, "We're just trying to do our job!"

"You'll shut your mouth and go home if you know what is good for you!" Colonel Devon pointed a finger in the janitor's face as he screamed.

"Fine, we're done up here!" the startled janitor said, as he stumbled backwards.

Two other janitors had slipped into the hallway to watch the commotion.

"Clear the floor people!" Alec yelled at them.

Struggling to stay on his feet, Colonel Mike Devon read *Mike Devon, PhD* on the door the janitor had motioned to.

It can't be, he thought, then opened the door. A quick scan of the office told him its owner was a technician of some type. He walked up to the desk and saw a picture of himself holding up an award. Colonel Devon felt the hair tingle on the back of his neck.

The cleaning man knew my name, the nameplate and now this?

Constant barrages of thoughts and images he didn't recognize made him nauseous. The Colonel dropped into the chair and sat with his eyes closed while the episode faded away. When he was sure he had regained control, he opened his eyes.

Nope, still here, wherever that is. He looked up at the clock, then down at his watch. *They match.* The Colonel glanced back at the picture of himself and knocked it over onto its face. "What are your objectives, Colonel?" He sat silent for a few moments, slowly rotating around in the chair until he was facing the desk again. "Identify where you are, friendly or foe."

The Colonel rested his hand on the butt of his sword. The engraved, titanium alloy looked more like a child's toy than a deadly weapon. Concerned, he removed it from the sheath and turned it on. The familiar hum and pulsing in his hand gave him confidence. He reached out toward the corner of the desk and lowered the sword until he saw smoke. The unseen blade slipped through and the corner fell onto the floor. *Can't be the Nazis. They would never leave me with this.* An imperceptible smile lit up his eyes. He loved watching his invention work. It was a clean, silent tool that was one of the finest in the SAF's small weapons arsenal.

Colonel Devon put the sword away and opened the top left drawer. He went through each drawer, poring over every item for any morsel of information he could glean. He put miscellaneous items and papers on the desk, tossing everything else across the floor to his right. The scattered mess grew until he had worked through the entire desk. Glancing over at the heap, the Colonel smiled at the thought of the janitor cleaning up. He hated the janitor more severely than he understood, but he accepted it.

The Colonel's head jerked up and he glanced off into the distance. *I'm Mike Devon—am I trashing my own office?* He looked around the room again, trying to find anything that looked familiar but found nothing. *No. Then what if Mike Devon, PhD, is doing the same in my office?* The Colonel felt rage starting to course through his veins as he realized the security breach that could be occurring. He was helpless for now and it infuriated him even further.

* * *

A confused and blind Mike Devon found himself lying on the uncomfortable floor. He could feel voices talking to him, but could not quite make them out audibly. Mike remembered the earplugs and pulled them out.

A still muffled voice demanded, "What are you doing, Michael? Screwing off? I think you have plenty to do, don't you? Wait a minute; are you drunk?"

"Hey, I'm sorry, but I'm not feeling so well. Something happened…" Mike tried to talk, but kept seeing visions that took over his entire consciousness.

Where is that place? It seems so familiar, but I've never been there.

"Are you listening to me?"

"No. I—"

"I said, you'd better believe something is not right here!" the man screamed.

"What I'm trying to say is I can't see. I can hear you, now, but I cannot see. I fell and—wait, Alec?"

"This is your boss speaking! If I find out you are on drugs, you are finished! It will be pretty difficult for you without my recommendation to find your next employer, what with your lack of position and all," Alec yelled.

What's up with that weird accent? Mike forced himself to remain calm. "I must have hit my head when I fell. Would you help me into a chair?"

"You'd better not be hurt!"

Mike was confused and worried, but the powerful visions were dulling and he was almost able to maintain his mental focus. "It might be a concussion, I think I may need to go to the doctor."

"Doctor? You must have hit your head pretty hard to think *you* could get to see a doctor. Especially when *I* am only allowed two visits each year," Alec replied. "And what are you doing out on the floor without your ID?" Alec asked, as he tugged Mike to his feet.

Mike stumbled along until he felt Alec push down on his shoulder. Reaching back, he felt the arms of a chair and lowered himself into it. Colors were starting to come out of the shadows now and he watched the mumbling figure walk away. Mike sat there confused. He recalled the test to find something to make sense of the situation. After a few minutes had gone by, he had mostly recovered from the episode, but was no closer to an answer. The floor came into focus as he finished thinking.

Wait, that's not the right flooring. Something went wrong! Mike sat up and looked around. *This isn't TAC!*

Looking down at his watch and struggling to focus on the tiny hands, Mike made out the time. It was almost ten o'clock.

"Michael, do you need me to help get you caught up a little? The boffins were nice to me today, so I'm ahead of schedule. Michael? Are you OK?" George called down the hallway.

"George?" Mike was completely confused now.

"Yeah, pal, what's up with ya? You look a bit peaked."

What's up with the clothes and the accent? Mike wanted to ask him, but thought better of it. *This can't be happening.*

"Michael? Are you sick or summat?"

"Sorry, George. Uh…yeah, I was running some tests in my lab and I fell, or something," Mike explained. "I can't remember what happened after that."

"We're at work, at BAE, remember that? You're not at home in your basement workshop now," George said.

"BAE? British Aerospace sold this branch to TAC in O-five, the year before I was hired." Mike looked closely at George. "I'm not *that* messed up." Mike tried to find his sense of humor, but could see from George's reaction that he wasn't joking.

"Tack? Not sure about that, mate, but I *am* sure you're in rough shape. Let's get you to the break room." George helped him to his feet.

"I'm a bit sick to my stomach, so go easy," Mike said.

"You need to hit the bog?"

"What?" Mike asked.

"The loo, do ya need to visit the loo?"

"Oh, right. No bog. Just some water and a few more minutes to recover."

"Were you using some nasty chemicals? Or maybe taking something you shouldn't?"

He really sounds British and this place isn't right. BAE? It isn't possible, is it?

"Michael?"

"Uh, no, nothing like that. I'll be fine in a few minutes."

"You tinker down in that lab of yours at home so much, you're probably just bollocksed," he said, as they entered the break room.

Mike looked around the room, trying to see something he would recognize.

"Let's put you here, by your locker. Put your feet up and take it easy for a bit."

"Thanks, George."

"No worries, Michael. I'll be back to get you in fifteen minutes."

This has to be a dream, it can't be real. Michael?

Mike's eyes focused on the locker in front of him. He felt agitated as he lifted the latch on the door, as if he knew something bad was about to happen. Mike saw a wallet on the shelf and reached for it, bumping a badge dangling from the hook above. It read *Janitorial, Michael Devon, 4th Class.* The room turned slightly, nearly causing Mike to fall over. *No, it can't be,* he thought as he opened the wallet and slid out an identification card. Hearing himself gasp, the reality of his predicament became clear. *Something went wrong with the test. Something went terribly wrong.* The world around him started to spin again and Mike grabbed onto the locker door. He closed his eyes and took several deep breaths. *How are you going to fix this? Think, Mike, think…*

* * *

Courtney felt an unexpected relief wash over her as she pulled out of the parking garage. She hadn't realized the stress that had been building, leading up to this day. It became clear to her now, as tears formed at the corners of her eyes and her throat choked with pain. It had been an emotional week, culminating in this near euphoric release, with the final departure upon her. Courtney had never let herself form attachments here and was surprised to feel loss, along with a host of other feelings, about this place.

She fought to regain her focus as she drove out onto the highway, speed-shifting into fourth gear and hitting the rev-limiter. She had to get to TAC, into the lab, before the Colonel Mike did something to interfere with her plan to return home. Someway, somehow, she was going to get him to activate the spud and Mike should return. For a brief moment her heart started to ponder what it would be like to lose Mike, but she willed it into submission.

If the return was successful, then it was possible to travel back and forth. If not, then…

Courtney would not allow herself to entertain the idea, not

even for a moment. She was going home, if she survived, that was all there was to it.

Courtney slowed down a few blocks from TAC, not wanting to raise any suspicion.

She knew there were regular visits from a host of agencies, from within and outside of the USA. These visitors would note the comings and goings of the guard shifts, employees as well as vendors. Preparing to make a variety of moves if necessary, for expertise or for information. Some of these visitors were assigned to several such high-tech facilities, moonlighting as vendors and collecting data to be sent home for processing. The DIA had regular updates on the players in the game and the likely repercussions. They needed to know who the bad guys were if TAC was ever compromised, or if they ever had to breach it themselves.

Courtney knew her best chance for a successful entry had about a thirty minute window. Everyone was busy filling out their forms and prepping to hand over their posts to the next person; they barely had time or energy enough to do their jobs in the tired rush to leave. After that, a fresh shift would be on duty and the likelihood of her success would go down. The timing was perfect.

She checked to see the Colonel sitting at Mike's desk one last time before pulling up to the gate. As her car rolled up, a familiar face looked out the window at her.

"Howdy Ma'am," the guard said.

She already had her pass out and laying atop the door mirror for the guard to see, like most of the employees at TAC did. As long as she acted like every other employee they would let her right on in, as they had a few times before. She had made a few visits over the past couple of years. It had been in rental cars every time and always dressed in similar, dark colored business clothes.

"Back again, eh?" he asked.

"I sure am. You certainly have a good memory!"

"Nah, it wasn't that long ago," he said with a grin.

"It was the last project, so that would have been at least a couple of months back." Courtney was not truly surprised he had recognized her.

"Yeah, but you're in your own car tonight I see," the guard went on.

Courtney felt her senses heighten. *He's too observant, military background.* "Hey, that's right, it is my car. Someone's on his toes!"

"Well, I just came on shift, but I wouldn't have known you by sunrise," he joked.

"Now it's my turn. You're studying criminal justice, working here to pay for school?"

"No ma'am, Army, six years. I'm just trying to get back into the swing of things here stateside," the guard finished.

"They teach that in the Army?"

"Rangers, Ma'am. Recon. Uh, reconnaissance, that is. Have to notice the details if you want to get the bad guys and stay alive," he said.

Courtney noticed the tone of his voice change. *He's getting suspicious.* "Well, thank you for your service, soldier. Have a nice night." *I have to watch out for that one. He's strong and well trained.*

Courtney drove into the visitor's parking area and backed into a parking space, obscuring her only license plate in the shrubs. Turning off the car, she sat quietly and opened up the security feed from the building behind her.

Let's see what you're up to now...

* * *

Mike was sitting in the break room, trying to decide what to do. He wanted to run away, but reason won out.

Breathing deeply, Mike walked over to the water dispenser, filled a cup and drank it down in one long drink, refilled the cup and emptied it again.

You need an accent, too, or he'll suspect something.

"You're a janitor tonight, Michael," he said, attempting a

British accent.

"Just figured that out did ya?" George asked, laughing.

"Geez! George, you scared me, sneaking up like that!"

He likes a good laugh like the other George, Mike thought. "How do you do it, George? How do you come to work for that piece of garbage night after night?"

"I wish I had a choice mate, but I don't. My family has been servant class since Egypt fell," George answered matter-of-factly. "We're in the same boat you and me. Only difference is you're smart and have something in the works at home. I have nothin' but a lazy cat and a portly wife waiting for me."

"You know me, always working on something at home," Mike said.

"Always the same, crazy invention. Lord knows we've tried to get you hitched, but none of them compare to that bird from your childhood." George leaned in and smiled, "We haven't given up on you yet."

"Good. I'm glad," he said, then a thought struck him. "Hey, don't you have a birthday coming up soon?" *He's going to be thirty this year. Say it, George...*

"The Missus talk to you about my surprise party?"

"I may have heard a couple of the guys talking in the loo the other day."

"The blokes are chatting up my thirtieth in the toilet now? Not sure what to think about that!"

Mike chuckled with him. *The year is right and that's definitely George. That only leaves one more question.*

"C'mon, we have to get back out there before Alec finds us in here," George reached out his hand and pulled him to his feet.

Just stick it out a few more hours and George can help you get to Michael's, Mike told himself. *That'll give you some time to figure this thing out.*

"Well?"

"All right, show me what I have left to do," Mike said.

George lead him out of the breakroom and down the hall,

then opened the door into the stairwell.

"I should take the elevator, I'm still feeling a bit shaky," Mike said.

Mike started for the elevator but George stood still and stared at him with a confused look on his face.

"George? Are you with me?" Mike's smile faded as he realized he had made a big mistake.

"Sure thing, mate. Sorry, just thinking about something. Actually, you don't have much left to do. I bet you can knock out the *loo* by the *lift* on the third floor, in an hour."

Hearing George emphasize the words told Mike what he had done. Even a few wrong words could cause big trouble and it made him feel even more threatened. *Keep the chatter to a minimum. No telling what he might do if he thinks you are a security risk.*

"Oh, I left your cart right outside the loo," George explained.

"Thanks man, I owe you one," Mike said.

"No worries. You're always helping me out, so it's about time I returned the favor," George replied.

"Now why do I get the feeling you don't really mean that?" Mike immediately regretted what he had said, but George's face lit up.

"Well, maybe you didn't hit your head so hard after all!" George laughed. "Meet me back here as soon as you get done, just make sure it's before midnight."

"Got it. See you in here at ten minutes 'til," Mike said as he entered the elevator. *I wouldn't live it down if Chilli and Ray saw me cleaning toilets.* Mike started cleaning the bathroom, but his mind was elsewhere. *Is it home, but changed? Or, is it a second version, parallel to home? If it is a parallel, can I get home?*

Mike took his frustration out on the porcelain, scrubbing himself into a sweat.

I either created a wormhole and changed the past, in which case I am stuck. Or, I moved between two realities and now Michael has taken my place.

Mike lifted his head and looked around, realizing he was

done. Startled, he checked his watch.

"Plenty of time. Nice work." Moments later, Mike loaded his cart into the elevator.

"Hold it, Michael," Alec called out. "I'm going down with you. Or, should we step into the loo and see how you did?"

Dang, he'll make me late, then how do I get to Michael's? I'd better make this good. "Sure, check it out, I think you'll be impressed."

"Oh?"

"Heck, I have been in there almost two hours," Mike replied.

"Shut up and get in the lift, I don't have time to listen to you brag about your lousy work and what's up with the stupid accent?" Alec demanded.

"Just under the weather, mate," Mike said.

"Mate? I am not your mate you lousy peasant! You are so far beneath me it makes me sick just riding the lift with you! I'm nearly two classes above you and don't forget it!" Alec screamed in Mike's face, then turned and faced the doors in silence.

If I have to go in there and get a bunch of lip from this jerk, I might hurt him. Mike glanced around. *I could slit his throat with my scraper,* he mused. *Wait, then what happens back home? If there is one.* Mike struggled to collect his thoughts.

Alec stood with his back to Mike the entire elevator ride. He shoved the cart backwards into Mike's hip as he stepped off.

"Hey! You did that on purpose!" Mike yelled.

"Of course, I did!" Alec called back over his shoulder as he walked away.

I've never liked him, even before I really got to know him. Could Michael's situation have caused that? Wait, if Michael is at TAC, then he might get to see Alec! Mike chuckled at the thought of Michael's reaction when he realized Alec wasn't his boss. He walked down the hallway and paused outside the breakroom to collect his thoughts. *I have the address on the ID but I need to find my car, if I have one. Find the keys, say as little as possible and stay calm.* He opened the door and saw George approaching with a determined look on his face.

"Come on mate, we have to get you out of here before he takes another swipe at you. I have your cagoule, wallet and keys. Oh, and I clocked you out." He grabbed hold of Mike's arm and lead him back out into the hallway, dropping Michael's things into Mike's hand.

No car key? Perfect. Wait, what's a ca-jewel? Mike cut a quick glance at George. *Oh, a jacket.*

"Alec is in there and he's tearing into the whole crew thanks to you. Why would you do something so foolish? You called him mate?" George asked, pushing the button on the elevator.

"He's a horrible person, George. It's all I can do to keep from —"

"Quit that!" George hissed. Quieting down even more, George whispered, "We can't have you going back to dreaming about slitting his throat with your scraper again, now can we? I swear, Michael, you start obsessing about the old man again and you are on your own."

Mike stepped on the elevator behind George.

Scraper? That was Michael's memory?

"Michael, are you listening to me?"

"Sorry, George, I know you don't need any extra worries. I'm just, well, not myself tonight," Mike said.

Mike noticed George cut a quick glance toward him and it made him uneasy. A few moments later, the elevator doors opened. Mike looked ahead and saw several sets of gates and scanners.

"You first. I'm right behind you," Mike said, as they reached the scanners. There was a black box with the template of a hand on the right side of each gate. George went through first, placing his hand on the scanner.

Mike was so focused on George's every move that he almost missed George glance back at him.

He's on to you. Mike's thought was instantly interrupted by a loud horn and a red flashing light. He felt the blood rush from his face and gasped for air. *Oh, no!*

"Stay there," said the guard, "you have been flagged. Let's see here…you're missing a scar on your hand? How did you manage that?" he asked.

"Impossible. It's just another scanner glitch," the second guard said. He walked up from behind the first guard and reached out with a portable unit. "Put your right hand on here," he ordered.

Mike slowly placed his hand on the smaller, portable unit. His heart was pounding and he was getting dizzy. The light blinked green atop the portable unit and Mike wanted to cheer.

"Fingerprints are good. Must just be from all of those healthy chemicals you boys use in the loo!" the guard laughed and slapped Mike on the back.

Mike flinched so hard the guard noticed and gave him a suspicious look.

"OK, get on now, we have work to do," the guard said, as his partner let Mike pass.

Mike could feel sweat on his forehead, then a trickle rolled down his back as he walked.

"George, I'm feeling worse, can I get a ride home with you?" Mike asked, as they stepped out of the building.

"Like you have a car? Yeah, I can take you home, like I always do."

Mike could hear the distrust in George's voice.

"You really aren't feeling like yourself tonight, are you?"

You should have been quiet just a few moments more, Mike thought.

In an overly calm voice, George said, "I should have bought the red TVR instead of the blue one, eh?" He motioned toward a sporty, blue car in front of them.

"Nah, red is overdone, silver is my favorite," Mike said and walked up to the right side of the metallic blue sports car. *Maybe being a janitor isn't such a bad gig here after all.*

Mike looked back to see George staring at him as if he'd seen a ghost. He quickly looked down into the car and saw the steering wheel was on his side.

"If Alec sees you touching his car, he'll have you fired for sure. Mine is the little red Fiat, over there," George said, pointing to a beat up little car.

"George, I know you think something is wrong and you're right. I can't explain just yet, but get me to my apartment and I will. Everything is okay, I promise. Please, just trust me on this," Mike said.

"Now there you go again," George replied.

"I understand, but—" Mike started.

"Your clothes are all wrong, you said *bathroom* and *elevator* earlier. You walked up to the wrong side of the car, the *wrong* car even and now your flat has become an *apartment*," George said.

"Yes, I know. Take me to my *flat* and I will explain everything," Mike tried once more.

"I don't know how you are doing it, but you look five years younger. You *do* sound like Michael, except for the ridiculous accent."

"I can explain."

"Even your fingerprints match, less a scar. Not yourself tonight? I'll say!" George was backing away.

"George, please stay. I can explain. I wanted to tell you later, but I'll do it here if I have to."

"No, mate, I've heard enough."

"Please, George, give me one more chance. I'm begging you…"

George stopped and stared at him for a moment.

"You have thirty seconds, that's it, so you'd better make it good."

Mike wanted to keep him completely out of it, but it looked like he had no choice.

"I'm not from around here, but I *am* Mike, or Michael. I know it sounds crazy, really, I do. I think it's crazy myself. I have a wallet, money, coins and keys to my other life. My life in America," Mike said, pulling the items out of his pockets.

The look on George's face told Mike he had caused some doubt.

"America? Are you kidding? Supreme Britain took out the Nazis, the Japanese and the Allies in the early forties."

"Supreme Britain won the war?" Mike asked.

"The Queen has pretty much owned the globe since Egypt fell. There's been no real opposition for sixty years now," George explained.

"But the atomic bombs—"

"Yes, Churchill used them on just about everybody and brought the world to its knees. Like Egypt before her, Britain will rule the world for a couple of thousand years," George said with pride.

"That's terrible!" Mike replied.

"Are you part of one of those underground spy rings working to overthrow the Queen?" George was visibly angry. "Are you after the visitors we have coming in from Washington, D.C., next week?" George demanded.

"Washington, D.C.? There is a Washington, D.C.?" Mike asked.

"Now you're going to tell me you have never heard of George Washington, the first American Prime Minister? The city was named after him and so was I."

Mike just stared at him, unable to think of anything to help his situation.

"I suppose you don't know about Thomas Jefferson or Benjamin Franklin either?"

George was becoming very agitated and Mike knew he had to act fast.

"No, I know who those men were, I just didn't think *you* would. So, who were Adams, Jefferson and Madison?" Mike waited in anticipation.

"The Prime Ministers who followed Sir George, of course."

"So, here goes." Mike carefully chose his words before

speaking. "George, I think I have come here from another place, well actually, another *here*. Our history is not the same, but many of the people seem to be."

George stared at him with an annoyed look on his face.

Knowing that he must sound like a lunatic, Mike continued, "I've developed a special device that transports, or shifts a person from one place to another. I'm not sure how it works, exactly, but me being here and these things prove that it does."

George was still listening, so Mike went on.

"I don't want to hurt anyone, I just want to go home. I don't even want to be here, really. Won't you please help me get home?"

Mike fought back the urge to cry. He was exhausted from all of the stress, fear and excitement. He was too tired to fight, his head hurt and he was dizzy again.

Mike reached out to grab onto a car to keep from toppling over and made a plea, "George, I know you, from my place, you're a kind man. You love your wife even though she has blamed you for the loss of three babies. I see you taking abuse from Alec several times a week and yet you still manage to smile. That's the George I need. The George that sees the good when no one else can. I just need to get to my, er, *Michael's* flat to see if there is anything there that can help me fix what I have done."

George looked at Mike in shock.

"Somehow, you know me better than your predecessor. I never told him about the miscarriages. Not that he would have cared. All he thinks about is that crystal machine and a dead girl."

Mike felt a fury inside him he had never known before. *Ignore it, you never even knew the girl. Focus, Mike, focus.* Struggling to hold his tone, Mike asked, "What crystal machine?"

"That string of prism-shaped crystals in the basement that you, well, Michael, is constantly messing with. I guess you wouldn't know about that either?" George asked.

Memories of the girl from his dreams flashed in front of Mike's eyes and he knew they were Michael's. "Uh, right, I don't know about that," Mike said, trying to focus his thoughts. "And, who's the girl you were talking about?"

"Courtney Lewis. Michael was in love with her when he was younger."

Mike was confused and his mind raced back to the conversation at Bella's. *Does Courtney know about all of this too?*

"So, the rumors about the ancient technology are true?" George asked.

"There are some things we know about the ancients that most people wouldn't believe."

"We have seen some unbelievable things in there and some scary things, too." George hesitated, but went on. "Occasionally, one of us comes across a photo or a drawing on a desk and share bits and bobs with the others. Some even read papers, like Michael, for instance. He'll slip out to the loo with stacks of paperwork under his shirt and read it."

"Pretty sloppy for the scientists to be leaving that sort of information out on their desks," Mike replied.

"They don't think any of us can understand what they're working on. We're beneath them."

"In social class?"

"Exactly, we're fourth class. Peasants," George said. "But, the best things have been retrieved from the incinerator rubbish—pictures of impossible acts."

"Like what?" Mike asked.

"I've already said too much."

"No, I understand. I don't need to know. What about Michael? Would you tell me more, about him?"

"I don't know if I…" George's voice trailed off as he stared off into the night.

"Look, George, I'm very sorry. I've always wanted to take more time to get to know you, back home, but I have been too obsessed with my invention. I'm not a good friend, here or there." Mike didn't know what else to say when George turned toward him, so he kept quiet and waited.

When the silence broke, Mike could hear George's voice waiver.

"Maybe not, but you're the only friend I have."

He reached out and George took his hand in a firm grip.

"Thank you, my friend, I will make this up to you," Mike managed to say as they shook hands.

"Michael is not like you. He carries a lot of hate that is driving him to a very bad end."

"I understand."

"But do you understand you're taking a huge risk stepping into his life right now?" George asked.

"Look, I took a huge risk back home, though it wasn't exactly on purpose. If I want to get back home, I can wait for Michael to send me back, or I can try to duplicate my invention and Michael's crystals might help."

"You shouldn't go there," George said, shaking his head.

"I don't have a choice," Mike said.

"You could get pinched by the police. He's always worried that they're watching."

"I understand, George, but that's a risk I have to take."

"All right then, I'll take you there."

George walked over to the little, beat-up red car and climbed in. The screech of the hinges made Mike cringe as he opened the other door.

Mike knew, somehow, that Michael's project was important. He didn't know how or why, but he knew.

* * *

Michael Devon found himself sprawled across a countertop, ears ringing and the stench of vomit in his nostrils. He lay there for several minutes, with one cheek smashed on the hard surface, waiting for the strange dream to subside. As his vision cleared, he could see walls around him, but couldn't recognize where he was. Barely able to carry himself on his wobbly legs, he made his way over to a chair and dropped into it. He slowly turned in a half circle, viewing the walls around him. He suddenly froze and stared in disbelief at a series of photographs. Michael felt tears trickle down his face as he studied the pictures of Courtney Lewis.

Sobbing, he leaned forward and placed his head on the desk. Memories of his childhood Courtney flooded his mind.

Keep your eyes down, don't speak unless spoken to, Michael recited over and over to himself as he walked across town.

"Are you really going to school with the rich kids?" his friend asked.

"Yeah, Mum said I have to," Michael said.

"All because that lousy kid died?"

"Sorta. Mum works for his parents. They think I'm smart, so they gave me his seat in school for the rest of the year," Michael explained.

"That why your gutties are so clean?" a dingy little boy asked.

Michael admired his clean shoes. "Yup."

"Think you can do it?" his friend asked. "Them classies are awfully smart."

"Yeah. But, I have to follow all their rules or they'll throw me out."

"My Mum says this is the chance of a lifetime," his friend said.

"I guess it is, I've never heard of anyone else going over there," Michael replied.

"But they're all second and third class kids. You're not even supposed to talk to 'em."

"I know. That's one of the rules, too," Michael said.

"Clean your shoes and don't talk to anyone? Are there more?" the boy asked.

"Well, the rule is *be very clean*. Oh, and I'm not supposed to look at anyone, either."

"You scared?" the boy asked.

"A little, but Mum says there'll be lots of good kids there, so I need to be on my best behavior."

"What's that supposed to mean?" the boy asked.

"Don't be stupid, stupid."

The boys stopped at the entrance to their school and Michael waved as he continued on.

Keep your eyes down, don't speak unless spoken to, Michael repeated to himself, until he entered the beautiful stone building. He walked straight into the classroom, just as he and his mother had rehearsed the day before. One by one, the other children filed into the room. Nearly every one of them made a comment about him, but Michael kept still. He kept his head down as best he could. He couldn't help but notice their nice clothes and shiny shoes. The bell rang just as two giggling girls scurried into the room and took two chairs just one row in front of him.

They smell so nice, like flowers and soap. Their hair is so long and pretty; now I know what Mum meant. Michael struggled to follow along with the teacher, but kept looking back at the long, flowing, auburn hair in front of him.

When the morning classes were over, Michael stayed in the back of the classroom and ate his lunch alone. After lunch, the auburn-haired girl returned before the other children.

"What's your name?" she asked softly.

"I'm Michael, but I don't think I'm supposed to talk to you. You're better than me."

"Don't be silly, you're just poor, that's all. No one is *better* than anyone else."

"Please don't get in trouble. My Mum says that kind of talk will get me beaten," Michael whispered, keeping his eyes looking toward the floor.

"She's right, I could get beaten for saying that as well, but

I know I can trust you."

"How?"

"I can see it in your eyes," she said.

Michael looked into her eyes for the first time and felt his heart race. *Wow, she's an angel!*

"Hey, you're kinda cute," she said.

"I…well…" Michael stammered.

"Courtney! What are you doing in class already?" her friend called out as she entered the classroom.

"Just wanted to get started on my homework for tonight. Come on, let's try to get it done before class starts."

Michael looked at his schoolwork and acted like he was reading. Every word she spoke was like music, so he just sat there and listened as the two girls worked through the assignment. When they finally caught up to where he was, Michael followed along and finished silently with them. Every day after lunch, Courtney would return to class early and sneak a smile at him, wrinkling her nose slightly. Her friend was usually right behind her, so Michael would pretend to stare at the chalkboard so he could see her. Neither of them spoke a word to the other in front of the students. Courtney would occasionally slip a hand behind her and secretly wave her fingers at him. Michael wanted to reach out and touch them, but knew he would never see her again if he got caught.

A girl like that will never marry me, I'm beneath her. Unless I do something heroic, or invent something amazing, she'll marry someone else, Michael reminded himself.

It drove him to study harder and he became determined to be more than his birthright. He was driven to prove his worthiness to the elites so he could obtain third, or even second-class status and openly befriend Courtney. She was beautiful, strong-willed and very bright. Perfect in his mind. He knew these traits were a serious problem for her; women were not to be opinionated or intelligent. Those who were got publicly flogged and even executed.

When she did not show up for school for nearly a week that spring, Michael heard rumors that she had a mental breakdown.

He was scared for her and every day that went by added to his worry. *Maybe they saw her say something to me? Wouldn't they beat me, too?*

She returned the following Monday morning, but the girl he knew was gone. The secret smiles, winks and waves never resumed. Day by day, Michael's anger grew as visions of her being beaten or tortured raced around in his head. He vowed to himself that he would get revenge on those who ruined his Courtney.

For days, she sat teary-eyed in her chair and stared out the window. She looked far off into the distance and refused to look at or talk to anyone. Finally, almost two weeks after her return, Courtney opened her mouth and began speaking. She was not kind and she did not stop. She told them she did not care if they beat her or drugged her again and that she would rather die than live like them. She informed the teacher that she was a barbarian, that they were all fools. Courtney told them of another place, where all people were equal, including women and that was where she belonged. She was taken from that place and she demanded they send her back.

The teacher tried to get her to be quiet, but Courtney refused to stop talking. She went on to tell them that Britain was a small country, the USA had saved them from Germany and that the Queen was just a puny little rich lady on an island far across the ocean. With that shocking statement, the teacher issued her a red citation and yelled at her. That only made matters worse. That was when the swearing began. Courtney called her names and even struck the teacher, as she grabbed Courtney by the arm to lead her out. The teacher ran back to her desk, hit an alarm button and the siren sounded. Within thirty seconds security was there. They dragged Courtney down the hallway, kicking and screaming the entire way.

Michael just sat in his chair as the event unfolded, without the slightest expression on his face, but felt as if a bomb had gone off in his gut. Three days later, there was a public trial held in the town square. She'd been beaten so badly her face was unrecognizable, but he would recognize that auburn hair anywhere. The magistrate read a long list of accusations, some true and some not. Fifteen-year-old Courtney Lewis was hanged in the town square for crimes against the Queen and God. The crowd cheered, her parents wept and Michael Devon ran.

Michael opened his watery eyes and tried to shake himself out of the dreary trance, but the room kept shifting around him. *I know I was late for work, running a test on the crystal harmonizer at home, but what happened after that? Was I successful again? Could I have changed the future, which was my past, this time?*

Michael felt as if he was dreaming, though his senses told him otherwise. The room around him became stable and he rose from the chair. He went over and took the pictures off the wall, one by one, then sat down at the desk. He sat there, holding them in his arms, mourning her loss all over again. The only real happiness he had known was those few months when she was in his life. That was when he had forgotten the shame of his position: the inevitable reality that he would never amount to anything, never know freedom and never truly be happy. As he held the pictures, Michael felt the bitterness and hatred drain from his soul.

***

Courtney wanted to free her country and knew she would have to take a few lives along the way. There were hundreds of millions who had been brutalized by the world dominating Nazi regime. A few thousand more innocent deaths, to turn the tide of power on the evil Hitler family, were of absolutely no consequence. Any that had it coming were a bonus.

Courtney took one last moment to go over her plan and search it for gaps. Confident she was prepared for most plausible contingencies, she headed toward the front door of Theoretical Applications Corp. Already aware of her presence thanks to the security cameras, the guards were both staring at the front door as she opened it. Smiling at the two of them staring like schoolboys— eyes wide and grins even wider—she knew she was going to breeze through phase one and reach the lab.

"Howdy boys, nice night, huh?" she asked with a smile.

Tripping over each other and their own tongues, they both managed a cool, "Yep."

"I'm Emily, here to see Mike Devon. He's having an issue with some very expensive equipment I sold him." She smiled and pretended not to notice their stares.

"Yeah, well, we need to get permission from his superiors since you don't have a blue badge," the first guard said.

"We need to check out both of your bags, too," the second guard added.

Opening her coat Courtney said, "Hey I think this is a blue one, isn't it?"

Clearly disappointed, the second guard said, "Can you swipe it for me, right over there."

"No sweat, I've been through before, but call them if you like. Oh, it is kind of late though," Courtney said, as she pointed to the clock behind them. "I've been in twice actually and don't need an escort, due to my clearance and confidentiality arrangements," Courtney said.

The first guard spoke up, "Maybe I should escort you anyway."

"Running an escort service, now are you?" she said and gave him an alluring smile.

"I, I, um…" the guard stuttered into silence.

"Nah, but thanks though, I should be back down in twenty or so. Will you still be here?" she asked as she turned toward the elevator.

"Yeah, I will. Well, *we* will be down here. I make another round up through the floors in about an hour, at one a.m.," he said.

That didn't hurt now did it? Courtney thought to herself. She could feel four eyes glued to her every move. *Stay out of my way for the rest of the night and you both might get to go home.*

She thought she could hear the two of them exhale as the elevator doors closed. It never got old. The power she had over men was intoxicating. Nature had been kind to her, though the world had not and she took full advantage whenever it suited her needs.

Courtney pulled up the video feed of the uniformed Mike Devon once more. *So, he's a Colonel in the SAF now? I bet he's proud of that.* She felt a smile trying to break through.

She stepped off the elevator and approached Mike's office. Looking through the windows, she saw the uniformed Devon had made two stacks of files on the desk. He looked up just as she had expected he would. Courtney waved and smiled at the Colonel as if she knew him, then opened the door.

"Good evening Colonel Devon, I see you're making yourself at home. My name is Emily and I'm here to help you get what you need before you return to the SAF." *Let him discover who you are.*

Visibly shaken and confused, the Colonel straightened himself up, placing one hand on the hilt of his sword. "Continue," he ordered.

"Well, I work for an agency that has been perfecting some technology that is, shall we say, very powerful? That technology is how we brought you here, to our world. We can't really predict exactly where our visitors arrive just yet, hence the lack of a welcoming party," she said, feigning an embarrassed smile.

"What do you know of the SAF?" he asked.

"I happened to work for the Special Attack Forces myself,

some years back. Not to mention that my parents dedicated the majority of their lives in service to the SAF and defeating the Nazis."

"Why bring me here?"

"I've been collecting information about weapons technology for nearly twenty years now, working to create an opportunity to return and help the cause. We brought you here so you could help me safely deliver that technology to the SAF."

She noticed the Colonel's eyes dart back and forth from her left to her right eye, then her nose and back to her eyes. He settled back in on her right eye and she noticed his eyes soften slightly as his pupils dilated, but he held his face perfectly still.

Bingo...recognition, Courtney said to herself.

"But, if you worked for the SAF and you have been here for that long, you must have been fairly young when you were brought here. Like, in your teens?" he asked. "The year was?"

Courtney could see his pulse pounding in his neck. "Yes, I was fifteen. I was helping with an experiment that got out of control and I found myself here, in this America. Here, the Nazis were crushed and nearly extinct by 1945. A version of us, with far better technology, managed to do what we could not. I still don't know the answers to the *hows and whys,* but I have been looking for them," she explained. *He believes you, don't push.*

"Your name was changed when you arrived then?" he asked.

"Why, yes, I was not sure if you would remember me, but you were there during the testing. We were so young and I was an ugly duckling of sorts."

"I remember you, though I don't remember you quite that way."

"Really?" *Oh, this is going to be good.*

"Well, you see, I convinced my father to offer you the job in the lab. I wanted to keep you safe and to get myself out of the killing to try to have a somewhat normal life."

"Oh, my, I didn't know that. Well, thank you, Colonel. I guess I didn't realize I was in that much danger."

"We were born into a very violent time…" The Colonel paused briefly and his demeanor stiffened slightly. "I need to be brought up to speed if I'm to be of any real help."

Courtney smiled. "That's exactly what I hoped you would say."

* * *

Michael systematically went through the drawers, files and books in Colonel Devon's office. He repeatedly stopped to look at the pictures of Courtney, but kept himself from daydreaming. Jammed between two books, he found a wooden display case with *Series Two* engraved on it. Inside was what appeared to be an electronic tool, or weapon. Michael pried the case open and removed the device. It was much heavier than he expected and had several switches. Michael carefully switched the larger, recessed switch forward and felt a soft thump. It had a strange vibration to it that made his fingers tingle.

There's a lot of energy here. Must be some sort of resonator. I suppose it could be magnetic. Either way, it definitely feels like a weapon.

Michael slowly and carefully moved the end of it downward, toward the thick black book on the desk. He watched in disbelief as the corner started smoking and then fell to the ground with small paper pieces fluttering down to the floor. He tapped the book several times with the invisible blade and watched as it effortlessly slashed through. Powering it back down, he placed it back in its holster, then strapped the holster on his hip with his belt.

"Why, Colonel Devon, you seem to have broken free from British oppression. If only I had been so fortunate," Michael said, looking at a picture of the Colonel in uniform. Suddenly, a thought struck him, "Could she still be alive, here?" He could almost feel her presence, but the lack of recent pictures worried him.

Over the next few hours, Michael poured over everything he found and pocketed a few items he thought would be of use. He sat back in the chair and tried to imagine what she would look like at thirty-three years old. Finally, when he was nearly ready to go, Michael took the pictures of Courtney out of their frames. Behind one of them was a folded newspaper clipping. He felt his heart race as he unfolded the article and read.

* * *

Terry and Bill both reached for their vibrating phones.

"Unbelievable!" Bill exclaimed. "Tonight of all nights!"

"Easy big guy, I doubt they're doing it on purpose," said Terry.

Glancing down at their screens, they read, *Secured incoming conference*. They jumped up from opposite ends of the table and left the two attractive girls they were with. Shoving his way through the crowd, with Bill in tow, Terry approached the restroom behind a pair of muscle-bound men strutting like roosters.

"Sorry, Pony-boy, we have an important call to take," said Terry as he reached past the long-haired man to grab the door handle first.

"I don't think so," replied his bald companion.

"Bill?" Terry asked politely as he stepped into the restroom with his ringing phone in one hand.

The first impact was fairly subtle and the bald man collapsed at his friend's feet.

"Don't do it Pony-boy," Terry said, as his phone rang again.

The man threw a punch at Terry, who twitched out of the way and gave Bill a nod. The pony-tailed man howled as Bill's roundhouse came from behind and caught him just under his right eye. The *crack* was unmistakable, a broken left cheekbone. The man reeled around to meet Bill's left uppercut. The second man fell, landing partially on top of the other.

"Go ahead," Terry said, as he accepted the call.

Bill dragged the two unconscious men far enough into the

restroom to shut the door, then latched it.

The caller said, "All parties are present. Code Lima Lima Bravo Echo. Full Authorization is granted. I repeat, code Lima Lima Bravo Echo. Full authorization granted. Response mandatory."

Bill and Terry stared at each other in disbelief, visibly shaken at the orders to take Courtney down.

Reading the secured message on his phone, Terry answered, "Orders received. We are both en route, ETA 30 minutes. Send all pertinent intel ASAP."

"Negative, we have a bird coming down on top of your building now. Use the fire escape on the west exterior wall for roof access," the voice directed. "We have gear on board."

"Roger that." Terry hung up and stepped past Bill to unlock the door.

Bill held the door shut with his right hand and used his forearm to firmly nudge Terry back. "Hold on. This isn't happening. We've gone over this scenario a dozen times and we always end up dead. This is a job for a full team, not just the two of us."

"Look, buddy, this isn't a death sentence and we darn sure *are* going to do our jobs. Keep your cool and let me take the lead on this one. You take her down when she's up to her elbows in my intestines. That's our plan. If she gets to me, you empty that cannon of yours into both of us if you have to. And you *will* empty it. Are we clear, soldier?"

"I don't know."

"You don't know? She's off the reservation. A bad guy. We do bad guys, or have you forgotten? That's what we signed up for and what we're expected to do. Besides, you know she'd drop us both without blinking, if she got the orders."

Bill thought for a moment, then answered, "You're right. Sorry." He lowered his arm and let Terry pass.

With that, Terry opened the door and walked out. Bill glanced down at the two men as he stepped over them. *That'll be us, before the night is over.*

The two men hurried out of the club, without a glance toward the two girls they had been talking with only five minutes before. The assignment to bring down Lima Lima Bravo Echo had completely overtaken their every thought.

* * *

"He studied time travel, wormholes and multidimensional math until he had exhausted every resource he could find. Michael even *borrowed* books from BAE, risking everything. He read anything he could get his hands on from Stephen Hawking, Albert Einstein, Isaac Newton and countless other mathematicians, physicists and scientists, but it was never enough," George explained, as he and Mike drove to Michael's flat.

"I know of all those men and have read many of their works myself," Mike said.

"Really? You should compare them with some of Michael's books. It would be interesting to know if they wrote the same things."

"You are thinking like a scientist. Did he teach you that?" Mike asked.

"The only part I really understood was that he was trying to find a way to go back in time and help that girl, Courtney. He would talk about dimensions and time for hours, rambling on even as I left the house. I thought he was barmy, dreaming that he would be able to see her again someday." George shrugged. "It looks like he wasn't crazy after all."

"Technology has a habit of making the crazies into visionaries," Mike said. *I just hope I survive long enough to experience it for myself.*

"Here we are—Michael's place."

"This is way bigger than mine," Mike said.

"It's been in his family for three generations now. Both sets of his grandparents and his parents bought it together so they could afford it."

"I see," Mike said, trying to imagine both sets of his grandparents living under one roof. "That must have been interesting."

"Yes, it must have been wonderful to have the family so close," George said.

"Well, I knew both of his grandmothers and I'm not so sure about that!" Mike laughed.

George gave him a confused look, then said, "I'll take you inside, but I can't stay."

"No, I'm fine, you should just go on home," Mike said and opened the car door. "Oh, is there anything I should know before I go in? Security system? Dog?"

"Well, there *is* one more thing I should tell you."

"Fire away," Mike said and pulled the door shut.

"So, after Courtney was killed, her parents spoke out and were executed a few days later."

"That's terrible, George."

"It was. Well, Michael broke into their house that night and stripped her bedroom. He kept everything boxed up in the basement of his parent's flat for years. When his parents had both passed on, he set her stuff up in one of the bedrooms. Kind of creepy, eh?" he asked.

"Yeah and tragic at the same time." Mike felt surges of anguish wash over him. He could feel what Michael had endured. Visions of the newly revealed event began playing in his head as Mike viewed in horror.

"Mike? Are you all right?"

"Oh, uh, yeah. Just imagining what it must have been like," Mike said. "I'm sorry to involve you, but I had no one else I could trust."

Mike felt terrible for putting the kind man at risk. Life had not been fair to George and he didn't want to make things worse.

"It's all right, mate. I know. But, understand that if something happens to you, I *can't* be involved. My wife is pregnant again and I have to be there for her," said George, as he looked off into the distance.

"George, I'm so happy for you and wish you the best. Here, take my watch. It should fetch a decent price. The platinum is rare even if this Swiss brand isn't known around here," Mike said. "Use it to get a good doctor, right away."

"Wow, that's quite a watch, but I can't," George said.

Mike climbed out of the car, tossed the watch onto the passenger seat and closed the door. Smiling at George's reaction, Mike crossed the street and walked up to the front door. He unlocked the door and stepped back nearly fifty years in time. It was unnerving to be in a new place that felt so familiar. The kitchen was a mess and the rest of the place was cluttered and dusty, except for one room. Courtney's recreated bedroom was immaculate, with pictures of several small groups of girls on the dresser. A young Courtney was in several of the pictures, which helped Mike clearly remember the face of the girl in his dreams. Her big smile and bright blue eyes were so happy and full of life in the pictures. It was hard to comprehend why she had to go through so much, at such a young age. Among the pictures was one of Courtney and what appeared to be her parents, at a lake.

Mike took several of the pictures out of their frames and stacked them on the bedside table.

These may not be Courtney, exactly, but they are a part of her. Maybe I can give them to her someday.

He lay down on Courtney's bed, collapsed onto her pillow and willed himself to dream about her.

* * *

"I'm not sure I believe this bull about a second set of them from a land far, far away, but it sure sounds like the big boys believe it," Bill said to Terry, over the chopper headsets as they watched various intelligence streaming in over their smartphones and a tablet.

"I know, but the feed clearly shows Mike stepping—or getting yanked—into nowhere. Then high-and-tight, Military Mike, in uniform, staggers into view a few minutes later?"

"It's a mind trip, you have to admit," Bill said. "I suppose it could be CGI, though."

"Absolutely, but it would have taken hundreds, if not thousands, of hours to produce two hours of the goofy footage."

"If it is real, this tech is just plain crazy. I can't believe we would let some punk civvy develop this! We should have cleaned it all out long ago! Who makes these decisions anyway? I'd like to beat his head in right about now!" Bill yelled loud enough that Terry could hear his voice carry inside the chopper.

"Easy, big guy. Remember, Courtney has been involved in the decisions for this project since the outset. It makes perfect sense that she would make sure it stayed civilian."

"Yeah, I know but do you really think she has been planning something the entire time?" Bill asked.

"I do. Too much of this is starting to click. I think we have to assume the worst for now," Terry explained.

Looking down at the tablet PC, he quietly read an instant message from their boss.

Need to know: Agent Lewis' mental instability—late teens. Ongoing delusions of being surrounded by aliens and parents replaced by impostors. Civilian authorities began the commitment process, but the parents died and delusions along with them. Psych division diagnosed likely abuse in the home.

"Thanks for the note, God, we read you," Terry said to the eavesdroppers he assumed were watching from the surveillance center, then held it up for Bill to read.

"Man, we're in for some freaky stuff tonight!"

"Affirmative. Courtney has never been straight with us, always seemed disconnected and this would explain so much," Terry reasoned.

"Watch, she calls him *Colonel Devon*, and see how his hand

goes to his hip when she startles him? This thing on his belt must be a weapon," Bill pointed to the screen.

"Agreed and if he goes for it, drop him."

"Roger that," Bill said. "I have a bad feeling about Military Mike. The dude looks tough."

"Courtney is the problem. She won't follow a military playbook like he probably will." Terry thought for a moment. "She's probably plugged in to the security feed at TAC. Heck, she might even be——"

Terry ripped the back off his phone, pulled out the battery and nodded at Bill to do the same. He pulled a piece of scotch tape from the inside and covered the terminals, then put the phone back together. *Courtney's precaution.*

"She'll try to get out as soon as she has what she's after. You go in through the lobby and bring the security team up to the lab," Terry instructed, as he slipped on a backpack.

"Ten-four," Bill said, shouldering his pack as well.

"Don't let them shoot me, either. I don't like getting shot, Kevlar or no Kevlar."

"We'll see what I can do," Bill chuckled.

"I'll be coming down from the roof, so that leaves all of the windows for exfil. Oh, and she *will* use deadly force, so keep your eyes open, "Terry said.

"We're here," the pilot said, putting them both on high alert.

In one fluid motion, Terry opened the door, dropped his chopper headset onto the seat and jumped out the door.

"I'm clear! Get those guards, then come save me from Colonel whack-job and She-Ra! Got me?" Terry ordered over the secured com.

"Roger that, give me 90 seconds, on my mark…go! Stay alive now, you hear me?" Bill said.

"Roger that. Quiet down so I can, *you hear me?*" Terry watched the chopper drop Bill in the parking lot, opposite Mike's side of the building.

"Copy. T-minus seventy seven," Bill replied, as they both entered TAC.

* * *

After a brief explanation of her plan, Courtney gave Colonel Devon a short list of final instructions.

"You've thought this out," he said.

"I would hope so. I've been working on it for a while." Courtney turned her jacket inside out, then said, "And act like you own the place, or we're both done."

"Courtney Lewis?"

His tone caused her to look him in the eye. Though his face lacked expression, his eyes told a different story.

"Yes, Colonel?"

His mouth opened but nothing came out for several seconds. Finally, he took a deep breath and said, "I have wanted to see you again for…for my entire adult life."

"I'm very glad to get to see you again, too," she replied.

"No…I mean, I've wanted to make it up to you, somehow… I blame myself for what happened."

"Don't. It was no one's fault. It just happened. For now, we have to focus on getting out of here alive," she said. Courtney noticed a hint of frustration on his face and knew he was not satisfied. "But, if it helps, I forgive you." Courtney felt her throat constrict slightly and turned around before she forced herself to swallow. Courtney headed down the hall, as if nothing was wrong. *Maybe I do, maybe I don't. Either way, he needed to hear it.*

Courtney felt her phone vibrate three times in rapid succession and tugged it out of her pocket. "We have visitors! Let's grab the device and get out of here," she ordered as she headed for the lab.

"What device?"

"The one we used to bring you here." Fumbling with her

phone as she reached the lab, Courtney said, "Bill and two security guards are arguing down in the lobby."

"Who's Bill?" the Colonel asked, as he reached her.

"One of my ex-partners. Very dangerous, too." She scrolled to the next alert on her phone and tapped it to bring up a video feed. Courtney could just make out a person, quickly passing the sixth floor. *Terry?* "One or two coming up the stairwell from two floors below and one coming down from the roof, three floors up. They'll come through that door." Courtney pointed toward the door marked *Stairs*.

The Colonel ran up to it, pulled out his weapon and made an adjustment. Courtney heard a buzzing sound and saw smoke rising past the Colonel. She saw molten metal splattering at the Colonel's feet for a few seconds, then he turned around.

"Done," he said, leaving two glowing stripes at the edges of the door, smoking as they cooled. "That will buy us some time while they find another way."

"Wow, I didn't know those could do anything but slash men, women and children. Well and explode occasionally," Courtney said, as she turned to enter the lab.

"We haven't had the exploding issue for several iterations. The current models are very stable," the Colonel said proudly.

No argument for the men, women and children.

Courtney held her tongue as she reached down and scooped up the spud, then rushed to the far corner of the lab. "Here, grab this case and load that up," she said, pointing to the spud base and power supply.

"This thing is going to weigh nearly a hundred pounds," he said, lifting it up.

"Should I carry the heavy one?"

"No, I'll be fine," he said.

"And, this is your pack. It has duplicates of everything I have in this one," Courtney said, as she separated the thin, laptop style bags. "One of these phones is inside. Push the button here to turn it on. The password is *overthrow*." She handed him the pack. "Intel I've been collecting for nearly a decade."

"Overthrow, got it."

"Touch this and it will open up a list of items numbered in order, touch the number one and read it first." Courtney opened the door, rushed out into the hallway and checked the security feed once more.

"Wait, I'm not following you."

"No time. Just touch item number one and read. Got it?"

"Yes," Colonel Devon said, hurrying to keep up.

"If something happens to me, the information in this phone, or the larger one in that pouch, is critical. It also has the info you'll need to get this system operational and return home."

"Do you think this will help the SAF?" the Colonel asked skeptically.

"The weapons systems documented in there will." Courtney realized he had become noticeably more focused and his eyes were dark and lifeless. She knew these eyes all too well. They belonged to every cold-blooded killer she had ever seen.

Courtney grabbed a communications headset and microphone from her bag, put it on, then tucked her locks into a dark blue baseball cap. She then pulled out her silenced P226 and stuffed two extra, hi-cap clips into her left rear pocket.

She started to feel a tinge of regret, then reminded herself, *forty caliber Hydra-Shok rounds, into Kevlar isn't deadly. Let's just hope I don't miss.*

* * *

Terry was first to arrive at the third floor and found the source of the smoke and fumes.   "Third floor exit is jammed and the door feels warm," he said softly.

"Roger that, we're almost there," Bill said, as he cleared the last few steps to Terry.

"Uh, Bill, they might have welded it."

"No fire alarms, though."

"Disabled?" Terry asked.

"Could be."

A winded security guard said from the landing below, "Couldn't be, we would get an alarm if someone tampered with them."

"Uh, yeah, we think someone may have disabled all of the alarms," Terry explained.

"Impossible, they would have to go through us first," the guard said.

"You stay down there and make sure no one comes up the stairs," Terry told the guard as he pulled off his backpack.

Bill reached out and slowly pulled on the handle. "Doesn't budge. I see what you mean."

"I'm going to blow it," Terry said as he pulled some putty out of an inner pocket and began rolling it between his hands.

"Wait, you can't use explosives in here!" the guard yelled.

"Fire alarms?" Terry asked with disbelief.

"It's against company policy and you could damage the building! Man, you aren't exactly the brightest guy, are you?"

"Do you see the look that doughnut-gobbler is giving me? I swear if he says—" Terry looked over his shoulder. "If you say another word to me, I'm going to beat you to death! Now shut up!" Terry hissed, as he placed four small charges on the door hinges.

"Easy there, *big guy*," Bill said.

"Very funny," Terry said.

"Come on up, we're going to the fourth floor. It's going to rain concrete on you down there," Bill warned.

"OK," the guard replied and slowly made his way past them.

"Thanks, we really need his help," Terry said shaking his head.

"You should have seen the other guy," Bill laughed and ran up to join the guard.

Terry followed him and said, "Cover your ears, squeeze your

eyes tight and open your mouth, or this will rupture your eardrums." Terry covered his ears with the remote in one hand and held up three fingers with the other. He dropped them, one at a time, then set off the shaped charges on the door.

Slightly disoriented, they headed back down to what Terry expected to be an easy entrance. Instead they found the door mostly in place, with a wide gap where the hinges used to be. Bill grabbed the edge of the door and yanked it back into the stairwell, leaving an opening wide enough to squeeze through.

"Me first," said Bill, holding Terry back with one hand. He pulled out his pistol with the other, then dove through the hole. A single shot rang out. "Clear!"

"You all right?" Terry asked as he slipped through the opening with his gun drawn.

"Yeah, sorry, that was an accident. I was so sure she was going to be waiting for me that I shot my reflection," Bill said as he motioned down the hall to the full height window.

"You've got to be kidding?"

"I know and I'm not going to hear the end of it for a long time," Bill said with a smirk.

The guard wiggled his way through the opening and said, "That's a rookie mistake son, you aren't supposed to put your finger on the trigger until—"

"Shut up!" Bill yelled.

Suddenly, their coms started making a strange static noise.

"Wait, that's—"

Terry was interrupted by a voice on their coms that sounded like his. "Get that bird ready, we need a lift!"

"No! No! No!" Terry screamed into the com. "She put a jammer in here somewhere! She's been monitoring our channel! Quick, down the stairs!" He barely got the words out when the building shook. Debris flew through the small gap they had just come through. Stumbling backwards, he turned and looked at Bill with a shocked expression on his face. "She's been planning this for a while." With that he looked over at the guard and said, "You'll be lucky to make it out of here alive."

"Never take the elevator? She beat that into our heads for years. She all but forced us into the stairwell so she could vaporize us! Are we *that* stupid?" Bill screamed.

Terry glanced over at Bill and saw a strange look on his face. He dove to the floor, against the wall and pointed his pistol in the direction Bill had been staring. Then, Bill took off running, firing shots at his reflection in rapid succession. The wild hail of bullets struck the glass from floor to ceiling. Terry lay with his pistol aimed in Bill's direction, confused as to what his partner had seen. Bill sprinted toward the large, damaged windows. When he was a few feet from the glass, he tossed his gun backwards. Terry jumped to his feet and watched in horror as Bill leapt out the third story window.

As the noise from the clattering glass quieted, Terry exhaled loudly. "The tree. He jumped into that tree. He's going for the chopper."

* * *

Mike opened his eyes, looked hopefully around the room, then disappointment set in. *Nope, not a dream.* He glanced at the clock. *Two a.m., I'd better get started.* Mike picked the pictures up from the desk, then headed into the basement. He noticed the stairs had been worked on recently and was slightly confused by the landing halfway down. As he looked around the lab, he was shocked at what he saw. "You really *are* messed up."

One wall was covered with grouped pictures of Courtney. Most were enlarged duplicates of those he brought from Courtney's room, surrounded by six, smaller ones. There were seven, mismatched bookcases lining another wall, filled with books and stacked to the ceiling. In the middle of the large room was a large, wooden table, missing one chair. On the far wall was a long workbench, covered with electrical devices of various shapes and sizes. In the corner adjacent the picture wall and the workbench was an array of devices hooked together with wire. Each device had a prism-shaped crystal on top, but no two crystals were the same size.

Mike counted seven of them, as he untangled the cords and strung them out on the workbench. He pulled on the wire from the first device and traced it back to a black box with three knobs and four gauges on the front of it. *Must be the power supply.* Looking up and down the oddly crafted system for a moment, he shook his head, then noticed a set of notebooks on the end of the workbench. Each of the notebooks had a date and a volume number on it, numbered in Roman numerals.

"Seven, huh?" He picked up the last volume. "You like the number—"

Mike spun around toward the strange staircase. He counted seven stairs above and seven below the landing. Looking at the pictures, he saw they were in groups of seven, then counted the chairs at the table. Feeling the hair on the back of his neck tingle, he said, "Seven. That's creepy." The sounds of his own voice helped ease him. Mike scanned for more oddities, but didn't see any.

He carried the notebook over to the table and sat down, then rechecked the room before he began to read. "Let's see what the kook has conjured up." The first page had him hooked and the further he read, the more excited he became. It took nearly two hours to get to the end, then Mike went for volume six. Over an hour later he sat up and stared at the crystal-topped array.

"So, you aren't crazy, but this just isn't possible." Mike felt guilty when he realized he felt the same way about Michael's project that scientists back home would feel about his.

He was into more advanced, dimensional math than Mike had seen before. The short notes Michael left scattered around the pages served as a guide as Mike struggled to fully understand the work.

"If this is right, then there is no barrier. This is far too dangerous for one—"

Mike suddenly felt awash with paranoia. He froze in his seat and listened very carefully for any strange sound. Several times, he thought he heard soft footsteps overhead. Mike remembered seeing a backpack by the stairs and quickly retrieved it. He dumped out a change of clothes and took it over to Michael's invention. He rushed to disconnect one of the crystal devices from the string and put it in the bag, then covered it with the seven notebooks and the pictures from Courtney's room.

Mike rushed upstairs to Michael's bedroom, hoping Michael would have a small stash of emergency money. There was some money in the wallet from the locker at BAE, but he didn't know how long it would last.

Looking around the room, his eyes lit on a book high atop a bookcase. *The Einstein-Rosen Bridge. Now why are you up there?*

Mike moved a chair by the bed to the front of the bookcase. He climbed up, grabbed the book and jumped down. The book rattled as he landed, causing Mike to smile. Inside, there was a small stack of paper money and a handful of gold and silver coins. It was likely a meager sum in reality, but probably a small fortune Michael had struggled for years to save. "Sorry, but this is for the both of us."

Mike curiously picked up one of the books on Michael's bedside table and scanned it. Suddenly, he felt everything around him become hazy and exhaustion overcame him. He held onto the chair to steady himself, his eyes burning and head pounding. *I need to rest for a few minutes, that's all.* Mike staggered out to the front room and dropped into an old, wing-backed chair. He had barely sat down in the chair when he fell unconscious.

* * *

Courtney lunged off the elevator the instant it opened. She grabbed a chair from the hallway and jammed the doors, rendering it useless.

"The stairs, quick!" she ordered, then glanced at her phone. "They're one floor up and our route is clear." They ran for the stairwell, with their cases in tow. "Close it softly."

Courtney opened the door then rushed down the stairs. Courtney paused at the door to listen for new trouble, then pulled her phone from her pocket. Checking the cameras once again, she opened her bag and removed a military-looking remote control.

"They made it into the lab. Cover. I'm blowing the stairwell at the third floor." Courtney watched the Colonel put his hands over his ears, squint his eyes shut and open his mouth. She did the same herself, then pushed the button. The beep of the remote was instantly engulfed by the concussion of an explosion and sounds of falling debris two stories above, in the stairwell.

Courtney motioned for Colonel Devon to check the lobby, but just as he was about to pull on the handle, she checked her phone and saw a guard running toward the door with his gun drawn. She waved the Colonel off and the two stood in silence.

"Can you read me? Are you guys OK up there?" The guard on the other side of the door called out.

The colonel drew his sword and nodded at Courtney to move up the stairs. She grabbed his case along with hers and worked her way up the first flight of stairs. The door began to open as the Colonel plunged his sword through the wall next to it. He planted his foot on the far wall for support and ripped the sword across the solid steel fire door, into the wall on the other side. The guard's repeated screams made Courtney wish she could end his misery. Almost instantly a hail of gunfire erupted, forcing Colonel Devon up the stairs toward Courtney. When the gunfire stopped, they made eye contact briefly, then one last round went off.

Courtney looked at her phone. "He's down."

The Colonel slipped back down the last flight of stairs, peering out through stray bullet holes as he went.

Courtney grabbed both cases and rushed down the stairs as he yanked the lower section of the wrecked door open. He ducked under the upper piece and entered the lobby with Courtney right on his heels. The gutted man was lying on the floor, tangled up in his own intestines, a pool of blood was growing around him. His gun was in his right hand, near his mutilated head.

"Honorable man," the Colonel said as he reached to take his case from Courtney.

She held up her finger to silence him and held her phone up to the com mic, playing a man's voice requesting an airlift.

"We're gonna take a little chopper ride," she said, in answer to his inquisitive look, then ran out into the lobby. She slid her case under the turnstile, then hopped over, reaching the front doors fifty feet ahead of the Colonel. "I'll go to the pilot's door, you go in the side. Colonel, I don't want to kill him if we don't have to."

She opened the door and the two headed out across the parking lot. The sound of gunfire and glass shattering was just barely audible over the sound of the chopper lowering in front of them.

Not slowing to look back she yelled, "The boys are making a try for us!"

The Colonel tossed his case in the side door and then jumped in. Courtney shoved hers in behind him, then ran around the chopper and opened the front door. The pilot's limp body flopped out in front of her and she grabbed his head to protect him as he fell. She checked his pulse, then yanked the headset off and tossed it inside. Courtney then grabbed the pilot's wrists and drug him off the skids before jumping in the chopper. Within a few seconds, she had spun the rotor up to full speed and they began to climb rapidly. Shoving forward quickly on the stick, she nearly clipped the tops of the first trees.

"Stay low!" he commanded. "Bogie on the floor at our six, another at our nine!"

She had seen the latter out of her side window; it was the guard from the gate. The unmistakable sound of bullets striking the helicopter fuselage could be heard over the noise of the wailing turbine. Courtney pitched the chopper over hard to the right side and dropped into a field past the tree line and out of sight from the shooters. After a few tense moments went by, she turned off the lights and transponder, turning sharply again to the right. To quiet the chopper as much as she could, Courtney idled the turbine down to maintain minimal lift. She kept the chopper just barely ten feet off the ground, taking advantage of the additional lift from ground effect. They flew across several fields like this, covering nearly two miles before she gently set it down, sliding to a halt in a field near an industrial complex.

She looked back at the Colonel and said, "We're at the substation."

* * *

Bill was more concerned about getting through the glass and reaching the tree, than overshooting it. Everything was in slow motion as he reached out, grabbed a branch with one hand and clenched the thirty-foot perch for all he was worth. He felt a massive jerk as the full force of his jump came to bear on his one hand, causing his legs to flip forward and his grip to fail. Unable to reach the branch with his free hand, Bill tumbled backwards, falling ten feet until his thighs hit a flimsy branch. He firmly grabbed on but it instantly snapped off. He fell the remaining twelve feet, face-first, into the flowerbed below. He reached out slightly with his arms and legs to absorb some of the blow but still found himself unable to breathe. Bill struggled to force the air out of his lungs and his body eventually took fresh air back in.

As life returned to normal speed, he looked back up at the third story window he had just exited, he saw the outline of Terry peering out. Raising an arm to let Terry know he was alive, Bill heard the sound of a chopper off in the distance. It was their chopper. Its turbine winding down after landing on the other side of the building. Beaten and bruised, Bill struggled to his feet.

"You OK?" he heard Terry call out.

Bill nodded and waved, then managed a meager, "Yep," as he stumbled off toward the helicopter. As he started to jog away, Bill heard the guard yell, "They're getting away!"

Wishing he was within reach of the guard, Bill held his pointer finger up long enough to be certain Terry would notice. "Give him one for me, Terry."

* * *

Mike was startled awake by a wailing siren. He leapt out of the chair and scrambled over to a front window. He peeked out and saw an ambulance scream through the intersection. Relieved, he flopped back down into the warm, comfortable chair and the pounding in his chest slowly subsided. *Still not a dream. So, now what? Modify Michael's invention? Or attempt to rebuild the spud from memory?* His stomach growled and he looked at the clock across the room. *Five? The little restaurant around the corner should be open now.*

He got up from the large chair and he walked to the bathroom. As he opened the door he was startled to see a large, crazy-haired twin of himself staring back at him.

Mike screamed out in surprise, grabbed the door jam and raised an arm to protect himself. His would-be attacker did the same.

"Dang it!" Mike yelled at himself in the oversized mirror on the far, bathroom wall. "Who does that?" Mike demanded. *Freaking nut-job! See what could happen if you don't get some balance in your life? Oops, talking to yourself is an early sign—*

He looked back at himself in the mirror and chuckled.

Clean and refreshed from a long, hot shower, Mike put on some of Michael's clothes and headed to the front door. He made sure he had everything he wanted to keep stuffed into the bag. Pulling the bag's strap up over his shoulder, he cautiously headed out the door, locking it behind him.

As he crossed the street, Mike noticed a plain, four door sedan. The tinted windows were down a little, but he couldn't see if anyone was inside. *That was on the other side of the street when George dropped me off.* Mike slowed and turned his gaze back to the car. It immediately started, then drove away. He had been fighting a strong sense of paranoia since he had arrived. *It's nothing. You're in a strange place. Lack of sleep and food. Nothing at all. Get a grip. and quit talking to me, would ya?* He smiled at his own joke.

Mike walked down the dimly lit sidewalk until he arrived at the little café he had envisioned. He couldn't tell if he was dreaming or not, until he grabbed onto the cold doorknob. He pushed slowly on the wooden door and it creaked as it tapped a bell overhead to announce his presence. The woman behind the counter was already looking in his direction or he might have run away.

Smiling at her, Mike forced out, "Good morning, how are you doing?"

"Not quite. Sun's not up yet. You related to that bloke down the street? Look a lot like him, you do." She stared at him with cold, unblinking eyes as she spoke.

"Well, yes, he's my cousin actually. Folks say we look like twins." Mike regretted choosing a place so close to Michael's.

"What folks?"

"Uh, just folks in general, that's all," Mike said.

"Ain't seen him in quite a while now. Stopped coming in here. Boy's a bit touched in the head, most folks think." She continued to stare, watching Mike closely.

"Yeah, he's different, that's for sure. You open for breakfast?" Mike was turning to leave.

"Course we are, can't you read? Sign says *Open.*"

Mike felt himself becoming extremely angry. *Lady, you'd better shut your mouth or I'll—*

Mike caught himself and took a deep breath to calm down. *This isn't normal. Must be lack of sleep or the stress. Or the trip.*

"Here's a menu."

"Thank—"

"Ya ain't from around here now are ya?" she interrupted.

"Uh, nope. Small town out in Maine. Is it that obvious?" He forced a smile as he reached for the menu.

"Maine? I always think of them as havin' a much stronger, Queen's English sorta sound to 'em."

Mike noticed her expression change slightly. She was clearly faking a smile now and looking straight through him. *If I wasn't so hungry I'd just leave. Why can't she just shut up and do her job?* Mike thought.

Barely seated at the counter, Mike quickly read the menu and stood back up.

"I would like a number four please." He requested.

Mike really wanted a number three, but he didn't want to answer the questions about how to cook the steak and eggs, so he settled for hotcakes and sausage.

"I'll have a seat at the window," Mike announced.

He wanted to look out the window and watch the cars go by. He had noticed several brands that he was not used to seeing very often, if at all. Brands that caught his eye were Austin Healey, Reliant and MG. There was an abnormal amount of Jaguar and Rover vehicles and very few American made cars. It was all far too British and Mike wanted to learn what had gone wrong, but he had to keep his focus on getting back.

"You won't unless you can prove you are third class or better. Show me your papers."

"I...they're back at the house. Shall I go get them?" *Better this way.* He turned once more to leave.

"Stay. Fourth class sits over there." She pointed off to a somewhat secluded corner toward the back of the building.

"Oh, of course." Mike said and walked obediently to the area she had directed him to. He sat down and glanced back to the front windows. He noticed the lady was talking on the phone now, with her back toward the glass. His instincts were screaming for him to run. *It's nothing. You're just paranoid. You'll feel better after you eat.*

When Mike's food finally made it to him, it was just barely

warm. After taking his first few bites, Mike glanced at the front windows again and saw the lady staring back at him. He quickly turned his gaze back down to his bland, lukewarm breakfast.

Don't run.

Mike shoved several more bites into his mouth, then placed the sausage into a napkin and slipped it into his pocket. He placed a ten-pound note under the edge of his plate and stuffed another large bite of hotcake into his mouth.

Getting up as normally as he could, Mike walked toward the door marked *Gents*. He stepped inside and it closed behind him. He spun around, slowly cracked it open and peaked out to see if she was approaching his table. Seeing she wasn't, Mike carefully slipped back out to the table, watching the glass for her reflection. He grabbed his things and rushed to the back door. Mike twisted its bell off and pulled on the handle, expecting another creaky door. It opened quietly and he rushed out into the cool, morning air. Mike felt momentary relief as he jogged down the shadowy alley, heading for Michael's. With every step he felt less at ease, until he was once again overwhelmed by anxiety.

Trust your instincts, Mike. Something is terribly wrong, but what? As Michael's house came into view, Mike saw two men in dark clothing, running out of the front door. *Oh, no!*

Looking around frantically, one of them spotted Mike and called out to the other; "Down there!" then turned and called out, "Halt! Don't move! Scotland Yard!"

Mike veered hard away from them, to his right, nearly falling down. Fear and adrenaline took over and he broke into a full sprint. *Scotland freaking yard!? That old battle-axe called them! I knew something was up!*

He could hear tires squealing behind him and glanced back to see his lone pursuer had slowed down.

All those workouts are paying off now, Mike thought. Knowing they were coming after him in the car, Mike zigzagged through alleys and backyards over and over to thwart his would-be captors. He could hear the roar of their engine off in the distance as he stepped back into the open. Mike saw a large store barely two hundred yards away. Within minutes, he was able to get a different shirt, a windbreaker and a larger backpack. He grabbed a bottle of water, bags of peanuts and jerky, then stopped at the aisles of books on his way to check out. He didn't want to stop, but knew he needed to learn about the culture to improve his chances to return home. Scurrying down the rows, Mike found three history books that interested him: *Supreme Britain's Colonization of The Underprivileged Western World, Hail to The New World Order* and *The War That Brought Peace and Civilization to The World*. Anxious to get back out on the street and put more distance between him and the detectives, Mike hurried to the front and paid for his items. He stopped just inside the exit doors, put his things in the new bag and put on the new jacket. He then stuffed the old bag into the garbage and walked out as fast as he could without arousing suspicion.

Mike caught himself wishing Courtney was with him and fought back the overwhelming feeling of loneliness. *You have to get better at this, or you're not going to make it out of here.*

His body exhausted to the point of collapse, Mike walked into *Mimi's Inn* to rent a room for the night. It was daybreak and he needed to get off the streets to figure out what he was facing in this strange place. The sleepy lady at the counter barely spoke any English and for the first time in his life, Mike was pleased to have the communication barrier.

Nearly running up the stairs with his heavy bag, Mike's stomach was growling and cheering him onward. Moments later, he was on the fifth floor of the old, rundown hotel. Looking out the window as he was closing the blinds he realized that he recognized the skyline. All of the major buildings appeared to be nearly the same as back home, though some of the minor ones had changed. Mike twisted the blind one last turn, but continued to stare in the direction of the view.

How could it be that so much is the same when a different government has been running the country for decades? Maybe the main players are still the same? Some of them were.

He tried to grasp the possibilities, but he was filthy and famished. He grabbed a handful of peanuts and a piece of jerky to eat while showering. The hot water relaxed him and by the time he made it out, Mike felt refreshed. He fell onto the bed and grabbed more food as he flipped through one of his new books. His eyes closed and he felt his body twitch, then sleep overcame him.

* * *

After the noise of the turbine had quieted down, Courtney pulled off the headset and said to the Colonel, "We have some time now so I would like to see if you can answer some questions for me." She watched closely to see the Colonel's reaction. "What do you know of my parents Court and Danni Lewis? Are they still alive?" His face didn't respond, but his eyes did. Courtney grabbed hold of the Colonel's arm. "My parents? Please, do you know anything about them? Are they still alive?"

"Yes, your parents are both alive. We have mourned your death since—"

"My death? They thought I was dead when I vanished? Wasn't there another Courtney like you and the other Mike Devon?" Courtney knew what had happened from Mike's dreams and was forcing the Colonel to admit to it. "I took her place here, she must have gone there, in my place."

"Yes, I know. There was another girl who took your place. One second you were there and the next second she was. Well, she looked like you, mostly. Her clothing and some other things she had were not from anywhere we could identify."

"That fits Mike's dream," Courtney said.

"What do you mean about *Mike's dream*?"

"Mike has had a recurring dream since June of 1994, the same time of our event. I think he really experienced it. I think that since you were so close to the altar, you were nearly switched with Mike. Somehow, he was brought into your world, well, partially. He remembers too many details, like colors, sounds and words for it to be a dream. He even had issues with his hip for some time afterward. I guess an SAF soldier struck him."

"I remember the strange, shimmering figure in a bed. We tried to kill it. Him." The Colonel's eyes darted around as he tried to make sense of the memory. "We tried to kill me? Is that even possible?"

"It appears so. What happened next?" Courtney asked.

"That was just before you...you...she died."

"What are you keeping from me? There is something else I should know, Colonel, what is it?"

"I thought it was you for all of those years. It never occurred to me that it could be another girl, how could it have? All of those years..." Colonel Devon said, as one lonely tear worked its way down his cheek. It dripped onto his lapel, disappearing into the fibers. "I was trying to protect your family. Your memory..."

"Mike said he saw the other girl get struck by one of the guards and he thought she died. So, he was right. Was she executed by you, Colonel?"

"She was frantic...screaming...completely crazy. It went on for some time. Then she struck one of the soldiers. He defended himself."

"A soldier defended himself against a fifteen year old girl? You expect me to believe that?"

"He overreacted and she...she fell. Her head hit on the floor. There was blood everywhere."

"You mean he struck her down, don't you?"

"We thought our experiment had driven you out of your mind, or that we had tapped into some demonic force. We never ran experiments like that again."

"I see," replied Courtney as she paused for a moment. "I see how you have justified your actions to ease your conscience after killing a young, innocent girl."

"Courtney, it wasn't like that, we—"

"So how did my parents hold up after you and your pals delivered the news that you had murdered their little girl?"

"This discussion is over," he said, as he reached across himself to grab the door handle.

"No, it's not over Colonel! I have a right to know!"

"You may have a right to know, but I'm not discussing it any further. I can't." He was barely able to speak clearly and tears were now dripping off both sides of his chin.

"So, it's that bad is it? So bad that a tough soldier like yourself can't talk about it?" Courtney saw it was of no use. Besides, she already knew the answer. "It's going to eat you alive, Colonel."

"It already has," he mumbled.

They sat in silence with Courtney staring at Colonel Devon, as he gazed out the window.

Finally, Courtney reached over and wiped the tears off the left side of his face.

"Colonel, that was a long time ago and we can't do anything to fix it right now. *Right now,* we have a mission to complete."

"I'm not ready."

"Yes, you are. You have to be. You owe it to her, as well as the others who suffered and died over this for the past twenty years. We're going to complete this mission, deliver these tools back home and put things right."

The Colonel continued to stare silently out the window.

After a long pause, Courtney asked, "Can we talk about other things for a while?"

The Colonel turned to look at her, struggling to maintain eye contact.

"Please," he managed to say.

"Excellent. We have twenty five minutes before we need to go. What can I answer for you?" Courtney asked.

"How can we be here, in this place? Traveling between our

two worlds?"

"I'm not a physicist, but as I understand it, the devices resonate the natural frequency of gravity and Earth's magnetic fields," Courtney explained. "As with any resonance, if you keep adding energy, in the proper frequency, it continues to accumulate. Eventually something gives under the immense strain of that oscillating energy. In this case, it seems the layers of our existence are breached and a door opens to allow movement between the layers. These layers are clearly connected since there are so many similarities—cities, buildings and even people."

"Thank you, I think I understand."

"Seriously? You do?"

"Well, partially. You see, my sword technology is based on resonance."

"Of course, it is. You and Mike have even more in common than I expected."

"Yes, we do. What can you tell me about the history of it all? Do you know of a convergence in our past?" he asked. "There must be a point when we fractured, or there wouldn't be so many similarities."

"Back in the early 1900s the Germans were fascinated by all things mystical and technological. They were hell-bent on using those things to dominate the world. Their own *Die Glocke* research eventually lead them to go after the ancient crystal altar, which they stole from Egypt, who had stolen it from Nepal. The same altar the SAF scouts captured from the Nazis. Here, in this place, it never made it to the Egyptians. Instead it remained hidden in Nepal until the Nazis found it around 1943. So, the crystal altar was actually destroyed in a bombing, here in this time line, long before I was born," she said.

"Interesting and confusing."

"It is. I'm not certain why it works, only the Einsteins of the world can explain that, but we mostly understand what it does." Courtney glanced back at him. "Colonel, you seem distracted, is there something wrong?"

"Not at all, please continue," he replied.

"Well, for a while I thought it may have changed the past and therefore our world had changed, but you coming here proved what I had hoped. We live in different versions of the same world and have traveled between them."

"What other proof do you have?" he asked.

"Well, our world history is very similar and some key dates are the same."

"Name something I would recognize, please."

"For example, on the fourteenth of July of 1942 there was The Battle of Britain. You believe Britain fell to the Germans on July fifteen, after only five days of fighting. Here, the battle lasted three months and three days and Britain won."

"Germany didn't take Britain?" the Colonel asked.

"No. The Nazis didn't take Stalingrad at the end of November in 1942, either. Here, the USSR launched a counter offensive on November nineteenth of that year and pushed the Nazis all the way back to Berlin," Courtney explained.

"That would change the entire war!"

"By 1943, almost nothing happens in the same year or the same way," she answered.

"Then Asia and Africa never fell?"

"Correct."

"This would be a far greater place to be then. Is the general population free and safe?" he asked.

"Many countries are much better for it, but some parts of the world still slaughter each other nonstop, so I guess that depends on your perspective."

"Are you a politician?"

"Far from it." Courtney looked at the Colonel and saw a masked grin. "Nice try though."

She saw a spark in his gaze, then he asked, "Have you been able to identify the point where we diverge?"

"I think I'm close, but I haven't found it exactly."

"It has to be with the Nazis or Egyptians, right?" he asked.

"I'm thinking it's the Egyptians. They somehow managed to keep their world dominating power much longer back home than here. Our histories vary less and less as you get back around 1500 BC, where they are basically identical. For you, the Nazis conquered them in WW1 and combined their knowledge with the Egyptian technology, but that never occurred in this history," she said.

"So even though our history is different, the key players, the elites and the rulers behind the wars, are mostly the same?"

"Yes, most of them are the same men, from the same bloodlines, controlling the masses throughout history."

"It's almost as if it was all decided before our grandfathers took their first breaths." The Colonel sat quietly in thought for a moment, then looked at Courtney and said, "I just don't know what to think about all of this."

"I've struggled with it for years and I don't know either. I do know that I want to go home. I want to help defeat the Nazis with technology I have collected from this place."

"There are many ways to defeat them, but I'm not sure you actually have to," he said.

"Who else would?"

"Look at it this way, if our histories don't match, then it would be safe to assume that our worlds have existed, back in time until the histories do match. Roughly thirty five hundred years, correct?"

"Yes, but our time is up for now," she said, seeing her phone light up. "We need to get back to the mission." She nodded at several people filing out across the parking lot off in the distance. "Those people leaving are the night shift. We make our move soon." Courtney opened a file on her phone and then held it out for the Colonel to see.

"Here's a video of the lab, the moment you and Mike switched," she said, handing it to him.

After the short video ended, the Colonel looked up, "That's when it happened?"

"Yes, and we're going to repeat it so you can deliver that pouch."

"This is amazing technology, but do you really think it will help that much?" he asked.

"The technical details and plans inside them will. They contain all of the information I could gather on rocket propulsion, laser technology, nuclear technology and electricity. Also, there is a variety of weapons, both mechanical and chemical."

"Any gravity tech devices, like the sword, or Mike's device?"

"Mike's device is mostly documented, but only he has all of it."

"But nothing else, more *futuristic* in nature?"

"More out there than Mike's device?" She was surprised by the informed look she saw in the Colonel's face. *You know something Colonel. What is it?*

"No matter, I can figure it out."

"Is there something I should know?" she asked and saw his expression dissolve. *Oops, he caught you peeking into his mind.*

"Nothing we have need of now," he said.

"Understood. Now, remember, these devices use the same code. If you enter a code incorrectly, three times in a row, you lose the information on that device forever."

"Got it."

"You remember the code then?" she asked.

"I do."

"If all goes well on this end, I will join you in thirty minutes. If Mike doesn't make it, or if my coworkers surprise me, I may be right on your heels."

"Roger that," the Colonel said.

"I'm betting on at least one of us surviving, with a set of the information intact."

"You have prepared well," the Colonel said. "we'll succeed."

"I hope so." Courtney felt a twinge of concern as she spoke, then reached into her bag. "Also, you made it through with the sword on your hip so I'm thinking we're safe with these Colt 1911 pistols and ammunition. They should use the same forty-five ACP ammo you have there, correct?" she asked, as she showed him a bullet.

"Yes, that looks just like the round we use, though I usually prefer my sword over a hand gun.

"Excellent. There are three extra clips, with fifteen rounds each, in these pockets here." She pointed to each of their bags, then pulled out another pistol. "And this is a twenty-two caliber, silenced pistol. It also has fifteen rounds but they are small and subsonic so you have to get up close and personal with this one to be effective. The upside is that the report is so slight you can barely hear it twenty feet away."

The Colonel answered with a disconnected tone, "Yes, quiet weapons can be very helpful."

The thought reminded the Colonel of a nighttime raid against the Nazis.

There were emplacements on each end of the Highway 101 bridge, crossing the Columbia River near the Pacific Ocean. The emplacement on the south end overlooked the bridge and the small town of Astoria. The northern stronghold sat alone, on a hill, looking four miles back toward the southern fort.

The Nazis had not seen their enemy coming. They were surrounded and overtaken without firing more than a few dozen shots at the SAF. Major Devon racked up seven kills with his pistol and five with his sword, before one shot had been heard. He received two awards for his bravery and leadership that night and made Lieutenant Colonel as well. It was deemed by the Nazis to be one of the most embarrassing events of the conflict, since all but a few of the six hundred and forty two Nazis survived with no SAF fatalities.

The Strategic Attack Forces had long since learned that there was no way for them to support POWs. Instead of torturing and enslaving them, as the Nazis did, the SAF tried and executed the Nazis after each battle. Ten to twenty at a time, the captured Nazi soldiers were interrogated and then shown footage of Nazi POW and slave labor camps, as well as war crimes from the previous seventy years. Most of the men pretended to be unaware of the heinous crimes though very few showed any surprise at their presentation. After a speedy trial, all but a select few were marched to a gravel pit a few miles away, up very steep hills and executed in the days that followed.

Though a major success for the SAF, it had scarred the Colonel and he knew it.

"Colonel?" Courtney saw sadness on his face.

"Sorry, I was distracted."

"I noticed," she said.

"Continue."

"All right, then. You and Mike sound alike, so it's possible that one of the technicians may recognize your voice. Just go along with it if they do. The two guards in the entry won't know either of us. They'll attempt to set off the alarms and lock down the facility, if they think something is amiss."

"Makes sense," he said.

"By that, I mean that we have to be on our best behavior when we go in."

"Roger that."

"As a last resort, I have two small vials of non-lethal gas I can use to put them down for a couple of hours. And—if everything goes south—I've placed large canisters of the same gas in the building air supply units on the roof." Courtney wanted to smile with pride, seeing the impressed look on his face.

"I like it, but why not gas them now?" he asked.

"We could lose the station if the operators are unconscious."

She reached into her pocket, pulled out a small pouch and dumped some pills into her hand.

"Not likely, but I suppose it is possible."

Courtney made eye contact with him and remained silent, showing her annoyance rather than voicing it.

"Right. Your op, sorry," he said.

"Take two of these orange and white pills." She reached out toward him. "They'll protect us if we have to use the gas." Courtney noticed he had a blank expression on his face. "Security will be our first of three objectives. The second is to capture a tech and make them help us connect the power supply to a transformer and the third is to operate the spud and send you back."

The Colonel swallowed the pills.

"We need one control room operator to run it and the electrical linesman to connect the power supply to the fifteen kilovolt transformer. Once that's done, we can complete our return trip home."

"You have done your homework, but let's hope you didn't overlook something," the Colonel said, in a condescending, military tone. "I'm sorry, I didn't mean that."

"That sounded too natural to be an accident," Courtney said in a playful tone. "I hope I didn't miss something myself." She noticed his eyes smile briefly.

"Either way, I don't mind a bloody, frontal assault first thing in the morning," he said, then winked.

"Let's keep the bloodshed to a minimum, all right?"

"Yes, ma'am."

"And remember, if you have to run the device without me, you have a video on your phone and the tablet computer. Take a minute to watch Mike operate it, then duplicate what he does. Got it?"

"Affirmative."

"OK then, here we go," she said, as she stepped out of the chopper.

Courtney jogged across the field and stopped at the edge of the parking lot, just outside the view of the surveillance system. She pulled her phone from her back pocket and checked the video feed.

"Only one guard at the entrance now; the second one will be making rounds for over an hour," she said. "Let's go." Courtney entered the lit parking lot with Colonel Devon right on her heels. She heard him chamber a round in the small pistol. "Colonel, why don't you put that away until we actually need it."

"Only if necessary."

"Inappropriate looks don't justify it." She glanced back at him.

"Really?" he said, smiling.

"I'm not even answering."

* * *

Terry walked the floor in sections, listening to the com for any communication from Bill. He stepped up the pace when he heard shots fired and narrowed it to an area within twenty feet of the elevator. Terry climbed a chair, poked his head carefully through an opening in the ceiling tile and shined his light into the darkness.

"Bingo! So, I'm the *buddy* you wanted to play a joke on with *my* scrambler? Well, I owe you one, *buddy*," Terry said, then jumped down from the chair. *That was dumb. She's listening and you just gave her a big laugh.* He slid the chair over two ceiling tiles and went back into the ceiling. He pulled the little black box down and switched it off. He immediately heard the huffing and puffing of his partner, accompanied by crackling brush.

"I need an update, big guy," Terry said.

"In pursuit. Our bird. I hit it a few times. Trying to get a visual," Bill said in short bursts.

"Where are you?"

"In the tree line. Heading toward a field," he managed.

"Where is the chopper?"

"Half mile east, heading due south. Doing forty plus."

"Bill! What was that? Talk to me, Bill!"

Terry heard a loud metallic clanking noise.

Bill groaned, "Just a chain-link fence."

Terry heard sniffling on the other end. "You crying?"

"Bloody nose," Bill answered, "thanks for your concern, though."

Terry held back a relieved chuckle, not wanting to aggravate Bill more.

"I'm heading back your way," Bill grumbled.

"Roger that. I sent your message and they're scrambling another chopper from...uh, backup is en route," Terry stopped himself from divulging anything more over the compromised radios.

"That was a rookie mistake," Bill said jokingly, "hey, Terry?"

"Yeah, yeah," Terry was not as amused as his junior partner seemed to be.

"Where exactly are you standing?"

A loud choking gurgle came over the radio and then a sickening grunt, followed by a thud.

Terry felt his heart sink. "Bill?" His mind was churning with images of Bill having his throat slit. *No, please, no!*

Choking, Bill managed to speak, "Yeah, I'm here. Just got clotheslined by a branch."

"Be careful, this is starting to get dangerous." Terry muted his mic to hide his laughter.

"Yeah, just starting...uh, Terry?"

"Yeah," he managed, then muted it again.

"I can hear you laughing clear across the parking lot," Bill croaked.

"Sorry pal," Terry said, as he wiped tears from his eyes.

The ding of the elevator arriving on the third floor announced Bill's arrival, as well as freedom for Terry and the guard. When the door opened, Terry got his much awaited look at Bill.

"Let's see you," said Terry, unable to hide his amusement.

"You first," the battered agent said smartly.

"Here's mine." Stepping aside, Terry happily exposed the security guard sitting across the hallway with blood all down the front of his shirt. The guard's nose and top lip were twice their original size and he was staring at the ground.

Bill burst out laughing and immediately wrapped an arm around his middle. He held his ribs with one hand and grasped his face with the other as he laughed in agony.

"What happened to him?" Bill finally managed to ask, after catching his breath.

"He opened his mouth one time too many." Turning to look at the guard, Terry said, "Come on *Sleepy*, let's get *Dopey* out of here."

"Yeah, about that, *Mufasa*. I think he should wait up here for a while," Bill said giving Terry a pained look.

"What? *Mufasa* isn't one of *The Seven Dwarfs*." Terry shook his head. "Anyway, we need to get down there, ASAP."

"Sure, he is. But why the big rush?" Bill walked slowly toward a chair.

"No, he's *not* in it, *Mufasa* is a lion. Because, *he* needs to get back to his post, that's why."

Bill sat down slowly, "OK, just give me a minute."

"The locals will be here any time and TAC has additional security on the way. This whole building is a crime scene and I'm not staying up here while the yokels mess everything up," Terry said.

"Just one more minute," Bill said, wincing as he leaned back in the chair.

"Thirty seconds. We have a score to settle." Terry heard a thumping noise in the distance. "Chopper! Hurry it up!" He ordered, running into the elevator. He turned around to see the other two struggling to catch up. Terry looked Bill up and down. "Nose, face, arm, ribs, neck. You miss anything?"

Bill stepped into the elevator and slowly turned to face the doors. He lifted up his right hand and showed two fingers missing their fingernails. "Left 'em in the tree, I think. I'm pretty good otherwise, though."

"Geez! Oh man, those look painful." Terry winced as he stifled a chuckle.

"Nah, but these are." Bill lifted up his shirt part way.

Terry pulled it up the rest of the way, exposing a red and purple blotch larger than his hand. "Um, those are broken, buddy. Looks like two, but maybe three ribs."

"Yup, I figured. Mufasa was one of the king's bodyguards. Remember, the short one?" Bill asked.

"He what?" Terry asked.

"Oh yeah, don't look over this way, your coworker's body is a mess," Bill said, as they stepped off the elevator.

"Wait. What?" Terry asked. "No, he wasn't. He was the father lion in—"

"Yeah, he was. I just watched The Seven Dwarfs the other night," Bill said.

"You are so wrong. Wow, they really did a number on that poor guy," Terry said, seeing the disemboweled guard's corpse.

"Yeah, bad deal," Bill said. "I hope the chopper has FLIR."

"*Their* birds always do," Terry said, as armed FBI agents started pouring in the front door.

"We're with you," Terry called out.

Terry and Bill held their breath while the leader of the inrush approached them cautiously with his gun pointed in their direction.

"I need to see some ID," the agent demanded.

"Pretty sure you don't," Terry said.

"Wanna bet?" he barked, moving his barrel in Terry's direction.

"Sure," Terry said, "ask your boss if Terry and Bill can go now."

"Dispatch, I have a couple of idiots here claiming they don't have to show ID and asking permission to leave," he said, turning his head slightly to speak into his com.

Terry looked over at Bill, knowing he was getting impatient

and gave him a quick wink.

"You are kidding me!" the agent said. "How can you know these yahoos are who they say they are?" The man's face fell slightly. "Sorry. Yes, I understand." He turned to the agents behind him, "they're cleared."

"We'll be going now. Oh and we'll return your bird when we're done with it," Terry said, patting him on the shoulder as he walked by. "Thanks for coming to the party. Elevator works, but the stairwell is blown from two to four," Terry called over his shoulder, as they reached the front doors.

"Time to clean their mess up!" yelled the officer. "Let's clear this building!"

* * *

Courtney lead the Colonel to the front door of the substation. Though security was much tighter than it had been and all of the key power facilities had installed updated security measures, it was mostly ineffective against her.

"Keep your eyes open," Courtney said under her breath.

The guard buzzed them through the front door and was clearly admiring Courtney as she approached.

Another creep with an HD scanner. You make it too easy for me. Courtney was annoyed, but did her best to approach him with a slightly seductive cadence. She maintained eye contact and blocked his view of the Colonel as best she could. She had been here once before to scope it out, in case she needed a backup energy source for the spud. "Well hey there, Chuck, how late are you working tonight?"

"Uh, I just started my shift, Miss?"

She kept her eyes locked on his as the Colonel approached the scanner. She heard a distinct *click* behind her. *Oh great, he pulled that gun out again.*

"Barbara James, I'm here to—" Courtney stopped when

Chuck's right eye disappeared in a cloud of spray and his head whipped backward. Courtney cut a sharp look at the Colonel.

"I was going to gas him when you set off the scanner, remember?"

"But you didn't even flinch," he said, clearly amused.

"I heard you flip the safety, do that in your pocket next time. and no more unnecessary killing."

"Only as needed," he said.

"Care to tell me the real reason you killed him?"

"I didn't like the way he was looking at you," said the Colonel, as he shrugged his shoulders. She jumped over the counter and took the guard's radio, keys and badge. "Thanks, *Chuck*," she said and jumped back over.

The Colonel stepped over the locked gate beside the scanner and waited as Courtney ran back and locked the front doors.

"Were you going to leave that brass on the floor?" she asked, picking up the spent casing and tossing it to him. The Colonel caught it and dropped it into his pants pocket.

"The pistol?" she asked, as they reached the elevator door. The Colonel slipped it into his pocket with an annoyed look on his face.

With the first objective behind them, they stepped onto the elevator and headed down to the basement to access some of the high voltage switchgear.

"Now remember, I have to convince the lineman to help or he could short out the spud and destroy it. So, absolutely *no* killing the guy in the blue, long sleeved shirt. Are we clear?" she asked.

"Clear."

When the elevator opened she saw the door they were after, about fifty feet down the corridor.

"That's the buss room, there, with the big steel doors on the right," she said.

Walking up to it, the sign on the door read, *Buss Room - HRC 4 Arc Flash PPE Required - Authorized Personnel Only.*

"Well, it sure is nice of them to label everything so well for us, don't you think, Colonel?"

"Where I come from, if you go somewhere you aren't supposed to then you deserve what you get."

"Hold up," she warned, then pointed through the window on their left.

Stepping sideways into the adjacent corridor, Courtney dialed her phone and handed it over to the Colonel, pointing at some text on its screen.

"Control Room," she faintly heard the voice say and leaned in to hear better.

The Colonel read the text to the caller, "Hey, this is Mike Devon, I just wanted to let you know we'll be running an experiment down here at TAC that will draw pretty hard on our high voltage transformer."

"Hey there, Mike, thanks for the heads-up. The sun's coming over the horizon soon, so we were going to spin the main turbine up for demand. Are you going to need the capacity for long?"

The Colonel looked at Courtney, who shook her head.

"No."

"Well, can you give me a few minutes so I can get everything ready?" the operator asked.

Courtney nodded.

"Yes," said the Colonel.

"Should I call you back on this number?"

Courtney nodded again.

"Yes," answered the Colonel.

"OK, we'll call you when she's stable," replied the technician.

"Thanks," said the Colonel, as Courtney ended the call.

She held the phone so the Colonel could watch with her, as she tapped on a folder marked *PS9*. Tapping on a link inside, Courtney brought up the surveillance cameras at *Power Station 9 and* opened the item marked *Main Control Room*. Zooming in on camera seven, they could look over the operator's shoulder and see the control screens he used. Standing quietly in the hallway, they watched the operator click on a turbine graphic, then make an adjustment.

"Let's go," she said and headed toward the buss room door, watching the camera feed closely. They could hear the whine of the forty three Megawatt, GE-6B gas turbine ramping up in the distance, as they slipped into the room. It was clean and cool. The noise of electricity humming and fans blowing filled the room. Two rows of tall, electrical cabinets ran parallel down the room, dividing it into thirds.

"Impressive. Everything has digital readouts I see. Is this a modern facility?" the Colonel asked.

"This is modern for the civilians, about twenty years old for government."

He asked, "Why do you say it that way?"

"The government here keeps a two generation tech gap between itself and the people. The civilians have no clue how far advanced technology actually is."

"Nothing unreasonable about that. If the people have it, then the enemy does too," Colonel Devon took on an air of command.

"There is a fine line between security and oppression, Colonel."

"I'm well aware of that and have crossed it more than once. There are too many variables to predict the results, so you have to constantly make adjustments."

"So, the SAF has been taking lessons on control and oppression from the Nazis then?" she asked, watching the Colonel closely.

"You are starting to sound weak, like an idealist. What you don't realize is that most people need to be lead about. They are weak, not strong and driven, like you."

"I see the Nazis *have* made an impression on you, Colonel. Dominate, oppress, control, legislate and murder——all tools to be used."

"Tools I'm sure you would use if you had them at your

disposal," he said.

"I believe in surgical precision—cut off the snake's head," Courtney said. "Enough for now, you're distracting me."

His face barely flinched but Courtney saw a spark in his eyes. *Nice, Colonel, you held your tongue, I'm impressed.*

Scanning the workers in the control room, Courtney said, "Just great. B-crew is on shift. All three of them are ex-military. The young lineman is fresh out of the Navy. This crew is going to need a little motivation."

"What now?" he asked, as she continued with her phone.

"I'm running a system diagnostic on the plant control computer. They can't change a thing for at least a minute. So, we'll have to—" Courtney felt her phone vibrate and read the alert on her display. "Scrambled signal nearby. They know we're here!" she said as she dashed out into the corridor and up to the control room door. "Locked!" she exclaimed, making eye contact with the lineman through the small window. "That's my guy."

Colonel Devon had his sword out and cut the bolt, before Courtney managed to get clear of the sparks. She stood back as he slammed through the door and drew his sidearm. "Move and you're dead!" he yelled at the three men inside. "You, put down that phone!"

Courtney stepped into the control room behind him and watched the operator slowly place the phone in its cradle. "Hello gentlemen. I don't have much time or patience, so I'll keep this short and to the point. We're here to test a device I acquired in a questionable fashion. We need to know if this device works before we can leave the city."

"We ain't helping terrorists," the man by the phone said.

"We are not terrorists, I assure you. We do not wish to harm you, or any of your equipment. We need to borrow it and you, for about an hour." Courtney smiled halfheartedly. "Now, I need the lineman to come with me and hook the device up to fifteen KV."

The only sounds were coming from the computer

workstation fans and the lulling hum from the generators, fans and pumps nearby. She purposely let ten seconds of silence pass, knowing she would have to escalate things. She stepped in front of the young man in a dark blue, long-sleeved, electrician's safety shirt. "You're the lineman, right?"

"No, ma'am, I'm just a tech. I have no clue about electrical circuitry and switchgear," he said, his voice wavering slightly.

Liar. You'll regret that. She quickly backhanded him in the face with her left hand, then punched him square in the ear with her right fist. As he tried to step backwards, away from her, she lightly kicked his left foot into his right and he fell over backwards. The Colonel lunged forward with his gun aimed at the other two men and his drawn sword in the other outstretched hand was pointed at the wide-eyed, young man lying on the floor. The operator in the office chair jerked forward in his chair, but did not get up. The other man stepped backwards, moving away from the operator, Courtney and the controls. Courtney walked up to the big man, sensing he was getting ready to try something.

"Are you the lineman?" she asked him, with a much more serious tone in her voice. He stared silently at the floor, as if mesmerized by something. She moved within a foot of him and yelled, "I asked you a question and I expect an answer!"

"I—I'm an operator. I don't know anything. I only turn things off and on," the man said.

"Colonel," was all Courtney said. She stepped back to her right side, toward the operator seated at the console.

Holstering his sword and handing her his firearm, the Colonel placed himself about a foot away from the big man.

"You heard me," said the man, clearly uncomfortable with his words.

The Colonel drove his left knee into the man's groin. As the man jerked forward, his head came down and Colonel Devon jammed his right fist into the man's throat. He tried to grab onto the Colonel as he fell forward, but the Colonel blocked his arm. The gasping man dropped to his knees; one hand on his throat and the other on his groin. Courtney nodded to the Colonel and he round housed the man in the side of his jaw. The big man crumbled onto the floor, wheezing and unconscious.

Courtney handed the pistol back to the Colonel and faced the seated operator. "Are *you* the lineman?" she asked, then drew her own gun. Looking down at it, she pulled the slide back enough to verify the marked round was in the chamber, then calmly released the slide with a crisp *click*.

He swallowed and said, "I'm an operator. I don't—" Courtney did not let him finish.

"I have already heard that—twice I might add. I need to hear you tell me how you can help me wire up my device. Understand?" Courtney spoke to him like he was a child.

"I can't help you," he said, his face white with fear. "Really."

"Then I don't need you, do I?" she said, as she pointed the gun at his chest and pulled the trigger.

She had the silencer off her Sig-Sauer for effect. It worked perfectly. The operator jerked back at the percussion. The chair had been used as a lounge for far too many years and offered no resistance as it lay back into a full, reclined position. The man's inertia carried him over backwards and his head made a dull thud as it struck the floor under the weight of his well-fed body.

Courtney was surprised at the force with which it all occurred, knowing the round was a blank. *Oh, that's too good! The lineman will be helpful now.* Smiling, she turned toward the young man seated on the floor behind her. She made eye contact with the Colonel who nodded. The lineman's eyes were wide and he was trembling.

"You are a sight! Look at you. Pretty ridiculous when you think about it, huh? I ask for a few kilowatts and people are willing to die for it? You too?" she asked. Courtney pointed the gun into his face, with her finger beside the trigger, then kicked his feet so he would look at her.

He shook his head slowly, but he didn't utter a word. As the expression on her face began to darken, his demeanor changed. "No, wait, I'll help you. I have a pregnant wife at home and think of all of the people living nearby. They don't deserve to die," the young man pleaded with her, tears in his eyes.

"Son, you have natural gas, condensing turbines here. Just how do you propose I harm the neighbors with what you have here?"

"Well…"

"The lovely people are safe, as you are, providing you are helpful."

"I will do whatever you want me to. I don't want to die," he said, wiping away tears.

"I don't want anyone else to die today, either. Now, let's go and I'll show you something really cool. It is pretty hi-tech, I have to tell you," Courtney said sincerely. She reached out her hand and helped him to his feet.

"I know too much, you have to kill me."

"If I kill everyone in a five-mile radius it does nothing to stop the authorities. They'll know everything soon enough. Colonel, put the bodies in that room please." She leaned over and whispered in his ear, "They are very close now, be ready to go."

The lineman pointed to his tool pouch on the table next to the door, "Should I carry these or would you like to?"

"No, you go ahead, I'm sure I'll be just fine." Courtney chuckled at the thought of him attacking her with a screwdriver and pliers. Looking down at her phone, she navigated to the building control screen and disabled the freight elevator between floors. She knew it would not stop a good team, but it would buy them some time.

* * *

Mike heard mumbling outside his door and his eyes opened

frantically. Confused, he looked around the room to get his bearings. He saw a book lying on the bed to his right and food to his left. *Mimi's Inn*. The doorknob moved slightly. Mike quickly stuffed his things into his new bag, along with the half eaten bag of peanuts. He left his dirty clothes on the bathroom floor, knowing they could come crashing through the door at any moment.

How could they find me? What did I do wrong this time?

Mike was furious with himself for making another mistake and for putting himself at risk once again. He could hear a doorknob being tried again, then more voices and a key clicked its way into the lock. Mike slipped out the window, onto the fire escape and closed the glass behind him. He glanced downward. *They'll be waiting for me down on the ground. Rooftop! It's my only chance,* he thought and scrambled up the ladder.

The old buildings were built very near or right against each other, so he was sure he could get two or three buildings away without much difficulty.

Mike was already halfway across the roof of the adjacent building, when back inside his room, the door opened slowly and a long, thin object slowly entered the room.

"House keepy," said the soft voice of the cleaning lady, her broom tapping on the doorjamb.

* * *

"I watched them head out this direction, then dive low below the tree line," Bill said, from the back seat of the chopper. "I don't have a clue where they went after that, but I would guess they went several more miles."

"It's a maze of fields and trees out on this side of town. Almost as if she planned it," Terry said, adjusting his headset.

"And that's impossible," Bill said sarcastically. "No trace of them?"

"We aren't seeing a thing in the night vision camera. Well, not yet anyway," Terry said, glancing back at Bill.

The pilot spoke up, "We're under an hour left in the tanks, so let's go up to five thousand, get a big picture, before we need to fuel up."

"How's the other pilot doing?" Terry asked.

"Seemed fine, but I only had a second to talk to him," their pilot answered.

"Yeah, I'd rather a bump on the head than the gut job they did to the guard inside. That was a bad way to go out," said Bill.

No one spoke for a moment.

"Hey Terry, you have any idea how they did it?" Bill asked.

"Yeah, I'll show you the video later, but we can't talk about it right now." Looking over at the pilot he went on, "I see what you mean." He pointed to the gauge with its arrow pointing just above the red portion of the dial.

"Yeah and the sun will be up soon. If we get fuel now, we'll be back in time for dawn," the pilot said.

"Roger that," said Terry, "and once the sun's up, I expect the Five-O will know where our missing chopper is."

"We need to be ready when that call comes in, so let's hurry," Bill added.

"He wants to give a little of what he got," Terry joked with the pilot.

"Can't say as I blame him," the pilot said. "We'll be on the ground in ten."

"You don't think they could be here do you?" Bill asked.

"It's possible, but that would have been fairly risky," Terry replied.

"Wait, what if she has sidewinders?" Bill asked. "Maybe she's getting ready to shoot us down!"

"Easy there, big guy. If she *really* wanted us dead, there are much easier ways to do it." *Also, she would have done it already.* Terry felt doubt rolling around in his mind as the chopper nosed downward, toward the airport. *She didn't kill us because she wants us alive. But why?*

* * *

"This is the device I want you to hook up for me," Courtney said.

"It's not a weapon?" the lineman asked.

"Absolutely not."

"Are you sure it's safe?" he asked.

"As long as you get us out of here quickly it is," she said. "I stole this from a private company that's a front for Chinese organized crime. The sooner you get us out of here, the safer it is for you," Courtney said, using one of the many stories she rehearsed for such occasions.

"I'll help you test it. But please, no more killing?"

"I swear, if you whine about that once more, I *am* going to shoot you! Do what I ask and I'll keep my word. Now hook it up!" Courtney had allowed herself to be a little frustrated, it helped with the theatrics, but now she was starting to really get angry.

"OK, OK." He looked at her inquisitively.

"If you open your mouth again, it had better be about the device."

"It is."

"Then speak!"

"I'm sorry, but are you sure this thing will take thirteen thousand eight hundred volts?" he asked. "Very few industrial machines even operate on it."

"Yes, I know it will. Open the cover on the power supply and see the primary connections for yourself. They're huge."

"All right then. We have a spare thirteen eight cabinet over there so all I need is some wire and I can hook it up."

"A one hundred foot spool of 15KV Primary URD cable, large cutters and a box of connector lugs were delivered Friday afternoon. It was sent to delivery point fourteen. That's right down the hall," Courtney told the surprised lineman.

"Oh. Well, let's go get it," he said.

"You lead the way," she said and the pair headed out the door. Within ten minutes the Colonel poked his head into the buss room. "Hey, are you about ready in here?"

"Impeccable timing, Colonel. You can take him back into the control room. Blindfold, tape and tie him. He was a big help and he doesn't want any trouble. Clear?"

"Crystal," the Colonel said, as he taped the man's hands behind his back.

"How are the other two?" she asked in front of the young worker, already knowing the answer would calm the lineman down.

"The big guy is doing all right. Still kinda wheezy, but sitting up now. The operator woke up and puked all over the place. Concussion. Seems your bullet missed him somehow. He did spring a leak though…big bladder."

"So, you didn't kill anyone?" the young man asked.

Seeing the frustrated look on the lineman's face, Courtney said, "You'll hear all about it on the news tonight, I suspect."

As the Colonel and the lineman walked down the hall, Courtney was already ramping up the spud. They had been in the substation for thirty two minutes and she knew time was running out. Within moments, the Colonel returned.

"Are you ready?" she asked.

"Well, I survived it once, so I guess I don't have anything to worry about."

"Here you go. One last thing for you to do to get back home. Turn this knob up to that blue line." She pointed to the power supply. "Easy enough?"

"Easy enough. Anything else I should know?" he asked.

"Just make it home with at least one copy of the data. It will all be worth it then."

"Got it."

"I won't be too far behind you, if all goes to plan. Secure the area so I don't get shot or something," Courtney said, smiling.

"I won't let anything happen to you, again," he said. "Oh, this can make you nauseous. You'll probably have some weird memory flashes, lose your hearing and sight," he explained.

"I saw you arrive."

"Oh, right," he said.

"Why do I get the feeling you are keeping something from me?" she asked.

"Because you're perceptive," he said.

"So, there *is* something I should know about?"

"Make it home and I'll tell you there," he said, reaching for her hand.

She took it, but felt uneasy and quickly pulled back.

"It's a deal. Now, when the meter hits the blue mark, the haze will appear over there." She pointed off the end of the spud. "You just walk right through."

"Roger that."

"I'll watch from back in the corner. That's a bit further than the closest tech was when Mike ran it at TAC. I should be plenty safe there," she said stepping back. She could tell he wanted to say more, but knew the time had come.

"Goodbye, Courtney."

"Goodbye, Colonel Devon."

The Colonel reached for the dial as soon as she was in place, then turned and looked back at her. He looked as if he were in pain, so Courtney smiled and waved, hoping he wouldn't change his mind. When the hazy area appeared, he turned and walked straight into it. She felt excitement course through her veins as she watched for Mike to return.

* * *

"What's up with that ridiculous uniform? Get up off that floor before I beat you senseless, you low class piece of garbage! How long have you been lying there, Michael, you drunken fool!

Wake up!" a man's voice screamed.

Unable to see, the dazed Colonel felt something metallic hit him repeatedly in the back. He grabbed for it, but missed. The object then struck the back of his hand, broke at least one bone and instantly cleared the fog in his head.

"I suggest you run for your sad life!" snarled the Colonel, as he rose to his knees. The attack paused long enough for him to stagger to his feet. In those few seconds, the ringing in his ears quieted enough for him to hear the next swing approach. It struck his head a split second later. The impact lit the darkness, filling it with a variety of colors. Blood streaming down the side of his face, the enraged Colonel lunged toward the direction of the barrage and took another hard hit across his back. Knowing the attacker was beside him now, the Colonel turned and started walking quickly away from the unknown assailant. He had one arm over his head with his palm facing backwards, protecting his head as best he could. He reached out in front of himself with his injured hand, feeling for any obstruction that might block his retreat. He walked nearly forty feet before he glanced off the wall. With his vision slightly returned, he pulled out his sword and turned back toward his attacker.

"You are fired! Go home and starve! Then you can be with your dead girlfriend and her parents!" the man yelled.

"You shut your mouth!" the Colonel screamed with all his might, unable to control himself any longer.

"I cheered at all three executions and I'll cheer when you're dead, too!"

The Colonel headed toward the shadowy figure and accelerated with each step until he was running.

"Stop! Do not approach me!" the man yelled, as he ran backwards. "Wait! Wait! You cannot!"

As the Colonel reached the man, he screamed, "Yes, I can!" then swung his sword.

There were two dull thuds as the man's forearms hit the floor. The janitor screamed in agony and dropped to his knees.

"Beg for your life, you piece of trash!"

The man continued to scream, with his eyes bulging and a crazed look on his face. Colonel Devon felt his anger leave as the blood chilling cries continued. "Courtney wouldn't want this, she would take pity on you. Out of respect for her I will end your suffering."

"No! Wait!" the man wailed, holding up two burnt stumps, as if to protect himself.

The Colonel raised his sword, then noticed a badge on the man's chest. "Well, Alec, you got what you deserved." He swung the sword again. Alec's dismembered head hit the floor behind him, then his body toppled backwards onto it. The Colonel calmly returned his weapon to its holster.

Alec's wounds were mostly cauterized, but there was a fine stream of blood pulsing several feet down the hallway. Alec's body shuddered and the headless neck gurgled on the floor as the Colonel walked past. He stopped, then turned back and kicked the writhing body off of the head. He stared into the frantically blinking eyes and smiled.

"You would have had about thirty more seconds to make things right with your maker, but I'm going to distract you for most of it," the Colonel said.

Placing the blinking head on the floor in front of the body, he slashed off both legs while Alec's head watched on in horror. Picking up one of the legs by the shoed foot, the Colonel clubbed the head as hard as he could. It rolled down the hallway and came to rest just above the stairwell at the end of the corridor. The Colonel dropped the leg and ran toward the head, which was on its left ear facing him. He arrived to see the dizzy eyes struggling to focus and kicked it. Alec's head tumbled down the stairwell, out of sight.

"You shouldn't have brought her into this, you evil little man! Look what you made me do!" he screamed down the stairwell. The Colonel shuddered as he thought about his heinous acts, then walked back to the elevator.

Courtney and her parents are dead? And then a thought struck him. *How could he know about her, unless this isn't home? And her parents… they're alive. But if they're all dead here…*

The Colonel's mind raced, trying to find a good answer, but kept coming up with the same conclusion.

There are three of us!

He felt himself go numb and stood staring off into space for several moments. Finally, he reached down and picked up the bag Courtney had given him. He got in the elevator and rode it down to the lobby, feeling as if he were floating. Never taking his eyes off his path, he walked through the lobby, past a yelling guard. He paused only to slash the arms off a turnstile. Visions of Alec flashed in his mind as the poles bounced on the floor. The Colonel walked through the still sparking, molten steel splatters, wondering if he would ever see Courtney again.

"You made it back!" Courtney yelled, but saw no response. "Mike? Can you hear me?"

The confused new arrival stared off into space, as he slowly sat up on the floor. He was wearing an SAF uniform and holding one of the Colonel's swords in his hand.

That's not Mike and it isn't the Colonel. Oh, no! Three? Courtney felt the disappointing reality hit her. *If there are three versions of home, then Mike is at our home now and the Colonel must be in this guy's place. I have to get him to turn it back on and rotate them once more to bring Mike back. A* sickening thought struck Courtney. *What if that brings number four? What if I can't get Mike back?*

It was far more complicated than she had originally thought and Courtney wasn't ready for it. She desperately wanted to rescue Mike, but returning home was far more important.

If Mike returns, I know the Colonel made it back. Then, we get the spud out of the States and hide out long enough to put a new plan together.

Courtney realized that she was planning a getaway with a man she felt she had known for years, but had only just met. Courtney's mind was spinning out of control with all of the questions, uncertainties and possibilities.

Focus, Courtney. What are you going to do with this one? Think...

The thinner Mike Devon was sitting up straighter and appeared to be more alert as a plan took shape in her mind. "Mr. Devon," she said, "it's me, Maria, can you hear me?"

His head turned in her direction, but his eyes didn't look at her.

How much longer? She checked her phone and noted the time.

"Who's there?" he asked very loudly, with a strange accent.

"It's me, Maria, can you hear me now?" she asked, much louder than before.

"Yes, of course I do. I don't feel well though. My eyes... everything is blurry." He felt around and touched the electrical cabinet behind him. "Do you know what just happened?"

"Well, you were running a test on your invention over there. It made a tremendous noise and you fell to the ground. Wait, you could have a concussion, what's your name?"

"Michael Devon, of course," he replied.

Sounds British.

"All right then, relax and catch your breath, Michael," she said innocently, as she walked up and assessed him further. *He's not military and not very athletic. A minimal threat.*

"Here, let me help you into a chair," Courtney said as she tugged on his thin arm.

"No, just help me to my feet. I want to stand."

The phone on the wall rang, startling them both.

"Oh," said Courtney, "that will be the power plant technicians calling to see if we need anything. Shall I tell them we're fine and have them reset the alarms?"

Michael held on to her arm. "Yes...uh, tell 'em to reset the alarms and that everything's fine," Michael said, as he looked around the room.

She could see that he was trying to act calm, but his eyes told a different story. He still had the sword clenched in his hand and it made her very uneasy. She realized that if she couldn't calm him down, she could be forced to defend herself. It was something she would have to do carefully, since Mike and the Colonel could be trapped forever. Her mind raced again to the thought, *could there be more than three?*

She felt him release his grip on her arm, allowing her to walk over to the phone. She felt his eyes on her and positioned herself to watch him as she talked.

"Hey, who is this? We have been trying to reach you guys, but no one is answering the phones."

She kept her gaze on him as she listened. "Did you try other extensions?"

"Yes, we have been trying other extensions, but we get no answer," the man on the other end said.

"Well, we were having a little retirement party for one of the operators. We must have been too loud to hear it ring." She tried to sound convincing. "Did you get an alarm I should know about?"

"Ya think? You guys bring your primary up to speed and nearly trip us offline. Then, you dipped to normal and immediately back to overload?"

"That does sound bad. Let me put you on hold for a minute. I need to ask Bob, the lead operator, what's going on."

"No, you *tell* Bob to idle his turbine down and to stop burying us in surplus! You guys are a modern facility and we're trying to do your job with the oldest gear in the district? You people are unbelievable!" The phone rattled and then went dead.

Courtney smiled and said, "Got it. Thanks for the help, we appreciate it." She turned and set the phone down, pretending that nothing was amiss. *Five minutes to get this guy to pull a lever. I can do that.* The door handle rattled and Courtney turned around to see Michael run out. *That one is a problem.*

Angry at herself, she glanced at her phone, knowing she was about out of time. Terry and Bill would be closing in and she was going to have her hands full trying to keep them at bay. She pulled up the security system and checked the alarms page. *They haven't entered the building yet. I still have a few minutes.*

* * *

Mike began to feel disoriented as he raced across the roof. The heavy bag jostling around on his shoulder made matters worse. He reached the far side where the adjacent building blocked his way. It was nearly eight feet higher, so he carefully tossed his bag up onto the adjacent roof. He stepped back and ran two steps up the brick wall to get a grip on top of it. He pulled himself up and over, cringing in anticipation of gunfire. Hearing none, he rolled over and watched. All was silent on the roof. No gunfire, not even a single agent in sight. He was breathing hard, partly from the exertion and partly from the nausea. The world around him started to shift erratically and Mike knew he wouldn't be able to go much further, then he heard it.

It's the spud! They are taking me back home! Mike was excited for a moment, then the sickening reality of his situation at home struck him.

As the world around him went black, Mike called out, "All right guys, you win. I give up." He hooked his arm through the straps of the bag, laid down and curled up in a ball to prepare for whatever came next.

The noise from this side is noticeably quieter. Why? Wait, is there a building here, back home?

Mike felt himself falling.

* * *

Michael ran out of the room when Courtney had turned to

hang up the phone. Tears were streaming down his face as he ran away. He had dreamed about this moment so many times, but just couldn't get himself to tell her. The flood of emotions overtook him as he rounded the corner at the end of the hallway and he collapsed to his knees.

She's alive! It's her! He screamed within himself. Breathing hard and fighting to maintain control, Michael wiped his burning eyes. He wanted to punch something, to scream, but all he could do was cry. The rattling of a door lever jolted him alert. *She's going to see you like this! Get hold of yourself, go back and introduce yourself!* He rose to his feet, but they carried him further down the hallway. *She's even more beautiful than I remember…I want to go back, but I need some time to collect my thoughts.* Michael heard a soft thud in the distance. *I hope she isn't coming down here.* He felt fear taking over. *Stop it! You're acting crazy! She won't like you if you act crazy!* He willed himself to relax and it helped a little. *You're right, I will, just give me a minute…*

* * *

UNIT 3: UNDERSTANDING

THE next thing Mike knew, he was back on a cold, hard floor. Deaf, blind and nauseous, Mike lay there waiting for the effects to wear off. It was surreal. No stimulus other than being able to feel his body breathing. He would have been unable to discern reality from dream, if it wasn't for the changing pressure in his chest.

Ah, there it is, finally, Mike thought, as light began to register. *I'm done traveling. There's no way this can be good for me.*

Strange smells had Mike confused for a few minutes and when he could finally see his surroundings, he realized he was not in a familiar place. Mike reached up, grabbed hold of a desk and pulled himself to his feet. A sick, helpless feeling washed over him as he read the nameplate at his fingertips.

Colonel Devon? Oh, no…What if I'm trapped forever? He turned around slowly, barely taking in his surroundings, then saw some plaques and awards on the wall.

"Colonel Devon," Mike said, as he read the name over and over. "So, you're in the SAF?" Mike felt his pulse quicken. "Then this is where Courtney came from!"

He stepped around the desk and dropped into the seat. Mike looked at the mess on the desk. *Someone recently ransacked Colonel Devon's office.* Mike flipped through the piles and uncovered several picture frames. He picked them up and found one still had a photograph in it. He immediately felt at ease as a young Courtney smiled up at him. *This really is her.* As he tried to collect his thoughts, he couldn't stop wondering, *what were you after? Weapons? Technology? What was it about the pictures?*

Then, the thought struck him. *It was Michael! He was here!*

What if she had Michael, or the Colonel run the spud again, trying to get me back? Who's there with her now? Mike felt uneasy thinking of the unstable Michael Devon coming face to face with Courtney. He closed his eyes and was struck by an overwhelming sense of déjà vu. The images, a mix of known and unknown moments, flashed in his head. They were a jumbled mess of events from different places and different times. He strained to make sense of them, realizing some were from Michael's life while others were from the Colonel's. Mike felt like he was being sucked into the memories and forced his eyes open. The images immediately stopped, but the emotions didn't leave as quickly.

Do something to fix this or you'll lose your mind! He could feel his identity melting into the other two and it scared him.

Mike looked back at the desk, grabbed the first file in reach and began to read. As he scoured the various articles his predecessor had sorted out for him, he was able to piece together what the Colonel had developed. Checking the upper, middle drawer for something else of interest, Mike reached in and felt the underside of the desktop. As he slid his hand back, he felt a hidden, metallic shelf. He grabbed the edge of a notebook with his fingertips and pulled it out.

Confidential? Hmm…

Mike slowly opened the pages then became lost in the entries. It contained many short, guilt-ridden comments about a girl he loved. As Mike read on, he froze on one specific line and read it several times with tears in his eyes.

"I saved her soul from eternal damnation. I know I did the right thing, but why doesn't it feel like it?" he read aloud, as his anger rose. "You killed Courtney? Then it was you I saw in the dream!?"

He was devastated, confused and angry. The room began spinning around him. Mike kept seeing flashes of the event that night, but they were not his own. The visions felt like memories and were so real he could almost feel her in his arms. He felt the excruciating pain of her death but knew he was somehow protecting her. Putting his head down, Mike's mind was flooded with memories of events he had never known before. Memories he knew he couldn't know, but somehow did.

Somehow, some way, we are all connected. We aren't choosing our environment, but can we choose how we act within it? If so, then it's all predetermined and we have to learn how to deal with the events. So, does that mean I'm in love with her because Michael and the Colonel love her? Is this why I've been able to do the things I've done? Or do we each feed off the others' emotions and memories? Then a thought struck Mike. *Michael hated Alec with a vengeance! That's why I've hated Alec since the first day I laid eyes on him!*

Amazed at the flood of understanding from this epiphany, Mike flopped back into the Colonel's chair and stared off across the room in thought. His eyes widened and Mike jumped to his feet and dove at the pile of books on the floor. He grabbed the phone book and flipped through the pages to the 'L' section.

Skipping back and forth, he read, *Linehan, London, Lewis!* "Court and Danielle Lewis are right here in town!"

Mike grabbed the phone from the cradle and dialed the number. It seemed to take forever, but finally he heard a ringing tone. Finally, on the fourth ring, a man answered.

"Yes?"

"Uh, hi. You don't know me, but I have some information for you. Can we meet someplace public and talk?" Mike was prepared to beg the man he believed to be Courtney's father. Several silent moments passed. "Sir? Mr. Lewis?"

"Yes?"

"I want—I want to talk to you about your daughter," he managed.

After an awkward pause the man said, "Meet us in the park in one hour."

"Thank you. Oh, which park?" Mike asked quickly.

"You're at the lab I see, so I meant the park across the

street. Unless there is a reason that won't work?" he asked.

"Not at all, that will be perfect, sir. Thank you again."

Mike was ecstatic and could hardly wait for the hour to pass. Uncertain of how secure the building was, he grabbed a jacket and hat off the back of the door. He used the internal camera on his phone to look at himself. He held the phone up next to one of the pictures of the Colonel. *Not grumpy enough.* Mike furrowed his brow and pursed his lips. *There you are, Colonel. All grumpy and bitter.* Mike smiled and saw the Colonel immediately disappear. *No smiling.* He pocketed his phone and picked up his bag. Mike slipped a stack of papers and the Colonel's journal inside the bag. As he reached for the door, Mike took one last look at the Colonel's awards. *What if you, Michael and I could have joined forces? We would have been unstoppable.*

Mike walked down the hallway and up to the elevator door. He reached out to touch the button, but the doors jerked open on their own. Mike paused slightly then stepped inside.

"Going down, sir?" a voice asked.

"Uh, yes, going down." Mike tried to sound serious but when the words hit his ears he was disappointed. *Get it right or you won't make it out of here!*

The elevator dropped rapidly, then braked just as hard and the doors reopened.

Mike stepped off the elevator to a pair of military guards saluting him.

"That's a fast elevator," he said, trying to cover the surprised look on his face.

"Sorry, sir. I will have them make sure to re-calibrate it in the morning."

Mike nodded and walked toward the guards, doing his best to look like the Colonel.

There was a buzz and a click and a glass door popped open in front of him.

"Have a good evening, sir."

Mike nodded and kept walking. *Almost there—*

"Uh, sir, aren't you forgetting something?" one of the guards asked.

Mike's heart was pounding as footsteps rushed toward him. He turned around to see a guard running toward him, holding a long, dark jacket.

"Right, yes." Mike reached out as the guard ran up to him.

"Good night, sir."

"Good night," Mike said, turning back toward the door. He felt a trickle of sweat fall down past his right eye as he opened the door into the night.

Mike saw a man and a woman sitting on a bench as he crossed the street. As he approached, the woman's likeness to Courtney become more noticeable. Mike saw that Court had a pistol on his lap, only partially concealed and Danielle appeared to be holding a weapon too. Court motioned for Mike to have a seat at the bench next to theirs, with himself between his wife and Mike.

"OK, we're not sure what you are up to—"

But that was all he got out. His wife gasped aloud and startled both of the men.

"Colonel? Is that you?" Danni asked.

"Yes, it's me, Mike Devon."

"But you look so much younger—and the hair. I barely recognized you out of uniform. Are you out of the service?"

"Colonel, I apologize for *this.*" Court holstered his gun. "It didn't sound anything like you."

"Well, see that's the issue. It's not exactly *me.*" Mike had struggled with the best way to approach them and finally decided to just lay it all out, but was still apprehensive. "I know this is going to be tough for both of you, but I need you to hear me out. Will you give me five minutes before you make up your minds?" Mike asked.

"No promises, Colonel," Court said, with a curious look on

his face.

"Please, just call me Mike."

"OK, Mike it is," Court replied, glancing at Danielle briefly. "I guess we'll give you the five minutes."

"Are you familiar with magnetic reconnection, the mechanism that launches solar flares from the sun?" Mike asked.

"A bit from physics class, but that was a long time ago," said Danni.

"The little I know is top secret and weapons related, Colonel. I mean, Mike. Yours and your father's, specifically, but we're not generally privy to such matters," Court said. "I don't mean to be overly direct, but what does that have to do with Courtney?"

"I understand, completely. Before I can tell you *what* I know, I have to explain *how* I know it, or you won't believe me anyway," Mike explained.

"Keep going, Mike, you have our attention," Danni said, looking past Court.

"OK. So, the way it works, basically, is a resonance that excites gravity and magnetic forces simultaneously, causing a massive buildup in energy over time. At some point, those forces are released and the magnetic fields guide all of that energy into a focused beam, releasing plasma energy. I've spent most of my career perfecting this technology." Mike leaned forward slightly to get a better look at each of their faces. "Are you both still with me?"

"We're keeping up, mostly," Court said.

"Well, I recently came across a blend of frequencies that resonates those same forces. But, I also discovered that it was capable of opening a pathway between our worlds."

Court and Danni looked at each other and Court opened his mouth to speak, but Mike interrupted, "I know, I know. Look, for the past two hundred years, scientists around the globe agree it is theoretically possible, but no one has discovered the mechanism, until now. Well, no one in modern times."

"Don't misunderstand us Mike; we've seen some pretty crazy stuff with all of the Egyptian technology the Germans have been developing over the past eighty years. Are you talking about wireless energy transmission, like the pyramids and the crystal altar?" Court asked.

"Actually, I've only read a couple of theories on wireless energy from the pyramids, like Nicolai Tesla did, but this is different."

"You're right, Tesla was one of the key German developers of that technology."

"Tesla was from Germany?" Mike asked.

"Well, the Germanic Republic of Russia, to be precise," Court said.

"Ah, I see. So, can you tell me about the crystal altar?"

"We only know that it's the size of a small bed, carved out of solid crystal," Court replied. "They believed it worked off wireless energy last I knew."

"And it had something to do with Courtney's disappearance," Danni added.

"Those were just rumors, Danni," Court said.

"I believe I know how the crystal altar functions and what it was used for, but I would need to test it to be sure." Mike opened his mouth to speak, but stopped himself.

"We're listening, but you're still off topic," Court said.

"Right, but I'm almost there," Mike said. "I think the ancients used the altar to travel from place to place, maybe even from time to time. Maybe."

"Mike, I have seen a number of devices we have confiscated from the Nazis and they usually have a lot of Egyptian glyphs on them. Last I knew, we still hadn't cracked the hieroglyph language of the ancient Egyptian scientists. No one has been able to move two hundred ton blocks about like toys except the ancients. If that kind of power was rediscovered, those who had it would be unstoppable," Court said.

"Using this technology, I was able to come here, from another world," Mike said quickly."

"The pathway between worlds you mentioned," Danni said.

"Yes. My world is very much like this one and many of the people and places are the same."

"Colonel, you really expect us to believe you?"

"I know I look like him and my name is Mike Devon, but I am definitely not the Colonel."

Mike saw the pair exchange uncomfortable looks, then Danni asked, "Do you have some news for us?"

Court gripped her hand, "Time's up. Let's hear what you have to say."

"I just don't think you will—"

Danni interrupted, "Yes, we will."

Mike took a deep breath. "Your daughter's alive. Courtney, she's alive."

Danni gasped and stared silently at Court.

Court's voice wavered as he spoke, "She's been adamant that something like this happened ever since that night. There were too many things that didn't add up. That girl's hair, the jewelry made in *Supreme Britain* and her hands were too soft. Danni knew it wasn't her."

"Where is she? Is she married? Does she have any children?" Danni asked.

"She's back in the USA, where I came from. I don't actually know if she's married, or if she has kids," Mike said, feeling sick to his stomach. "I never thought to ask, but I will as soon as I see her." *If I see her.*

Court asked, "Is she healthy?"

"Yeah, she seemed perfect to me, but I barely spent an hour with her before I left."

Danni gave Mike a strange look, then asked, "Is she smart? Pretty?"

"She's a bright girl. Beautiful and athletic." Mike saw she was watching his face and faintly reflecting some of his emotions. "Sorry, I really don't know that much about her."

Danni sat up straight, eyes puffy and her face covered with tears but joy in her eyes. "When can we see her? Can we go to her? Or is she coming here?"

"Danni, be careful," Court warned.

"I think you can see her, but not sure how or when. That's why I asked you here. I need your help to get back," Mike said.

"What can we do to help?" Danni asked.

"The crystal altar," said Court. "He wants us to take him to the crystal altar, right son?"

"I think that may be our only hope at this point. I can't carry my device with me, so I'm only able to travel when one of the other Mike Devons operate it back home," Mike said.

"How does that work?" she asked.

"Somehow, the person at the device forces the others to travel into the next world, kind of in a circle. At least that's the way I hope it works."

"This *other worlds* talk sounds just like those crazy Egyptians. Maybe they weren't crazy after all?" Court asked.

Mike nodded. "They might have been doing far more than everyone realized."

"So how many *versions* are there?" Court asked.

"I know of three already. There's the Colonel, Michael, from Supreme Britain, and myself. I just came from Supreme Britain, but I don't know if my next stop will be the USA or not."

"Danni and I have been retired from intelligence for a while now, so we can't go in alone, anymore. If you can get us into the lower labs, we can take you to the crystal altar."

"I just walked out of there, so I think I can get us back in," Mike smiled.

"Years of fighting the Nazis has made the SAF fierce and inflexible," Court warned.

"I understand," Mike said.

"They'll shoot you on the spot if they think you're an imposter," Court said.

"I figured as much. My only other option is to wait around indefinitely while my device is captured or destroyed, if it hasn't been already."

"If you're fine with it, then let's go to the Colonel's apartment, get your uniform and prep you for our little op."

"I'm ready," Mike said and stood up.

"Well, gentlemen, I do believe you just took twenty years off my life!" Danni said, as she rose and tugged Court to his feet. "Now, you have to tell us about our girl!"

As they walked across the park with Danni in the middle, Mike told the story of meeting Courtney. He watched Danni's face light up, looking years younger than when they met. *This is what Courtney could have been like, if all of this hadn't happened. I wonder if she can ever get past it?*

* * *

Courtney walked softly down the hall and heard Michael breathing as she neared the corner.

Not wanting to surprise him, she said, "Michael?"

"I'm right here," he answered.

Sounds like he's been crying—find the sword. Courtney reached for her pistol then changed her mind. *A round in the chamber, thirteen in the magazine, safety on.*

"What should I call you?" he asked when she came into view. "I know your name isn't Maria."

Still looks unstable. She looked into his eyes. *He knows.*

"You can call me Courtney, what should I call you?"

"Michael Devon," he managed. "We were in the eighth grade together, don't you remember?"

"I don't recall much from my childhood, I'm sorry,"

Courtney said, as a thud sounded from the hallway behind her. *The guys must be getting restless.*

"What was that?" Michael asked.

"Something to do with the generators I assume."

"Oh—I was the poor kid in the back, fourth class. We talked, remember now?" he asked, almost pleading with her to remember.

I almost remember. "I'm sorry, Michael, I don't remember fourth class." *Oops, he twitched. I said something wrong.* "Tell me something about fourth class," Courtney said.

"I was talking about my *social* class."

"Oh, I misunderstood." *Agitated, tense, eyes darting around.*

He glanced down at his uniform, then back at her and asked, "What do you know about the SAF?"

"Michael, I have almost no recollection of my childhood, something happened to me when I was young. I was taken from my home and brought here, to this place, just after my fifteenth birthday."

"The SAF, please?" Michael said, as he fidgeted with the sword.

Slipping a hand onto her SIG Sauer before she spoke, Courtney eased the safety off. "My parents worked with the SAF when I was young." She saw Michael's face change suddenly.

"Your accent, she had one just like it. I remember now," Michael said.

"Who did, Michael?"

"Courtney. Well, the Courtney just before..."

"That was the American Courtney."

"You know what happened?"

"Well, I think the girl you knew pushed me here, to the USA, taking my place and I must have pushed this Courtney to your world."

"So, you were *never* in Supreme Britain?" he asked.

"No, Michael, I wasn't. I was working in an SAF lab one

minute and the next minute I was in a strange bed in a new world…this world," Courtney maintained eye contact, but noticed he was touching the sword again. "Tell me about her, please?"

Michael's eyes continued to dart around. "I figured she was the girl in that article, working with the SAF. It was just that when I saw you—well, I just thought maybe—"

"Were you friends with her?"

Michael remained silent.

"She would have been raised by my parents, I suppose. They took great care of her, I'm sure of it."

"Really? You think so? Well just a few minutes before I came to this place, a newspaper article I read, well…"

"What was in the article?"

"Well, the *amazing* Colonel had it framed on his wall. It was all about how *Courtney Danielle Lewis* died a *hero*, giving her life working at the SAF to *secure freedom for her people*. It was dated June 1, 1994!"

"I…" Courtney tried to talk, but strange images flashed before her eyes and she felt fear.

"It looks like they kept *my* Courtney safe for a whole week!"

Courtney shook herself out of the dreamlike state. She felt the butt of her Sig in her hand as she noticed Michael's face had reddened and his neck was pulsing. She looked at his eyes and they were staring back.

"You know something you're not telling me!" he yelled.

"No, I'm not sure—"

"Three sets of parents lost their girls over this and one of those little girls lost her life!"

Courtney was sick to her stomach. "Your Courtney died in my place, Michael. For that I am sorry and grateful. I will do my best to make it right, but I cannot go back in time and fix it."

Courtney noticed Michael's eyes were red and swollen.

"*Two* girls died over this, Courtney. My people hanged the

American girl about ten days after the exchanges. I loved them both, but couldn't save either one. I just sat there and watched..." His voice cracked as he went silent.

Seeing an opportunity, Courtney slowly leaned up against the wall beside Michael and put her hand on his arm.

"You can't change that now," she said.

Michael's eyes met Courtney's for a moment then quickly down to her shoulder.

"That's where you're wrong."

"What is that supposed to mean?" she asked.

"I was getting close, before I came here." Michael kept his eyes away from hers.

"Close? To changing the past?" She leaned her head down and he briefly made eye contact. "Michael?"

"I was fine-tuning my *septi-circular*, crystal resonator. The vibration was intense and it was unstable. Like Einstein and Rosen had suggested," he said softly. "I can't leave it on for more than a minute at a time or I risk being detected."

Courtney remained silent, hoping he would continue.

"I couldn't even run it long enough to figure out how to cali—"

Michael's face changed and he cut a suspicious glance at Courtney.

So, did Mike cause this alone, or was it the pair of them, unknowingly working together? she wondered. "Michael, that's amazing. Were you using it when you came here? Maybe you caused this?"

"No, it was powered down. I was at work," Michael said.

"I see." Her phone chimed a GPS warning. *Looks like the boys are close.* "Michael, I can't imagine what you are feeling right now. I just want to help the SAF secure freedom and safety for my people. Will you help me?"

Michael's eyes lit up for a moment. "I'd like that."

"Then come with me, quickly. I have something to show

you." Courtney turned and headed back to the buss room. *Do this right and get Mike back,* she rehearsed silently as they walked. Courtney held the door open for him and said, "This is a device your American counterpart, Mike, developed. I am guessing it may be similar to your invention. Also, when that sword Colonel Devon developed is buried in steel, it makes a similar sound, only much quieter," Courtney said.

"So, the three of us are developing similar technology, in three different existences? What are the odds of that happening by chance?"

"Exactly. And all three of you have had ties to all three Courtneys. I think it proves there is some unknown connection."

"There is something wrong with all of this."

"Why do you say that?" she asked.

"This can't just be a fractured time line, or they would have gone off in three unique directions. Similar, sure, but not so connected for so many years. Something, or someone, is keeping them synchronized. But how?"

"Maybe it's just the way it works."

"But what's the law behind it? The principle that guides it all?"

"Michael, it is all very interesting, for sure, but I need you to help me operate Mike's device and put things back in place." Another thought occurred to her. "The future is possibly at risk as long as the three of you are not in your rightful places."

"I'm not so sure it matters. Someone altered the past and we are living in three, adulterated futures. We need to fix the past, that is the real problem."

Courtney said, "But, you shouldn't all be here. You should return home, or it could get even worse."

"I have no reason to go back!" Michael yelled.

She felt her phone buzz again and checked it. "Michael, please, I need your help."

"I already told you I'm not going back!"

"Not that, I need you to disable the elevator, down the hall where you were, while I gather my things. There are some men after me and they're heading in this direction," she said, holding up her phone.

"Oh. I thought you meant—"

"Go, slash a zigzag pattern through the elevator doors so they can't open." She opened the door for him again.

"That will stop them?" he asked, as he entered the hallway.

"No, but it *will* slow them down a little," Courtney said as Michael walked off.

She quickly went over to the panel on the far row of electrical cabinets and pulled the large breaker from *Tripped* to *Off* and then back to the *On* position. *Now, I just need to get him over here,* she thought, as she pulled out her gun.

In moments, Michael opened the door to the buss room. "Got it!"

Courtney watched his excitement fade to sadness, then anger.

"You turned it back on. I can hear it!" he said. You're... you're trying to get rid of me!"

"Michael, when those men get here they'll kill both of us, this is our only chance." Courtney held her pistol behind her leg so he couldn't see it.

* * *

"I'm not positive I can drive you straight to the Colonel's building," Court said. "I only stopped by once, to deliver some information we acquired."

"If we can't find it right away, we should head back and take our chances," Mike said.

"Understood," Court said.

"Knowing the truth about Courtney, helping her and possibly getting a message to her, is priceless to Court and I."

Danni reached up from the back seat and put a hand on Mike's shoulder.

"I hope we can figure this out," Mike said, glancing back at her.

"With Colonel Devon on our side, we should be just fine," Court said.

"So, how well do you know him?" Mike asked.

"We've worked around and for him numerous times, but there has always been a wedge between us."

"Since we lost Courtney," Danni added. "Wait, Court, I think you're close."

"You aren't going to believe it, but this looks like my neighborhood," Mike said. "And, we *are* close. Take a right at the next intersection and it is halfway down the block, on the right."

"Are you sure?" Danni asked.

"Yep. Well, that's the street I live on anyway."

"You don't seem very surprised," Danni said.

Smiling at her, Mike said, "Ma'am, after everything I have seen, not much surprises me anymore."

As the building came into view, Mike saw images of the inside of the building.

"So, what do you think it means if he lives in the same apartment?" Danni asked.

"What if he doesn't?" Mike replied. "Michael, in Supreme Britain, lives in an old house, in a completely different part of town."

"What is he like?" Court asked.

"He's working on something similar to my device and he's pretty bright. He knew Courtney and had a bit of a fixation on her."

"He did?" Danni asked.

"Yeah, that's why he took the executions so—" Mike stopped as Danni gasped.

"Who was executed? Courtney? Who else?" Danni asked.

"American Courtney was and her parents in Supreme Britain."

"What on earth for?" she asked, her voice cracking.

"She gave them a piece of her mind. Went off on some government types there," Mike said.

"That sounds like something our Courtney would have done," Court said with admiration. "Why did they kill her?"

"They called it treason."

"Was Michael there?" she asked.

"Yeah and he's been plotting revenge ever since. Trying to —let's say, he's chosen to apply the technology a bit differently than I have." *Not that he could have kept it together long enough to get it working.*

Court said, "Meaning?"

"We're talking about gravity and magnetic fields. They hold entire galaxies together in perfectly synchronized ballets," Mike said.

"But, I thought the real energy was in the atom," Court said.

"That's true, but these forces are interrelated on a galactic scale. These fields extend for millions of miles and can be used in ways we are only just beginning to understand."

"OK, professor," Court chuckled. "We'll have to table this for another discussion."

As the car came to a stop, Mike felt uneasy and regretted coming.

"Son, we can't let this device of yours get into the wrong hands or the entire world could be damaged."

Mike looked him in the eyes, "What if someone already did? That could be the reason for having three variations."

"Who are you referring to?" Danni asked.

"Well, the Egyptians did some amazing things in my world, but here they went so much further. The vast power production and wireless transmission networks that Nikolai Tesla demonstrated thousands of years later are a perfect example. If they used that power on the crystal altar, maybe they caused it all to happen."

"There are more incredible things, unbelievable things, occurring in antiquity," Court added.

"The ancient Egyptian power and control are what Supreme Britain built off of to dominate the world. That's basically what happened here, except the Nazi's managed to get it. None of that happened in my world. Egypt was conquered by the Romans in 332 BC. In the early 1940s, the USA helped destroy the Nazis, while Britain was in ruins."

"That is hard to fathom," Danni said.

"My question now is, which world is the true world? I just can't believe there has always been a *trinity* of realities, flowing along together."

"One thing at a time, Mike. Let's try to fix the little things first. We need to get you back home to this *USA* you talk about and see where fate takes us," Court said.

"I'm with you on that, sir," Mike said. He climbed out and opened the rear door for Danni. "If my hunch is right, he's in the same flat as me, on the third floor."

"Flat?" Danni said.

"I meant *apartment*." Mike chuckled.

"Well, let's go find out," Court said.

"Everything is laid out the same, but the decor is completely different," Mike said, as they entered the building. "Strangely enough, it's all familiar."

"Familiar?" Danni asked.

"Well, I recognize it, but I know I've never seen it," he said as he lead the way over to the elevator. He reached out and a vision of Jillian sitting across a table from him briefly filled his thoughts. Mike felt his hand jerk back from the button. *Don't be on there, please, don't let her be on there,* he thought as reality came back to him. Mike noticed Court and Danni exchange glances as he reached for the button a second time. "Think I'm crazy?" he asked.

"Not crazy, but I wouldn't talk too loudly, either," Court said with a grin as he stepped into the elevator.

As the doors closed, Danni asked, "Is it much safer where you come from, than here? I mean, is there *real* freedom?"

"Many countries have some level of security, their freedom on the other hand, well that's debatable. The same goes for the USA. It's arguably the best place in the world to live, maybe the best in history," Mike said.

"Do you think your world is the best of the three?" Court asked.

"I think so." *But I'm not sure they want me back.*

"Do you know if her parents are alive, there?" Danni asked.

"They died right after she got there, but she's a strong girl," Mike replied, as the doors opened to a well-lit corridor.

"I know this world is unfair, but I still have a hard time understanding why," Danni said, with her eyes tearing up.

"People have the freedom to make choices, that's why," Court said.

"I've heard that one before," Danni said.

You know she's crying, don't look at her. Don't do it—

Mike felt a pain in his throat after he saw Danni's face. *Told ya.*

She tried to hide her emotions and winked at Mike.

Mike was immediately back home, sitting across the living room from Court and Danni. She was teasing Court about something he said, then winked at Mike. He smiled back then looked over at Courtney. The little girl sitting on her lap—is that —

"Something is wrong, Court," Danni said. "Mike? Mike?"

Mike felt a slap on his arm and realized he was still standing in a hallway of the Colonel's apartment building. "I—did you?"

"Are you all right?" Danni asked.

"Yeah. It's just, well, I had a sort of memory," Mike said. "Something I didn't know before, but I guess I do now." Mike swallowed hard.

"You sound confused," she said.

"Yeah, I guess I am. Or I was. But I don't have time to be confused right now. Let's see if the Colonel's apartment is down here," Mike said, then headed down the wide hallway. "I'll bet you breakfast this is his place."

As they reached the door. He pulled the keys from his pocket and tried the key in the lock. It wouldn't fit.

"Of course not. That would be too weird if my own key worked, even if he does live here," Mike said.

"Shouldn't we just knock? Or maybe try the building superintendent? They'll recognize you, right?" Danni asked.

"Hold on," Mike said, turning around. He reached out for the fire extinguisher mounted on the wall, released the latch and a key dropped to the carpet.

"How did you know?" Court asked.

"I guess we dated the same girl," said Mike.

He turned the key in the lock and a solid clunk told them it worked. The heavy door opened quietly, showing empty blackness. Mike reached inside and turned on the lights. Seeing Court's already exposed weapon, Mike stopped. "After you, sir."

The light exposed a bachelor's apartment. Though orderly and clean, it was definitely lacking a woman's touch. As the armed couple made their way into the living room, Mike followed quietly and locked the door behind them.

"Colonel, it's Court and Danni Lewis. Are you here? Sir? Are you all right? Hello?" Danni asked, as she walked slowly into the living room.

"I'm pretty sure he isn't here," Mike said. "Actually, I don't believe he *could* be here."

"Why?" she asked.

"I think that if you tried to put us in the same dimension you could have a fission reaction, similar to an atomic bomb. You would be trying to put the same matter into a place it already existed and that's not possible."

Court asked, "Couldn't you just combine into a large blob?"

"Court! That's terrible," Danni said.

"OK, say it happens," Mike said. "All of those atoms have to instantly move away from each other, colliding into other atoms doing the same. You could be a small fusion reaction—a star. Fission or fusion. Either way you risk everyone and everything in the vicinity."

"I guess I don't want to find out what happens," Court said, as he walked up to a large, wooden bookcase and pulled down a book. "History, advanced weaponry and a bunch of physics books. He's even less fun than I remember."

"Sounds about right," Mike grinned. "Though, I'm afraid you'd find similar at my place."

Danni knocked and opened a door, calling out, "Hello? Anyone here?" She walked in.

Mike walked across the room and joined her. "Wow, this guy is an overachiever and proud of it. Look at all of those awards, plaques and medals." Mike pointed to the wall behind the large, mahogany desk that faced the door. "Oh—" He saw the large picture just as Danni gasped and rushed up to it.

"Court, come quick! You'll want to see this," she called out. "He has a picture of our girl. I told you he was in love with her."

Mike made himself keep silent.

"He came by our house several times, afterward," Danni said. "Court thought he would tell us what really happened but he never did. When Court demanded to know more, *Captain* Devon quit coming by to see us. We only saw him professionally after that." Danni's voice cracked and she went silent.

"Let's see if this apartment has something else mine does,"

Mike said. He lifted the picture off the wall, exposing a safe. He unsuccessfully tried his own combination. Then, on a whim, he tried Courtney's birthday, but it failed as well. Looking back at the couple, Mike suddenly realized he hadn't tried the most likely numbers.

"Six, fourteen, nineteen, ninety-five," he said softly, as he rotated the dial back and forth. Mike glanced back at Court and Danni and saw them exchange a glance.

"You remembered the exact date?" Danni asked.

"I watched as the girl that took your Courtney's place was beaten. I was scared and confused as I just sat in my bed while it happened." He pulled down on the lever and the door opened. "A young soldier dove at me with one of these and hit me in the hip." Mike said, holding up one of the Colonel's sword handles.

"Careful, that's not a toy," Court warned.

Mike turned and looked at Mr. Lewis, pausing as images of a battlefield flashed before him.

"Are you all right, dear?" Danni asked.

"Uh, yeah, I am." Mike walked over to the Colonel's desk and sat in his brown, leather chair. "This chair is just right," he said, jokingly.

Danni laughed. "I suppose that *is* to be expected."

"Goldilocks?" Mike asked.

"And the three bears," Danni said.

"Here's something else in common," Mike said, as he looked down at the desk drawers. "Military spec, biometric locks? Pretty fancy for home." Placing his thumb on the reddish black oval on the face of the drawer, Mike felt a solid *clunk* come from inside. "This drawer safe is heavy," he said, as he pulled on the handle. "It must weigh over a hundred pounds."

"Mike, I don't think you should do that. What if it's alarmed? Or booby trapped?" Court asked.

"You're probably right, but it's too late now," Mike said, as he removed the contents of the drawer. "Just some classified files, a gun and some money. Oh and a few sealed envelopes." Mike read aloud, *"In the event of my death.* The Colonel won't mind, I'm sure of it." He removed a rubber band from one bundle.

Court looked at him sternly, "Son, you should put it all back and lock the drawer."

"I would tend to agree with you, but these are mine, in a way. Oh, and this one is yours," Mike said, reaching out with an envelope.

"He's not dead, well, that we know of," Danni said.

"The Colonel *is* gone and we aren't certain he's alive. Besides, there may be something here that can help all of us."

"Well ..." Court said, looking at the letter.

"We need every advantage we can get," Mike said, as he watched Court slowly reach for it.

"Is there one for Dr. David Lowen, or maybe Captain Steven Kaide?" Danni asked.

Mike flipped through and saw both names. "Yes, how did you know that?"

"When I was trying to learn what happened to Courtney, I came across two other families who lost children to mysterious circumstances under Colonel Devon's watch. We thought that collaborating would get us better results. We were wrong. All six of us were taken in and interrogated, one after the other for three days."

"Sounds like you were getting close to the truth," Mike said.

"We thought so, too. At the end of it all, we were told that our children died fighting for our freedom and—should we want to disgrace their deaths further—we would be considered enemies of the SAF."

"And executed?" Mike asked.

"Or put on the front line in Asia for a tour or two," Court said. "Basically, a death sentence, especially at our age."

Mike looked down, slowly opened the first file in the stack

and began to read. He knew he would have no more objections when he heard their letter tear open.

"Interesting, but nothing we need in this one," Mike said, glancing up to see tears running down both of their faces. He quickly looked down and opened the next file to read through its contents.

"Well that explains everything. He did it. He killed that innocent girl with his bare hands. Trying to save her soul?"

Court was starting to sound angry so Mike kept reading.

"Court, things were much worse back then. The SAF was just starting to make progress against the Nazis. Those were very desperate times."

"The end always justifies the means for these warmongers," Court grumbled.

"Darling, he was so very young and foolish. He did it out of love for her and to protect us." Looking over at Mike, Danni said, "There wasn't even enough food to go around, so the sick and elderly were encouraged to commit suicide."

"He did it for his precious military," Court said.

"Sure, he was protecting the SAF, too, but don't you see what it cost him? His personal life was ruined by that one act."

"*His* personal life? What about *hers*? *Ours*?" Court asked, almost snarling as he spoke.

"Court, he was fourteen years old."

"So?"

"And, he's a product of the world *we* created."

"The Hitlers created it, not us. Not everyone in the Colonel's generation is as cold and ruthless toward their own people as he is."

"Court, you don't mean that."

"I do. I'd kill him, but I want him to suffer."

Danni made a disgusted face and shook her head.

"All he had to do was tell the truth," Court said.

As Mike picked up the Colonel's pistol he felt a queasy

sensation. "Oh, no! Get back! Quick! Run! Get away from me now!"

Court drew his own pistol, pointed it at Mike and shoved Danni toward the door.

"Put it down!" Court screamed.

Danni screamed, "No, Court! No!"

"Hurry Court, get back! It's happening again!" Mike dropped the files, letters and money onto the desk. He stuffed the pistol into his pocket, grabbed the sword and hurried into the middle of the room. "I'm sorry, I don't mean to scare you, but they're running the machine back home. I don't know where I'm going, or what will happen if you're too close to me!" Mike explained, as he felt the power of the spud growing. "I'm so happy I got to meet both of you."

"Goodbye, Mike, be careful!" Danni called out.

"I'll try to find a way to get Courtney here, somehow." He jammed the sword into his pocket and covered his ears. The loving look on Danni's face made Mike want to reunite the family even more. The noise overpowered every other sound in the room. "Thank you," Mike moved his lips, but realized no sound was heard.

Danni nodded in acknowledgment from the doorway, as she watched on with wide eyes. A hazy curtain opened in the middle of the room and slowly engulfed Mike as he went down to his knees, sliding into the fog. He arched his back in agony, screamed a silent plea and was ripped from view. The room was quiet and clear within a few seconds.

Almost knocked off her feet in the final overpowering seconds of the tremendously violent event, Danni struggled to regain her footing. Grabbing onto the doorjamb, she peered into the office and saw Court staring back with surprise on his face.

"What is it? Is he gone?" she whispered.

"Yes, he's—uh, no he's—he's not," Court stammered.

Easing back through the doorway, Danni tried to see what

had shaken him up so badly. From the look on Court's face, she wasn't sure she wanted to see.

Lying face down on the floor and groaning, only a few feet away from where Mike had gone down, was a man with a military haircut. He attempted to lift himself up and began gazing blindly around the room.

"Colonel Devon!" Danni exclaimed.

* * *

"I don't want to leave."

"Yes, you do, if you want to help your Courtney," Courtney said as she turned up the power. The room immediately began to fill with the hum of the spud. Courtney looked at Michael as he stared back. *You, my friend, need to go home.* For a moment, she felt guilty. *It's not much different than how I feel about Mike—a sort of misplaced love.* Courtney's mind wandered to what might happen when he returned home and she felt doubts start to rise. *Focus, Courtney! You are so close! Focus!* She waved at Michael, certain the system had reached its full operating power. She then pointed to the haze and motioned for him to walk to it.

Michael's head drooped slightly as he walked into the haze, then out the other side. He turned and looked back at her with an inquisitive look on his face.

Nothing happened! She felt anger and frustration flash across her face, then Michael darted out of the noise filled room. *You let him see your reaction! You're losing control of yourself and the situation!* She quickly checked the tracker app and was pleased to see the SIU team was getting further away. Courtney relaxed slightly and her thoughts went back to Michael. *I wonder why? Wait! The sword was on!* Courtney realized she had seen sparks when Michael went through the doorway. *That must be why he didn't travel!*

She grabbed the breaker handle and pulled down. As it snapped loudly into position, the noise in the room died out. *So, what now?* Courtney looked across the room and saw a man, in unfamiliar clothes, lying on the floor.

Mike? It looks like him, or another...

As she approached, she could see he was breathing. She crept up slowly, then lowered herself down to get a better look at his face. *No watch, or rings.* Courtney reached down to take his hand in hers, keeping her other hand firmly on her gun.

"Mike? Can you hear me? Mike?" She spoke softly at first, then louder.

"Yeah, just barely, but I can't see anything yet. Give me a minute and I'll be all right," the stranger said, with a faint British accent.

Her hopes immediately fell and Courtney pulled back slightly.

"Where are we?" Mike asked.

"We're in a power substation—"

"Wait, in America?" The man's accent disappeared, as he quickly lifted his head., exposing his face.

"Yes! Mike? Is that you?" *Of course, his name is Mike.* "I mean, who's your employer?" Courtney was still skeptical.

"Well, *Emily*, I would like to know who *your* employer is first," Mike said, as a huge smile crossed his face.

Courtney dropped onto her knees, on the floor beside him, stuffing the pistol in her pocket. She wrapped both of her arms around him. "It is you! Mike, so much has happened! Your invention worked! Well, you know *that*. Tell me where you've been and what you've seen!"

"First things first—are you married?" Mike asked.

"*That's* your first question?" she laughed.

"Well?"

"No husband, just me," she said, watching his eyes.

Mike pulled her around in front of him and kissed her full on the lips.

"I have been wanting to do that since lunch at Bella's. Wow, have I missed you!"

"Well, funny enough, I've missed you, too." Courtney kissed him back.

"It's crazy, I know. I don't even know you, *Courtney Danielle Lewis*. However, I *do* know your parents," Mike said, as he kissed her again.

Struggling to get back onto her knees, Courtney righted herself.

"That's enough there, Mr. Devon. Let's have it. I want all the details!" she said, barely holding back her emotions.

"Strange, it's starting to slip my memory," Mike said.

"Hey now, that's not fair!" Courtney laughed and delivered another kiss. "I'd like to hear some news about the parents I haven't seen in nineteen years if you don't mind!"

"That did it. My memory—its back!" he teased. "Danni and Court send their love."

"You talked to them and everything? They're OK? How did you find them? Tell me everything you know!"

"Yeah, well I've picked up a few tricks along the way," he said. "First, I looked them up in the phone book, then I called them." He smiled.

"Wow, that *is* impressive! A *phone book*, huh?"

"Yep. Then, they drove over and met me in a park." Mike's face became serious. "They broke down when I told you you were still alive."

"But they believed you?" Courtney asked.

"Well, I did have to warm them up a bit. They were told you died that night, but never completely believed it. Your mother had tried to get to the truth, but *Colonel Devon* kept it locked up."

"That must have been horrible for them, wondering all of these years."

"Like what you went through?" Mike asked.

Courtney shrugged.

"Wait, why aren't you surprised about Colonel Devon?" he

asked.

"I met him and Michael, too."

"How did that go?" he asked.

Courtney smiled at the concerned look on his face. "Strange, that's for sure, but I learned a lot, too."

"Tell me," Mike said.

"There will be plenty of time for that later, since neither of us has a job anymore."

"I missed those beautiful eyes while I was away," Mike said.

"I might have missed you a little," Courtney teased.

"I wish I could have taken you with me, but I didn't even know I was going away."

"It's fine. I was busy anyway," she said.

"Yeah, you had to get the Colonel and Michael to operate the spud. I'm impressed by the way."

"It was nothing. They were pretty easy to outsmart, too," Courtney said.

"Whoa! So, *I'm* easy to outsmart?"

"I never said *that.*" She winked at his boyish grin. "Now, what else do you have to tell me about my parents?"

"Well, they're both healthy, recently retired from low level spying for the SAF and would love to see you. Wait, why do I get the feeling that you're formulating a plan, beautiful maiden from a land far, far away."

Courtney felt at ease with Mike. He was good at making her feel human. He could look through the mask and see *her.* Many times she had focused the cameras in on his face to watch him and always felt a closeness she could not logically explain.

"You know we might be able to make that happen, don't you?" he said.

Mike kept looking into her eyes and she liked it. "Are you trying to get rid of me?" she asked.

"What? No, not at all, I was—"

"It's all right, I was joking."

"You're hard to read!"

"Sorry, it's an occupational skill set." She smiled. "I figured you could come up with a way to make it happen, but I'm not sure it's worth the risk of getting stuck with Michael, or the Colonel."

"So, you prefer my company then?"

"Well…"

"I see." Mike said, pretending his feelings were hurt.

Courtney squeezed his arm. "Of course, I do. Seriously though, the likelihood of this technology being misused is high."

"I know you're right, but I'm sure I can do it without additional risk," he said, patting her hand.

"I'd like for us to get to know each other better, before we do anything else crazy," Courtney said.

"Then, I have a question. How long have you known about our connection?"

"I guess the first time I really understood just how entwined our lives were, was when I read the transcripts from your dreams." Courtney leaned her head on Mike's shoulder and they sat quietly for a moment. *Not long after that I started to fall in love with you,* Courtney thought.

* * *

"Hello? Is someone there?" the Colonel asked.

Court looked at Danni and nodded toward the door with an inquisitive look on his face. She shook her head 'no' and he turned back toward the Colonel.

"I know someone is there. Who are you?"

"It's Court, sir."

"I can't hear what you're saying."

Court walked up to the Colonel and placed his hand on his arm.

"Court, sir. Court Lewis. Are you hurt?" He looked back to

Danni who nodded approvingly.

"I can feel you said something but I can't hear or see much," the Colonel said loudly, as he attempted to rise.

Court quickly moved a chair next to him and placed the Colonel's hand on it. He steadied the chair as the Colonel worked his way into it.

Once the Colonel was seated, Court leaned over and spoke loudly, "Sir, this is Court and Danni Lewis. We just met with Mike, from the USA, and we're up to speed."

The Colonel jerked his head toward Court, "Courtney! She's alive! She's trying to come here!"

Court moved back slightly. "Yes, we know."

"We have to stop her! Get me to the lab, ASAP!"

Court looked at Danni. "We can't let you do that, Colonel," he called out as he stepped toward her.

"Court!" Danni exclaimed. "Courtney thinks she's coming here, but it doesn't work like that! She'll get stuck in the other place!"

"What if—" Court stopped himself.

"We have to go to the lab. The crystal altar is our only chance! Hurry!" Danni ordered. Danni darted out the door. "I'll have the car waiting out front!" she yelled over her shoulder.

"We're right behind you!" Court called out, rushing to the Colonel's side. "Let's move out, sir!" said Court, as he nearly dragged the Colonel out of the chair.

"I'm doing better, just let me hold on to your shoulder," the Colonel said.

The pair hurried out of the apartment and into the hallway as the elevator chimed. They half jogged, half ran to it and climbed in.

"Perfect timing," the Colonel said.

"Danni must have slapped the button on her way to the stairwell."

"Of course, she did. That's an amazing lady you have there,

Court."

"Thank you, sir."

When the doors opened at the ground floor, Danni was waiting for them. "You look better, Colonel," she said.

"I feel better and it's nice to see you, Mrs. Lewis," he said, as he hurried off the elevator. "Now let's see what we can do to help Courtney."

Danni turned and ran to the front doors, with the two men on her heels.

"Get in, sir," Court said, opening the front door for the Colonel as Danni jumped into the driver's seat.

"Buckle up, gentlemen," she said, as she started to pull away from the curb.

"Are you certain our Courtney is in danger?" Court asked. "If you're here, then doesn't that mean Mike is back there?"

"I don't know. When I woke up in Supreme Britain, I was being beaten. I dealt with the issue, but that would have left Mike in a bit of a situation when he arrived."

"How many people did you—?" Court asked.

"Only one, but it was a bit, well, messy," the Colonel said. "From what I gathered, he's a lab rat and not a soldier. He won't likely get out of anything difficult."

"Wait, Mike was just here. That means he went home. Doesn't it?" Danni asked as she took a quick glance over at the Colonel.

"All I know is that I went from here to the USA, to Supreme Britain, then back here," the Colonel replied.

"Mike went to Supreme Britain, then here, so he should be back in the USA now," answered Court.

"I see what you're saying," the Colonel said. "He could be back there. But then Courtney might end up in the middle of the mess I left behind."

"Court, do you know how or why it happens in that order?" Danni asked.

"No."

"Colonel?"

"I'd have to see it happen a few more times. I'm not willing to risk something happening to her—again," the Colonel said.

"We're not far now, Colonel. Are you sure this is what you want to do?" Danni asked.

"Absolutely, I have to try."

"Colonel, I'm not convinced the crystal altar will work," Court said from the back seat.

"If not, Courtney could be trapped in Supreme Britain," the Colonel said.

"Then Mike will get shifted to Supreme Britain and could get in trouble. What then?" Danni asked, as she shifted gears firmly.

"I don't have the answers, but I know I'm not going to sit here and wonder what happened to her for another eighteen years."

"I think you knew," Court said.

"What is that supposed to mean? Are we going back down that path again?" the Colonel asked.

"We know the truth. Mike opened your desk drawer and found a letter addressed to us."

"What? My desk? There are classified documents in there!"

"True, but you have no right to be angry with *us*," Court said.

"You committed treason!" the Colonel snapped, turning slightly in his seat.

"We were trying to get to the crystal altar ourselves and Mike thought you may have something in there to help us," Court explained.

"So, you read classified documents? Did you read my personal files, too?" The Colonel grabbed at the seatback to turn and face Court.

The sound of Court's pistol chambering a round was

unmistakable.

"I suggest you calm yourself before something bad happens," Court said.

"I advise you to—"

"No! I advise you! I advise you to shut your mouth for one minute and listen to me! *You* are responsible for what happened to Courtney and the other girls, whether you admit it or not!"

"I am well aware—"

"And, your current plan pits you *against* the SAF. So, let's not forget who's who in this game!"

The silence in the car was interrupted only by the clank of a manhole cover.

"Colonel, I don't want to be disrespectful, nor do I wish to hate you for the rest of my life." Court struggled with the words, then said, "We're willing to let the bad memories die, if you are."

Court was surprised the Colonel didn't retaliate. As the seconds ticked by, he knew he had gotten through. He found himself struggling to hold back a grin as the anger and hatred left his body. *If only I could have done that twenty years ago.*

Finally, the Colonel broke the silence by taking a deep breath. "Court, in my position it's almost impossible to be wrong. No one allows it, no matter what the facts say. I should have told you the truth. I know that now and I'm truly sorry."

Court could see a tear forming in Danni's right eye and he wanted to comfort her, but forced himself not to.

Finally, the Colonel went on, "I believed I did the right thing when she went crazy that night. When that other girl went crazy, I mean. I've hated myself all these years. It's what drove me back into battle. It's why I dove headlong at death, over and over again. Many times, I would step off the battlefield angry that I'd survived. All of that killing only made my rage grow and made me hate myself more."

"Colonel, we understand, you don't have to—" Danni began.

"Yes, I do. You have waited years for the truth and I am going to give it to you. All of it." He paused for a moment. "Seeing her now has shown me that I can't continue pretending to live. I have nothing to live for except putting things right and I won't rest until I've returned her to you, or I'm dead."

"Son, you have done a lot of horrible things in your life. Horrible things that were necessary. Our generation brought yours into an evil situation and we needed you to save us from it. We made you what you are. Don't forget it and don't you regret it. We're proud of you." Court reached forward and placed his hand on the Colonel's shoulder.

All three sat in silence as they drove the last few blocks.

"We're here," Danni said quietly, as she pulled up to the curb.

"All right then, let's do this," the Colonel said.

One by one, they climbed out of the car and felt the first rays of sunshine warming their faces in the early morning air.

"No matter how this day ends, it will always be one of the best days of my life. Thank you, Colonel," Court said, as he shut the car door.

* * *

Terry watched the first sliver of the sun disappear behind a distant hill as the pilot set the chopper down.

"Be back in ten and we'll get back up there," the pilot said.

"Roger that," Terry said. He and Bill hopped out, hunched under the slowing rotor, then scurried toward the small terminal.

"I hope these machines take plastic, I only have three ones," Bill said, checking his wallet as he jogged up to the door. He flipped the door open wide and walked in with Terry right behind.

"Some people keep cash on themselves, in case." Terry opened his wallet and tipped it toward Bill as they approached the machines. "See? Mine's not full of receipts and claim checks."

"No problem, these are the new ones." Bill slipped his card in one and started pushing buttons. "I'm loadin' up!"

"Wow, that *is* exciting. Too bad they don't have a hotdog machine, too," Terry said as item after item fell to the bottom. Bill didn't say anything, so Terry knew his comment had the desired effect.

"I don't know about you, but this glorious physique needs lots of carbs and protein to keep going," Bill said, as he selected an energy drink.

"You sure you can carry all of that garbage?" Terry asked, as Bill collected the last of his items. He bought an energy drink for himself and immediately started drinking it.

"You think we'll find her?" Bill asked.

"If we don't pick up her trail soon, then I doubt it will be us."

"I think I'd prefer it that way," Bill said.

"People are going to die either way," Terry said, then turned and looked out the windows. "Oh, the chopper's ready. Come on, He-man, we have to get back up there."

The pair walked up to the chopper as the fuel truck driver walked away.

"That was pretty quick," Terry commented to the pilot.

"Yep, it pays to radio ahead," he said. "Jump in."

When the fuel truck was clear, the pilot started the turbine and within moments the rotor was roaring overhead. "Hang on, boys." The chopper shot straight up for a hundred feet, then dipped forward and they were back on the hunt.

Terry felt his phone buzz in his pocket and pulled it out. "It's the office." He pressed a button, held it tight to his head and covered his other ear. "Go ahead," he said loudly, then listened for a moment. "Roger that. Next to a power plant? Great news. Send the coordinates to the chopper." He looked back at Bill.

"Yeah, yeah, I heard," Bill yelled, shaking his head. "Just

marvelous!"

The flight navigation GPS unit chimed and the pilot banked hard to the right. "We'll be there in five minutes," he said.

"Remember, if we engage, don't stop shooting until you're out of ammo," Terry called out over his shoulder.

"Let's hope we don't," Bill said.

Terry had thought the same thing, but hearing Bill say it out loud made him angry. "Grow up, soldier, or we're both dead!" he yelled at his junior partner.

Bill straightened up slightly, "Roger that, sir."

Keep your head and the kid will make it out alive, Terry reassured himself.

"That's it up ahead," the pilot announced.

Terry instantly felt his stomach turn. *Has to be that drink.*

* * *

"Do you know what's going on with the war?" Courtney asked as she lifted her head off Mike's shoulder.

"Your parents told me a little."

"Give me the short version."

"Well, about fourteen years ago, there was one last big Nazi push into North America to eradicate the Special Attack Forces. The Hitler regime miscalculated and overextended itself when the SAF faked a retreat. They lured them into the mountains and used a new, high energy EMP on them. The SAF had the high ground and shot the Nazis up for days."

"No air support?"

"They zapped everything the Nazis threw at them, over and over. Your dad said the entire valley stunk of death for months."

"I can imagine…"

"It took weeks for the Germans to come up with a defense to the weapon, but by that time they had lost portions of Africa,

Asia and Europe."

"All of their existing equipment would still be vulnerable," Courtney said.

"Exactly."

"If it was that bad, I am surprised they didn't nuke the SAF."

"The SAF has hundreds of missile bases."

"Mutually assured destruction…"

"Yeah, but the Hitler family is crazy so they had to pull back in case they went scorched earth."

"So, the war is almost over?" Courtney asked.

"Well, the balance of power has shifted, but it's at a standstill now."

"A Cold War with the Nazis, then?" she asked.

"All of those deaths; tens or hundreds of millions wiped out. If we could just go back in time and take out the men behind the wars."

"But there are always others waiting to take their place," he said.

"True."

Mike watched her face go cold again. "Hey, what's wrong?" he asked.

"I need to know that the Colonel delivered the package. It could help end the war sooner and save lives."

"If I'm home, then he is too," Mike said.

"I think you're right, but I need to be certain."

"Then, we'll have to figure something out," he said.

Courtney smiled. "Why do you want to help me, after all of this?"

"I guess I don't know what you mean."

"I've pretty much turned your life upside down. Ruined your career and your future. Don't you want to strangle me or something?"

"Oh, I plan to kill you, sure, but not until I get what I

want." Mike pulled the small pistol partially out of his pocket.

"I see. Well in that case I suppose I should warn you about this." She looked down at her own gun, with its silencer near his ribs.

"Dang, you're good," Mike said as he tucked it back into his pocket. "Yours looks tougher. Is that a silencer?"

"Yep. For those occasions when a girl wants to be seen, but not heard," she said with a smile.

"Wow, you're even cuter than I remember," Mike said. He slid his hand around to the small of her back and pulled her closer.

"You might change your mind once you get to know me." Courtney kissed him.

"Can I ask you a question?" Mike asked.

"Sure," she said their lips still touching.

"Are you free for lunch?" He laughed first and then she joined him.

Thinking back, Courtney realized she had not connected with anyone in her life. No one had seen the real her, or truly known her and yet Mike had broken her barriers with so little effort.

It has to be—he has to be.

"Well? Aren't you going to say something?" Mike asked.

"Mike, you have done so much for me. I want to see my parents, it's just…"

"I understand. No lunch." He squeezed her arm and winked. "It's all right. Tell me."

"I've been in love with you for a while now. I know this sounds creepy and weird, but sometimes I dream about us. The dreams are so real, like we know each other, really well."

"Yeah, I know what you mean."

"I guess what I'm trying to say is, I know who you are, but I realize you don't know a thing about me."

"Courtney, I understand exactly what you mean and I feel

the same way."

"You do?" she asked, looking into his eyes. "Yes, then let's leave it at that for now."

"Agreed," he smiled. "So, tell me about Michael and Colonel Devon."

"That's a long story. Let's compare notes on them tomorrow," Courtney said.

"But, Michael was working on a mag-field and gravity resonating device as was the Colonel—some type of sword. I think all three of us are actually inducing an Einstein-Rosen bridge." Courtney was silent, so Mike added, "An X-point, or wormhole, linking the dimensions."

"I have been studying physics my entire life, Mike, and I think that's about the only plausible explanation for what we have seen. You're doing what NASA has been watching for with the four MMS Program satellites they launched back in 2015."

"I know, it's pretty impressive, huh?" Mike said.

"*You're* pretty impressive. And kinda cute, too."

"Hey, knock off the flattery, you're embarrassing me."

She smiled. "The other two Mike Devons aren't nearly as cute as you are, especially after one of your workouts," she said, as she stood up and reached out for his hand.

Slapping her hand lightly as he grabbed it, Mike replied, "Hey! That's not even right!" he said and chuckled as she helped him to his feet. "You seem so well adjusted for having been through so much."

"Let's just say I haven't always been happy." She smiled. "You're seeing a newer me, but I have another side that I'm afraid you'll see before tomorrow."

"Now, it couldn't be that bad," Mike said. "Oh, you have to see this!" he said. "This is one of the crystal resonators Michael was developing. He was trying to go back in time to stop the executions." Mike's tone and expression got serious. "He was really on to something with this, I have to tell you."

"Well, I only spent a few minutes with him, but I'm certain there's something seriously wrong with him."

"He didn't hurt you or anything did he?" Mike asked.

"No, though I think he might have been scared of me, the way he ran out of here," she said with a smile.

"Ran out? When?"

"Right as you arrived." Courtney's smile faded.

"Did you see us both at the *same* time?" he asked. "That wouldn't be good."

"No, but he couldn't be here if you are, right?"

"It's not possible, at least I don't think it is," Mike said. "Did he enter the opening?"

"He ran through it, then out the door."

"How? It's too powerful. Unless he could interrupt the fields—"

"He was carrying one of Colonel Devon's sonic swords," she said.

"One of these?" Mike asked, as he pulled one out of his backpack.

"Exactly."

"Oh, dear God, please help us," Mike said. He saw Courtney's expression change as she read his face. She instantly yanked the pistol from her pocket and spun around.

"I'm still here, *Courtney*," Michael growled.

"Get back! Get as far away as you can!" Mike yelled, stumbling backwards. "This can't be. This is bad, Courtney! Michael, this is really bad!"

"I swear, I didn't know—he—I thought he went back. Michael," Courtney stammered.

"What are you two doing? Are you trying to rewrite history?" Michael demanded.

"Absolutely not! Do you know what you've done? How dangerous this is?" Mike asked.

"I don't care! I want to know why you're doing this to me!"

Michael nodded in Mike's direction. "So, you could bring *him* back here?"

"Michael, I'm sorry. I was trying to put the three of you back where you belong," she said.

"What did you do to *my* Courtney? Is this why she changed so much? What did you do to her?" Michael demanded.

"Look, Michael, we didn't have anything to do with that. Your Courtney went to another place and didn't survive. I'm very sorry," Mike said.

Courtney watched on, raising her pistol then lowering it. Mike was much stronger than Michael, but Courtney knew that one wrong move could kill him by mistake. Maybe it would kill them all.

"So, you knew all along! It's you who's been watching me, isn't it? How do you do it? With that thing?" Michael demanded, approaching Mike with the sword outstretched.

"Hey! Get back!" Mike said, as he moved back between two electrical cabinets and drew his own sword. "Don't you know what can happen if we touch? Or possibly just get too close?"

"You think I'm a fool? *I've* been working to rejoin the layers! All you have done is move between them! I was getting too close to a solution, so you stopped me! That's it, isn't it? Well I'm not going to let you!"

Michael lunged at him, slashing downward toward Mike's head. Mike ducked and jumped to the side, swiping his sword at Michael's. The invisible blades made a dull thud as they struck. Michael swung again, slashing low in front of Mike, then hitting a cabinet to his side. Sparks flew as Michael pulled his sword up to strike again.

"Michael! Stop or I'll shoot!" Courtney yelled, as he brought his sword up for another strike. She lay her finger on the trigger as her sights aligned on her target.

* * *

Colonel Devon strode up to the guard at the security station and ordered, "Get someone down to lab seven immediately and make sure he has the second key." He turned toward Court and Danni, then motioned to the elevator. "After you."

"Sir, this says Captain and Lieutenant Lewis are retired," the guard said.

"They're with me. Now hurry up and let us through," Colonel Devon ordered.

The guard reluctantly obeyed and picked up the phone. As they entered the elevator, the Colonel placed his thumb on the panel, then tapped his password into the keypad.

As soon as the doors closed, Court said, "He'll be punished for that."

"I don't like it either, but we don't have the time," the Colonel said, turning around to face the rear of the car. The elevator went down to the third basement level, stopped and a tiny seam in the back wall opened up. As the doors opened, they could see two armed guards standing behind a tall desk at the far end of the bare hallway.

"Holster the weapons boys. This is an emergency. Call Dr. Bernabie Lujan and tell him he's needed in lab seven, ASAP."

"Sir, this is against protocol. We cannot permit you to enter without another senior staff member." The young guard almost choked as he said the words.

"Which is why I need Dr. Lujan."

"But…protocol…" the guard stuttered.

"Son, who do you think wrote that protocol?" demanded the Colonel. Pointing at the other guard he commanded, "You, place him under arrest!"

The older guard reached for his cuffs.

"Don't try it, sir. This is a violation—"

The Colonel yelled, "Shoot him if he doesn't holster his

weapon immediately!"

"Sir?"

"That's an order soldier!" the Colonel screamed.

The older guard turned and stuck the barrel of his weapon to the younger guard's head and screamed, "Drop the weapon soldier!"

"He's in violation—"

"And you're refusing a direct order from your commanding officer!"

The younger soldier quickly reached for the weapon at his head. One deafening report filled the narrow hallway, as another immediately followed.

The Colonel felt a moist spray engulf him as a searing pain shot through his body. He looked down to see blood oozing from his shirt as he stumbled and dropped to one knee.

"Colonel!" yelled the older guard, holstering his weapon as he rushed to help.

"Get me back on my feet, I don't have time for this right now!"

Court and the older guard tugged the Colonel to his feet, shuffling their feet to keep from slipping in the fluids that had spilled from the younger guard.

"Soldier, do you have the second key, or do I need to wait for Dr. Lujan while I bleed to death?" the Colonel asked, staggering toward the tall desk with the two men helping.

"I do, sir," the ashen-faced guard said, his voice wavering.

"Then what's the holdup?" the Colonel asked.

"Sir, will you please take my key?" the guard asked.

"Certainly. I accept full responsibility," the Colonel reached out his hand and the guard dropped the key into it. The guard then opened one of his leg pockets and pulled out a first aid pack. He tossed it to Court as he walked away, pulling his pistol from its holster once more. The Colonel watched the guard cock the hammer. He turned to the Lewises and put his hands over his ears. The couple quickly followed suit. As soon as the shot rang out, the Colonel lowered his hands, slipped both keys into their locks and entered the lab.

When Court joined him in the lab, the Colonel said, "We haven't had this thing on in a number of years." He turned the main power on and the panel lit up. "It's coming back to me, though." He looked at Court and Danni standing in the doorway, staring at him. "Are you two going to come over here and help me or not?"

"Colonel, we don't find it as easy to ignore a murder-suicide as you seem to," Court said.

"Is that what you saw? Unbelievable! Those soldiers gave their lives for their country and you dishonor them like this?"

"I didn't see it like that," Court said.

"A young man is put into an impossible situation and bravely stands his ground. Another follows the hardest order any soldier will ever get, but you don't see the honor and bravery they showed?"

"I—" Court said.

"Both of you would be dead right now if it wasn't for brave men like them."

The Colonel turned back toward the controls to the crystal altar and began making adjustments.

"I hate this place Court. I can't—" Danni began.

"Not right now, Danni," Court said.

"Hurry up. I have to get back before I bleed to death. Danni, get me some procoagulant please."

Obediently, Danni fetched the red and white packet for the Colonel. Lifting his shirt up to show a black hole right above his navel, Colonel Devon squeezed the contents into the wound. With a shudder and forced exhale, the Colonel then took the hemostatic bandage Danni offered and placed it over the wound. He then swallowed the two pills she gave him and glanced at the Lewises. "That's the fifth and hopefully the last time I get shot."

"Colonel are you sure you don't need medical attention?" she asked.

"Of course, I do. I'm bleeding internally and have one or more punctured organs, but I don't have time for surgery at the moment."

"We understand," Court said, "but—"

"Good." The Colonel laid down on the altar and said, "I think it's ready. Just slowly turn that dial on the left. It'll get loud, but keep turning the knob until everything goes silent," he said. "About one mark every five seconds. Got it?"

"Got it," Court said and reached for the dial.

Almost immediately, the room began to reverberate with the rapidly building energy.

The intense noise became unbearably loud, then the room suddenly went quiet. A haze surrounded the altar and the Colonel was gone.

Barely able to move, Court turned the dial down until he was able to grip Danni's arm. He nudged her toward the altar but Danni resisted. He watched her silently mouth the words, *I can't go without you.*

Court nodded and felt her grip clamp down on his wrist. He twisted out of her grasp, spun the dial and simultaneously shoved her with all his might. He felt Danni slap his arm, then her fingernails dug in and they both fell toward the altar.

* * *

Mike was the first to notice the reverberations in the room.

"Michael! Put the sword down, Michael. Now!" Courtney screamed.

Michael faced the barrel of her gun, then slowly lowered his sword.

"Wait!" Mike yelled and lunged to protect Courtney. He held his sword up, guarding against Michael's, as he passed within a few feet.

Mike asked, "Courtney, do you feel that?"

"Yes," she said with her eyes going wide. "Do you think it's the Colonel?"

Michael backed away. "How are you doing that?" he asked.

"I think it is," Mike said to Courtney.

"It has a different feel to it," she said.

"Quit ignoring me!" Michael screamed.

"The spud is different from the other side, too," Mike said.

"Answer me!" Michael screamed again, raising his sword.

Both men stood on opposite sides of the electrical room with their swords up, eyes squinting from the loud noise, unable to move.

Mike looked at Courtney and noticed she had a grin on her face. *We must look ridiculous.*

The room went silent and then a haze appeared. A shockwave broke the silence, knocking the three of them to the ground.

When Mike stood up, he saw the Colonel roll over, struggling to get to a knee. As he steadied himself, two tangled bodies collided with him, knocking him back to the floor.

"Help me!" the woman screamed.

Mike watched Courtney pull the Colonel off her parents, leaving a trail of blood on the floor.

"Careful, he's bleeding!" Court yelled.

"Mom? Dad?" Courtney asked, "It's you!"

Mike yelled, "Watch out! Michael ran behind the switchgear!"

Courtney lunged over toward the door and looked down the far side of the metal cabinets. "He's on the other side!" she yelled, as she rushed back to look down the middle row.

Mike screamed, "Here he is!"

He lowered his sword to protect Court and Danni. Mike turned and saw Courtney's gun pointed just above his head. He jumped over the Colonel, to give her a clear shot at Michael. He watched in horror as Michael dove at the Colonel. *We're all going to die.*

Courtney's gun fired three times in rapid succession. Michael screamed in agony as his body took hit after hit as he fell. Michael swung the sword at the Colonel's legs, cutting through his left shin.

"Brace yourselves!" Mike yelled, as the Colonel swiped back at Michael with his own sword, missing by inches.

Michael flopped over to his back and floundered away from the Colonel, which put him in striking distance of Danni.

"Colonel! Quick!" Mike yelled.

The Colonel clawed at the floor and managed to grab hold of Michael's pant leg.

"Don't touch him! Use your sword!" Mike screamed. The Colonel pulled him away and Michael spun around, raising his sword above the Colonel's chest. Mike saw the Colonel's expression change, as if he had found something. Mike watched in horror as the Colonel's hand slipped around Michael's ankle.

An intense light filled the room.

Mike felt his body being sharply compressed but he heard no sound. His thoughts went to Courtney as everything around him went black.

* * *

Terry and Bill were nearly knocked to the ground from a powerful reverberation that shook the building.

"What blew up?" Bill asked.

"No clue," Terry said, then touched his com. "HQ, we need emergency services for roughly a dozen casualties."

"Roger that. Hold for backup, team one," the agent replied.

"Negative, we are going in now. Teams two and three, do you have a copy?" Terry asked.

"Affirmative. ETA four minutes, over," came the reply.

"Roger that," Terry replied, switching off the com as he jogged over to the elevator. "That's too long. Catch my six." He worked his fingertips between the doors and forced them open, exposing the shaft and cables.

"Hold on," Bill said, opening a small packet. "Pain killers."

"Where—"

"The kit in the chopper," Bill said, flipping a tiny pill into his mouth.

Terry nodded as he slid his hands inside the arms of his jacket, reached into the shaft and grabbed a cable in each sleeve. "Go for a soft landing."

With that, he stepped out and placed his left arch against the left cable for a guide and hopped into the shaft. It was a slow thirty-foot slide down to the top of the elevator car below. Terry pulled off his greasy jacket, stepped to the side and Bill landed easily in front of him.

"That wasn't too bad," Bill whispered.

"My greasy jacket might disagree."

Terry placed it at his feet, then knelt down and lifted the escape hatch. He looked through from several angles.

"You hear that?" Bill asked.

"Yeah, probably just an aftershock," Terry said. "It's clear down there, but the doors are damaged."

He lowered himself inside. Terry pulled out his pistol and carefully inspected the doors as Bill eased into the car with him.

"Same device," Terry whispered, feeling the edge of the cut. "Still warm." He eased his face and pistol up to the cut to peek through. "Can't see much."

"Step back and cover me," Bill said. He laid on the floor of the elevator, placing his feet on the left door jamb for leverage.

Terry watched Bill's body shake from exertion as the mangled right lower section slid open nearly a foot. He dove headfirst, over Bill, through the narrow opening. Terry scanned the hallway with his pistol as he scurried to the far side of the corridor. He motioned for Bill to join him and got to his feet. Terry covered the hallway while Bill crawled through the gap and joined him.

He lead the way down to the corner and slowly leaned his head over to look down the adjacent hallway. He leaned back and whispered, "I heard voices."

Then, the building started to vibrate. Terry waited for a few moments after the vibration stopped, then checked the hallway once more.

"It came from down there," he whispered. "Cover me, I'm going to take a look."

Terry read the sign on the door ahead of him. *Buss Room.*

***

UNIT 4: THE NEXT STEP

MIKE was dazed by hundreds of images overpowering his mind. Some were Michael's life. Some were from Colonel Devon's, but they all felt strangely familiar. He could feel them becoming memories, but somehow separated from his own recollections. The pressure inside his head began to build until it was unbearable. There was a bright flash, then it ended just as abruptly as it had started.

What a peaceful place. I must be dreaming.
I'll wake up soon.
It's time to wake up…
Wake up!

Mike fought with all his might to move any muscle in his body and eventually one twitched. *That's it! Move!* As his limbs thawed and relaxed, Mike stood up and looked around.

Lovely place, but where am I?
It's not warm, or cold.
Too quiet.

He glanced down and saw his body lying flat and stiff on the floor. By a great force, he was sucked back inside his body—trapped once more.

No! No! No!
Get me out of here!
I can't see!

I want out!
I want to live!

Mike felt exhaustion setting in. He was barely able to get enough air into his lungs and thought he would pass out. He gave up and lay there, waiting to die, until he felt his left eyelid twitch. Then it twitched again.

Wait, you felt that!
You did it once, you can do it again!
Fight, Mike, fight!

Every part of his body was frozen, rigid. Bit by bit, Mike was able to regain control of his extremities. Finally, his eyes opened and he could see once more. Mike felt the sweat running down his sides as he sat upright in his bed. He wiped the sweat off his face, then turned and placed his feet on the floor.

Strange, the floor is warm.
Well, not warm, but not cold.
Oh, no!

Mike looked down, saw his body lying on the floor and was instantly sucked back in. He started laughing, but within moments it turned to crying, then wailing. He screamed with every breath he took in, but it did no good.

It's evil, it has to be.
It's trying to suck the life out of me.
If only someone would make me wake up.
Please, why won't you help me?

Despair overwhelmed Mike once more and he started fighting to move something—anything. Once more, he felt his body struggling to get enough oxygen. His lungs burned so badly he thought he might die, but he refused to stop.

Then…a bright light interrupted his thoughts, followed by another and another. Off in the distance, Mike could hear voices calling his name—yelling his name. The next bright flash was accompanied by a stinging sensation on his face.

Hit me again!
Again!
Do it again!

Mike screamed inside.

He felt another strike and his body responded with a twitch. Mike gasped in all the air he could and he smelled Courtney. His hand moved and he felt the cold, smooth floor under him. He saw another bright flash and the opposite side of his face felt like it was on fire.

Ouch!
That hurts!
I'm almost…

Mike's eyes opened slightly and he saw Courtney standing over him. He cut his eyes to the side and noticed her hand poised over him, ready to strike again. Then, he glanced into her eyes and saw her expression change.

"I won't hit you anymore!" Courtney smiled, as she lowered her hand.

Mike didn't want to blink, but his eyes closed against his will. He struggled for a moment and they reopened. Courtney's raised hand quickly dropped out of sight again.

"Were—were you going to hit me again?" he managed.

"You had another second or two," Courtney said with a wink. "You had us worried."

"Are you hurt?" he asked.

"I'm fine," she said.

Mike rolled his head to the side and saw Court and Danni. "You OK, too?"

"We're fine," Danni said, "but you gave us quite a scare."

"The implosion…" Mike said.

"Yes, we saw it," Courtney said.

"Do you know what happened?" Court asked.

"They touched," Mike replied. "I didn't think they—we—could be in the same world, but I was wrong."

"You weren't too far off," Courtney said.

"I suppose," he replied, returning Courtney's gaze.

Her phone buzzed and he saw her eyes go assassin cold.

"The boys are here and they won't show restraint. I think we should destroy the spud and surrender," Courtney said.

Mike felt a surge of adrenaline. "Help me sit up."

Courtney pulled him to a seated position.

"Court, would you help her get me up?" Mike asked. He then looked at Courtney, "I suppose you have a plan?"

"It changed recently and I haven't come up with one that ends with all four of us alive and free."

"What if all of us go to Supreme Britain?" Mike asked, as they got him to his feet. "It won't be easy, but I think it's our best chance."

"If we do, we lose the device and you know *they* can't be trusted with it."

"Then someone has to stay here and slip out with the spud once the other three have gone," Mike said. He kept an arm around Courtney and started to walk.

"No one would make it," she replied, stepping with him.

"Not even you?" Mike asked.

"I can't handle more than one or two of them with what I have here," Courtney answered.

Court asked, "Is there any way we could take it with us?"

"No, it doesn't have a portable power supply," Mike replied.

"We have a power supply that might work, in your sword," Court pointed out.

"I'm afraid we don't have time, but I think you're on to something," Mike said. "Wait, I think I know how we can do it!"

"Seriously?" Courtney asked.

"The portal takes a second or two to close after it powers down. That might be enough time for the last person to get through," Mike said. "It has to work!"

"Mike, I'm sorry, we shouldn't have come," Court said.

"Not at all, sir. We're glad you're both here," replied Mike, walking faster. "You can let go now."

Courtney stopped where she was, but Mike kept walking. "You three go through first. I'll cut the umbilical with the sword, grab the spud as I shut off the sword, then jump into the portal. Piece of cake."

"Piece of cake?" Courtney asked.

"Well, maybe not *cake*, but if I'm right, I should have a second to spare."

"That's not much. Besides, we may not be safe there. Remember, the three of us were convicted of treason and hung," said Courtney.

"Yes, but that was a long time ago. Besides, we don't have another option," he said.

"Mike, you're not safe in Supreme Britain," said Danni quickly. "The Colonel killed a man there."

Mike looked at Danni and then over at Court, realizing the magnitude of her words.

"Are you sure you can get there?" Courtney asked as she checked her phone to see how close the others were.

"Pretty sure," Mike said, jogging back toward her.

"Will you be able to get it running again? That is, if you make it to Supreme Britain with us."

"I think so," Mike said, hopping up and down. "Everything

is working again. Let's do this."

Courtney glanced at her phone again. "Good enough. Hurry and fire it up then. Courtney looked directly at her parents. "Mom, Dad, I love you both."

"We love you, dear," Danni said, putting her arms around Courtney.

"Good luck, Mike. We'll see you on the other side, son." Court reached out to shake his hand, then pulled him closer and gave him a hug, with his other arm around Courtney. "Thank you for putting my family back together," Court said.

Danni stepped up to Mike and kissed him on the cheek.

"Quick, they're in the elevator!" Courtney warned.

Mike ran over to the controls and Courtney turned on the breaker. The room came to life with power vibrations once more.

"One at a time, five seconds apart!" Mike yelled over the noise. "Be ready. It pulls hard!"

Court lined up first, with Danni a few feet behind him and Courtney brought up the rear. When the hazy portal showed itself, Court glanced inquisitively at Mike.

Mike nodded and Court lunged into the opening. Mike smiled as he watched Danni shuffle her feet toward the haze then get yanked from view.

Courtney was the last to make it to the portal. She glanced back and gave Mike one last look, smiled and then jumped at the portal, tucking into a ball.

This is it—you have to get it right or you won't see them again.

Mike visualized the timing of his actions repeatedly. He practiced the motions twice before he turned the spud back up and powered on the sword for the real thing.

This will work...One...two...three!

Mike ran toward the spud and the portal. Holding the sword in his left hand, he slashed the umbilical to the spud in a blast of sparks and instantly switched off the sword. He could feel the energy in the room slowing him down. He grabbed the spud with his right hand and dove at the dissipating haze with all his might. Mike felt his body strike something hard.

Oh, no, the wall!

He struggled to see or feel, but everything was dark and silent.

* * *

"Something moved in there," Terry whispered, as Bill joined him at the doors. "Remember what I told you."

Bill nodded.

Terry heard a metallic sound and motioned for Bill to get back, pointing at the slowly turning handle. A man's head started to come into view and Terry kicked the door, hitting the man in the head. Terry then yanked the door open and rushed inside.

"Don't shoot! Don't shoot!"

"Where is she?" Terry screamed.

"We don't know! She left at least a half hour ago!" one of the men yelled, cowering at Terry's gun.

"She's not in here, watch your back!" Terry called out to Bill. "Three hostages coming out with me."

Terry opened the door for three battered and worn out men to exit.

"Teams two and three?" he asked, into the com.

"Go for two. Go for three," they each responded.

"We have the workers with us, all healthy," he said. "Wait, could you repeat that intel please?"

"Copy that. The bad guys are still down there with you."

"Are you certain?" Terry asked.

"We viewed the security footage. Your people never left the buss room, it's across the hall from you." The agent continued, "We have two guns coming your way from each elevator."

"Roger that. Coming out," Terry said. He carefully opened the door and saw four guns pointing in his direction. Terry pointed at the doors across the hall and the four men in riot gear rushed toward him. Terry opened the door and knelt down as the men breached the buss room.

"Clear!" the team leader called out.

"Check the ceiling and all of the cabinets," Terry called out, "and watch yourselves!"

"Who's Terry?" a man asked.

Terry walked into the room. "That's me."

One of the men pointed to a note left hanging on the switchgear cabinet.

Terry walked up to it and read, "I wish I could have explained the operation but it's above TS. Maybe someday, C.D.L."

"If it was *above top secret*, that would explain a lot," Bill said.

"There's no way they got out! They're here, somewhere! I want every ceiling tile, closet, cabinet and sewer pipe searched!" Terry yelled, slamming his fist into the steel cabinet.

Bill walked up to him and asked, "Still think she's a bad guy?"

"Yes. I'm not buying that ridiculous note! Now, keep your eyes open, we have a big building to clear," Terry said.

* * *

Mike strained to see Courtney kneeling over him.

"Mike? Can you hear me now?" she asked.

"Just barely."

"You did it! We all made it!" Courtney exclaimed.

"We did?"

"Obviously! Here, let me help."

Mike accepted her hand and stood up. He looked around at the calm surroundings and saw people going about their everyday lives. He felt the fear subsiding as the reassuring touch of Courtney's hand energized him. "

"We need to get off the street before we attract attention," Mike said, noticing the others had there belongings. "We're a little conspicuous with all this stuff out in broad daylight."

"Good point. I have everything I need," Courtney said, holding up her bag.

"Most of what I need is at Michael's, if they haven't stripped it already."

"How far is that?" Court asked.

"Not exactly sure," Mike said, looking at the houses around them. "We need to call George."

"The janitor from TAC?" Courtney asked.

"Well here he's from British Aerospace. He'll take us someplace safe. Then I can make this thing portable," Mike said.

"Sounds good to me." Courtney smiled at her mother and said, "He's cute, huh?" Then leaned over and gave Mike a kiss.

"I think mine's cuter," said Danni.

"That's enough fighting, ladies. We need to go," Mike said, tucking the spud in his bag.

"It will be nice to spend some time together," Danni said.

"Yeah, and some much needed rest," Court added.

"If things stay quiet, I suppose I could convince you to reconsider our situation?" Mike asked Courtney.

"I think so," Courtney said. "As long as you stay focused on getting your project completed."

"Deal," Mike said.

Mike took Courtney's hand and started walking down the sidewalk.

***

—THE STORY CONTINUES—

EPILOGUE

MIK3 D3VON: Disclosures

"George, wake up. Michael's on the phone, and it sounds important."

"What? How long have I been asleep?" the groggy janitor asked. "Wait, who?" he said, as he lurched up in bed.

"Well, it sounds like Michael, but he's trying to disguise his voice with a silly accent. Said he was an old friend in town for the day," his wife answered, and turned to leave the room.

George jumped out of bed and passed her before she could get to the door of their small bedroom.

Grabbing the phone off the kitchen counter, he said, "Hello?"

"Hello there old friend. I know I told you yesterday that I didn't want to cause you any trouble, but can you do me one last favor?" Mike Devon asked.

"Do you have any idea what's happening, mate?" George asked and turned away from his wife's inquisitive look.

"No, are they after Michael?" Mike asked.

"Maybe, but they have bigger problems right now. Someone hacked our boss to pieces, in a hallway at work. We are all under house arrest while they finish the investigation." George closed his eyes as he listened for Mike's reaction.

"Someone hacked Alec up? George, that's awful! The smell must have been horrendous," Mike said.

"Yes it was. The entire building had the stench of burned flesh. Whatever they used cut right through the flooring as well." Why did you mention the smell?

"I can imagine."

"You don't know anything about it?" the janitor asked.

"Me? How could I?"

"No, you're right. How could you?" George answered.

"Do they have any suspects?" Mike asked.

"Not yet, and no one at work will say a word about what went on with Michael for fear of being arrested themselves. We had one chance to turn him in; when we learned about the insubordination and crimes against a higher class. No one did, and now they're all scared." Remembering that Scotland Yard could be listening in, George changed the subject. "What do you need from me?"

"Well, I need a ride. We need a ride; four of us came to town this trip."

"Four of you?"

"Yeah, I'm sorry, George, I shouldn't have called. I don't want to cause you any more problems."

"It's fine."

"Thanks, I owe you, again," Mike said.

"No worries. So, well, do I know any of your friends?"

Mike replied, "No, but you'd recognize one, from old photographs. If things settle down, I'll introduce you."

"I'd like that." George tried to sound calm, but his mind raced, Is it the girl? Old photographs – that must be Courtney! She's here? "Give me an intersection near you and I'll send my brother-in-law right over. I'm too tired or I'd come myself."

"Looks like Seventh Street and Rollins Avenue?" Mike read.

George replied, "You aren't far at all. Hold tight."

ACKNOWLEDGEMENTS

PRIMARILY responsible for the existence of this first book is Mark VanTassel, who single handedly taught me how to write a novel. He was brutally honest (and I do mean BRUTALLY) when he read early revisions; driving me to work harder and get better (after I got over the embarrassment of his revelations). Once, he told me, "Whatever you do, don't show this to anyone else. Seriously, I'm not kidding." I still remember the first time he gave me a good review, it went something like, "I actually enjoyed a couple of parts, but all the rest of it was drivel." Much to my delight, his training got me to the point I could critique his work and critique it I did! As you read along, watch for the phrase 'Strength of the Soul' where I tip my hat to Mark's own work.

Also, if it was not for my first readers, our oldest three children, enjoying this first book so much, the next two books would not exist. I hope you also enjoy the stories ahead.

Lastly, I would like to acknowledge Google, Wikipedia and NASA for their contributions as well. Details on magnetic reconnection, satellites, history, etc., were verified and made more accurate by web research and white-papers on topics inside which you will mistakenly identify as 'Science Fiction'. Now, I don't want to scare anyone, but there is more 'Science *Faction*' going on in the pages ahead than you may realize…

ABOUT THE AUTHOR

JW COUCH was schooled in the field of industrial maintenance & engineering by his father, from an early age. As an adult, he continued in the field, working regularly with technologies that include thermography, vibration & sound analysis and structural resonances, which appear in his books.

The MIK3 D3VON books are his first series and based in part on the real-world tech he works in.

Born on a farm and raised on *Star Trek,* he has always shared his father's fascination with technology and time-travel.

Made in the USA
San Bernardino, CA
18 January 2020

63243431R00153